229

S0-AJX-694

The Vampire Hunters

The snow ceased shortly after sunset, and the ensuing night was bitter cold. My enemies made camp in the open—their own fears and perhaps the consciences of some of them would hardly have let them rest inside the walls of Castle Dracula that night. They built up a fire against wolves—my disturbed children were still howling in the distance—and planned to take turns standing watch. But one by one they all sank into fitful sleep around the ebbing flames, till one person only remained awake, she who had begun to learn to make the night her day.

"Can it be that we've unfairly maligned Dracula? We're almost convinced of it after reading these clever, wry (and you thought the Count was humorless), imaginative, maybe occasionally self-serving transcripts of his tapes in which at long last he breaks his silence about those dark events at Castle Dracula and in London involving Mina and Jonathan Harker, Drs. Seward and Van Helsing, Lucy Western, et al. Quoting liberally from their respective journals, Vlad, as he likes to be called, shows how at variance their accounts are with what actually went on. The Count is not quite as full of the milk of human kindness as he'd like us to believe, but he's a persuasive devil. He'll have you cheering each time he outmaneuvers his pursuers."

—Publishers Weekly

FRED SABERHAGEN

THE DRACULA TAPE

TOR HORROR

A TOM DOHERTY ASSOCIATES BOOK
NEW YORK

THE DRACULA TAPE

Copyright © 1975 by Fred Saberhagen

A TOR Book
Published by Tom Doherty Associates, Inc.
49 West 24 Street
New York, NY 10010

Cover art by Glenn Hastings

ISBN: 0-812-52581-7   Can. ISBN: 0-812-52582-5

First Tor edition: May 1989

Printed in the United States of America

0 9 8 7 6 5 4 3 2 1

The following is a transcript of a tape found in a recorder in the back seat of an automobile belonging to Mr. Arthur Harker of Exeter, two days after the freakishly heavy Devon snowstorm in January of this year. Mr. Harker and his wife, Janet, both suffering from exposure and exhaustion, were admitted to All Saints Hospital, in Plymouth, on the morning following the height of the storm. They spoke of abandoning their auto on an impassable road near midnight, but seem never to have given any convincing explanation for leaving the relative security of their vehicle at an hour when the storm was at its worst, nor of exactly how they reached Plymouth. All Saints Hospital is some thirty kilometers from where their car was found in a drift on the Upham Road, just outside St. Peter's Cemetery and virtually on the edge of Dartmoor. The Harkers' physical condition and the state of their clothing

1

*upon arrival at the hospital suggests that they may
have walked across country. Their car was undam-
aged when found, and although all its doors and
windows were locked the key was still in the
ignition, which had been turned off. The petrol tank
was approximately one-third full.*

*The voice on the tape is masculine and rather
deep. It speaks English with an indefinable slight
accent. Three linguistics experts consulted have
given three divergent opinions regarding the speak-
er's native tongue.*

*The general quality of the tape, and the back-
ground noises detectable thereon, are, in the opinion of technical experts, consistent with the
hypothesis that the tape was in fact recorded in an
automobile, engine running at idling speed, heater
and blowers operating, with gusts of high wind
outside.*

*The Harkers dismiss the tape as "some joke,"
profess no interest in it, and refuse all further
comment. It was first played by rescue workers who
found the car and thought the recorder might hold
some emergency message from its occupants. They
brought the tape to the attention of higher authorities because of the references to violent crimes
which it contains. No external evidence has been
found to connect the tape with the alleged vandalism and grave robbing at St. Peter's Cemetery, now
under investigation.*

. . . this switch, then my words will be set down
here electrically for the world. How very nice. So,
if we are going to tell the truth at last, then what
real crimes can I be charged with, what sins so
utterly damning and blastable?

You will accuse me of the death of Lucy Westenra, I suppose. Ah, I would swear my innocence, but what is there to swear by that you would now believe? Later, perhaps, when you have begun to understand some things, then I will swear. I embraced the lovely Lucy, it is true. But never against her will. Not she nor any of the others did I ever force.

At this point on the tape another voice, unidentifiable, whispers an indecipherable word or two.

Your own great-grandma Mina Harker? Sir, I will laugh like a madman in a moment, and it is centuries since I have laughed, and no, I am not mad.

Probably you have scarcely believed one single thing that I have said to you this far. But I mean to go on talking anyway, to the machine, and you may as well listen. The morning is far off, and at present none of us have any place to go. And you two are well armed, in your own estimation at least, against anything that I might try to do to you. Heavy spanner clutched in your white-knuckled right hand, dear Mr. Harker, and at your good wife's lovely throat hangs something that should do you more good, if all reports are true, than even such an estimable bludgeon. The trouble is that all reports are never true. I'm the last stranger you'll ever welcome into your car out of a storm, I'll wager. But I intend you no harm. You'll see, just let me talk.

Lucy I did not kill. It was not *I* who hammered the great stake through her heart. *My* hands did not cut off her lovely head, or stuff her breathless mouth—*that mouth*—with garlic, as if she were a dead pig, pork being made ready for some

3

barbarians' feast. Only reluctantly had I made her a vampire, nor would she ever have become a vampire were it not for the imbecile Van Helsing and his work. Imbecile is one of the most charitable names that I can find for him. . . .

And Mina Murray, later Mrs. Jonathan Harker. In classic understatement I proclaim I never meant dear Mina any harm. With these hands I broke the back of her real enemy, the madman Renfield, who would have raped and murdered her. *I* knew what his intentions were, though the doctors, young Seward and the imbecile, could not seem to fathom them. And when Renfield spelled out to my face what he intended doing to my love . . . ah, Mina.

But that was long ago. She was an old, old woman when she went to her grave in 1967.

And all the men on the *Demeter*. If you have read my enemies' version of events I suppose you will tax me with those sailors' lives as well. Only tell me why, in God's name why, I should have murdered them. . . . What is it?

At this point a man's voice, conditionally identifiable as that of Arthur Harker, utters the one word nothing.

But of course. You did not realize that I could speak the name of God. You are victims of superstition, sheer superstition, which is a hideous thing, and very powerful indeed. God and I are old acquaintances. At least, I have been aware of Him for much longer than you have, my friends.

Now I can see you are going to wonder whether the crucifix at the lady's throat, from which you have begun to derive some small measure of

4

comfort, is really efficacious at all in present company. Do not worry. Believe me, it is every bit effective against me as—as that heavy spanner in the gentleman's right hand would be.

Now sit still, please. We have been cut off alone in this snowstorm for an hour now, and it was half an hour, not until you tried to watch me in the rear-view mirror, before you even began to believe my name, were convinced I was not joking. Not pulling your legs, as I believe the idiom has it. You were quite careless and unguarded at the first. If I had wanted to take your lives or drink your blood the gory deeds would now be done.

No, my purpose in your car is innocent. I would like you just to sit and listen for a while, as I try once more to justify myself before humanity. Even in the remote fastnesses where most of my time is spent, I have caught wind of a new spirit of toleration that supposedly moves across the face of the earth in these last decades of the twentieth century. So once more I will try . . . I chose your car because you happened to be driving here tonight—no, let me be strictly truthful, some arrangements were made to cause you to come along this way—and because you, sir, are a lineal descendant of a dear old friend of mine, and because I have learned that you habitually carry this tape recorder in your car. Yes, and even the snowstorm has been arranged, a little bit. I wanted this chance to offer this testament, for myself and others like me.

Not that there is anyone else quite like me. . . . Sir, I perceive by the condition of the ashtrays that you are a smoker, and I would wager you would like to smoke. Go ahead, put your spanner down in handy reach, and puff away. The lady too might like a cigarette, at such a trying time as this. Ah . . . thank you, but I do not indulge, myself.

We are going to be here for a while . . . I have seen few snowstorms heavier than this, even in the high Carpathians. Without doubt the roads will be impassable until sometime tomorrow at the earliest. Lacking snowshoes, it would take a wolf to get about in snow like this, or something that can fly. . . .

I suppose you'll want to know, or others will, why I should bother with this *apologia pro vita sua*. Why, at this late date, attempt to defend my name? Well, I change as I grow older—yes, I do—and some things, for example a certain kind of pride, that were once of great moment to me are now no more than dust and ashes in my tomb. Like Van Helsing's desecrated fragment of the Host, which there went back to dust.

I have been there myself, there in my tomb, but not to stay. Not yet to stay beneath the massive stone on which the one word's carved, just . . . *Dracula*.

TRACK ONE

Let me not start at the beginning of my life. Even penned in here, listening at close range to the words from my own lips, you would find the story of those breathing, eating days of mine too hard to believe. Later on, it may be, we will have some discourse of them. Had you noticed that I do not breathe, except to get the wind to talk? Now watch me as I speak and you will see.

Maybe a good point to start from would be that early November day in 1891, at the Borgo Pass, in what is now Romania. Van Helsing and the rest thought that they had me, then, and brought their chronicle to its end. It was snowing then, too, and my gypsies tried, but with only knives against rifles they could not do much when the hunters on horseback caught up with me at sunset and tipped me out of my coffin, and with their long knives went for my heart and throat. . . .

No. I have the feeling that I would be telling too much backward if I began there. How's this? I'll start where the other chronicle begins, the one that you must be familiar with. It starts early in the previous May, with the arrival in my domain in Transylvania of one Jonathan Harker, a fledgling solicitor sent out from England to help me with the purchase of some property near London.

You see, I had been rousing myself from a period—somewhat extended—of great lethargy, quiescence, and contemplation. New voices, new thoughts, were heard in the world. Even on my remote mountaintop, green-clad in the forests of centuries, well-nigh unreachable, I with my inner senses could hear the murmurings across Europe of the telegraph, the infant splutterings of the engines of steam and internal combustion. I could smell the coal smoke and the fever of the world in change.

That fever caught in me and grew. Enough of seclusion with my old companions—if one could call them that. Enough wolf howlings, owl hoots, bat flutterings, half-witted peasants hissing at me from behind contorted fingers, enough of crosses waved like so many clubs, as if I were a Turkish army. I would rejoin the human race, come out of my hinterlands into the sunlit progress of the modern world. Budapest, and even Paris, did not seem great enough or far enough to hold my new life that was to be.

For a time I even considered going to America. But a greater metropolis than any of the New World was nearer at hand, and more susceptible to a preliminary study. This study took me years, but it was thorough. Harker, when he arrived at my castle in May of 1891, took note in his shorthand diary of the "vast number of English books, magazines, and newspapers" I had on hand.

Harker. I have rather more respect for him than for the others of the man-pack that was later to follow Van Helsing on my trail. Respect is always due courage, and he was a courageous man, though rather dull. And as the first real guest in Castle Dracula for centuries, he was the subject of my first experiments in fitting myself acceptably back into the mainstream of humanity.

Actually I had to disguise myself as my own coachman to bring him on the last leg of his long journey from England. My household help were, as some of the wealthy are always wont to say, undependable, even if they were not so utterly nonexistent as Harker was later to surmise. Outcast gypsies. Superstitiously loyal to me, whom they had adopted as their master, but with no competence as servants in the normal sense. I knew I was going to have to look after my guest myself.

The railroad had brought Harker as far as the town of Bistrita, from which a diligence, or public stagecoach, traveled daily to Bukovina, a part of Moldavia to the north and west. At the Borgo Pass, some eight or nine hours along the way from Bistrita, my carriage was to be waiting, as I had informed my visitor by letter, to bring him to my door. The stagecoach reached the pass at near the witching hour of twelve, an hour ahead of schedule, just as I, taking no chances, drove my own caleche with four black horses up close behind the diligence where it paused in the midnight landscape, half piny and half barren. I was just in time to hear its driver say: "There is no carriage here, the Herr is not expected after all. He will now come on to Bukovina, and return tomorrow or the next day; better the next day."

At this point some of the peasants on board the stage caught sight of my arrival and began a timorous uproar of prayers and oaths and incantations; I pulled up closer, and in a moment appeared limned in the glow of the stagecoach's lamps, wearing the coachman's uniform and a wide-brimmed black hat and false brown beard as additional disguise, these last props having been borrowed from a gypsy who had once traveled as an actor.

"You are early tonight, my friend," I called over to the stagecoach driver.

"The English Herr was in a hurry," the man stammered back, not meeting my eye directly.

"That is why, I suppose, you wished him to go on to Bukovina. You cannot deceive me, my friend; I know too much, and my horses are swift." I smiled at the coach windows full of white, scared faces, and someone inside it muttered from *Lenore:* "*Denn die Todten reiten schnell* [For the dead travel fast]."

"Give me the Herr's baggage," I ordered, and it was quickly handed over. And then my guest himself appeared, the only one among the passengers who dared to look me in the eye, a young man of middle size and unremarkable appearance, clean-shaven, with hair and eyes of medium brown.

As soon as he was on the seat beside me I

cracked my whip and off we went. Holding the reins with one hand, I threw a cloak round Harker's shoulders, and a rug across his knees, and said to him in German: "The night is chill, mein Herr, and my master the count bade me take all care of you. There is a flask of *slivovitz* underneath the seat, if you should require it."

He nodded and murmured something, and though he drank none of the brandy I could feel him relax slightly. No doubt, I thought, his fellow passengers in the coach had been filling him with wild tales, or, more likely and worse, just dropping a few hints about the terrible place that was his destination. Still, I had great hopes that I could overcome any unpleasant preconceptions picked up by my guest.

I drove deliberately down the wrong road at first, to kill a little time, for that chanced to be the night, the Eve of St. George, on which all treasure buried in those mountains is detectable at midnight by the emanation of apparent bluish flames. The advance arrangements for my expedition abroad had somewhat depleted my own store of gold, and I meant to seize the opportunity of replenishment.

Now you are doubting again. Did you think that my old home was much like any other land? Not so. There was I born, and there I failed to die. And in my land, as Van Helsing himself once said, "There are deep caverns and fissures that reach none know whither. There have been volcanoes . . . waters of strange properties, and gases that kill or make to vivify." English was not Van Helsing's mother tongue.

Never mind. The point is that I took the opportunity of that night to mark out a few sites of buried wealth, of which there were likely to be several, as we shall see. My passenger was quite naturally curious at these repeated stoppings of the carriage, at the eerie glow of faint, flickering blue flames appearing here and there about the countryside, and at my several dismountings to build up little cairns of stone. With these cairns to guide me on future nights when I was alone, I would be able to recover the treasure troves at my leisure.

I had expected Harker's natural curiosity at these events to break forth at once in questions, whereupon I, in my coachman's character, would be able to demonstrate irrefutably that marvels unmet in England existed here in Transylvania. Thus he would be led by degrees into a frame of mind receptive to the real truth about myself and vampires as a race.

What I had not reckoned with was the—in this case—damnable English propensity for minding one's own business, which in my opinion Harker carried to lengths of great absurdity, even for a discreet and tactful young solicitor. There he sat, upon the exposed seat of my caleche, watching my antics with the cairns but saying nothing. He called out at last only when the wolves, my adopted children of the night, came from the darkness of the forest shadows into the moonlight close around the carriage, staring silently at him and at the nervous horses. And when I came back from marking my last trove of the evening, and with a gesture moved the wolves away and broke their circle, Harker still had no questions, though I could sense his stiffness when I climbed into the driver's seat again, and knew that he was quite afraid. Harker's tenseness did not ease during the remainder of our ride, which ended when I drove into "the courtyard of a vast ruined castle, from whose tall black windows came no ray of light, and whose broken battlements showed a jagged line against the moonlit sky," as he was shortly to describe my home.

I left Harker and his baggage at the massive, closed front door and drove the horses on back to the stables, where I roused with a kick the least undependable of my snoring servants to take care of them. Ridding myself on the way of false beard, hat, and livery, I sprinted back through the clammy lower passages of Castle Dracula to resume my own identity and welcome in my guest.

As I paused in the corridor outside the rooms I had made ready for his lodging there came into the dark air beside me a shimmering that would have been invisible to eyes any less attuned to darkness than my own; came voices tuneful as computer music and no more human; came the substantiation in the air of faces three and bodies three, all young in appearance and female in every rich detail, save that they wore without demur their clothes a century out of date. Not Macbeth on his moor ever saw three shapes boding more ill to men.

"Is he come?" asked Melisse, the taller of the dark pair of the three.

"How soon may we taste him?" Wanda, the shorter, fuller-breasted one inquired. With the corner of her smiling ruby lips she chewed and sucked a ringlet of her raven hair.

"When will you give him to us, Vlad? You've

promised us, you know." This from Anna, radiantly fair, the senior of the three in terms of length of time spent in my service. *Service* is not the right word, though. Say rather in terms of her endurance in a game of wit and will, which all three played against me without stop, and which I had wearied of and ceased to play long decades since.

I strode into the rooms I had prepared for Harker, poked up the hearth fire previously laid and lit, moved dishes that had been warming on the hearthstone to the table, and sent words over my shoulder into the dim hallway outside. "I've promised you just one thing in the matter of the young Englishman, and I'll repeat it once: If any of you set lip against his skin you'll have cause to regret it."

Melisse and Wanda giggled, I suppose at having irritated me and having gotten me to repeat an order; and Anna as always must try to get the last word in. "But there must be some sport, at least. If he stray out of his rooms then surely he shall be fair game?"

I made no answer—it has never been my way to argue with subordinates—but saw that all was in readiness for Harker, as far as I could make it so. Then, an antique silver lamp in hand, I dashed down to the front door, which I threw open hospitably, to reveal my now-doubtful guest still standing waiting in the night, his bags on the ground beside him.

"Welcome to my house!" I cried. "Enter freely and of your own will!" He smiled at me, this trusting alien, accepting me as nothing more nor less than man. In my happiness I repeated my

14

welcome as soon as he had crossed the threshold, and clasped his hand perhaps a little harder than I ought. "Come freely!" I enjoined him. "Go safely, and leave something of the happiness you bring!"

"Count Dracula?" Harker, trying to unobtrusively shake life back into his painfully pressed fingers, spoke questioningly, as if there might still be some reasonable doubt.

"I am Dracula," I answered, bowing. "And I bid you welcome, Mr. Harker, to my house. Come in, the night air is chill and you must need to eat and rest." I hung my lamp on the wall and went to pick up Harker's luggage, overriding his protests. "Nay, sir, you are my guest. It is late and my people are not available. Let me see to your comfort myself." He followed as I carried his things upstairs and to the quarters I had prepared for him. One log fire flamed in the room where the table was spread for supper, and another in the large bedroom where I deposited his bags.

With my own hands I had prepared the supper that awaited him—roast chicken, salad, cheese, and wine—as I did most of the meals that he consumed during the weeks of his stay. Help from the girls? Bah. They affected to be like infants, who can sometimes be stopped from doing wrong by threat of punishment but cannot be forced to do things properly. It was part of the game they played with me. Besides, I did not want them ever in his rooms if I could help it.

So with my own hands, hands of a prince of Walachia, the brother-in-law of a king, I picked up and threw away his dirty dishes and his garbage, not to mention innumerable porcelain chamber pots. I suppose I could have brought myself to scrub the dishes clean, like any menial, had there been no easier way. True, most of the dishes were gold, but I was determined not to stint on my guest's entertainment. Also, should I ever return to the castle from my projected sojourn abroad, I had little doubt of being able to recover the golden utensils from the foot of the three-hundred-meter precipice which Castle Dracula overlooked and which provided an eminently satisfactory garbage dump. The dishes would be there, dented by the fall no doubt, but cleansed by the seasons and unstolen. I have always had a dislike of thieves, and I believe the people of the villages nearby understood me on this point, if probably on nothing else.

In the month and a half that he was with me my increasingly ungrateful guest went through a sultan's ransom in gold plate, and I was reduced to serving him on silver. Toward the end, of course, I might have brought his food on slabs of bark, and he would scarcely have noticed it, so terrified was he by then at certain peculiarities of my nature. He misinterpreted these oddities, but never asked openly for any explanation, whilst I, wisely or unwisely, never volunteered one.

But to return to that first evening. When my guest had refreshed himself from his journey and rejoined me in the dining room he found me leaning against the fireplace and awaiting him in eagerness, as hungry for intelligent conversation and first-hand news of the great outer world as he was for good food.

I gestured him to the table, saying: "I pray you, be seated and sup how you please. You will, I trust, excuse me that I do not join you; but I have dined already, and I do not sup.''

Whilst Harker attacked the chicken I read through the letter he had handed me. It was from his employer, Hawkins, who described his young deputy as "full of energy and talent in his own way, and of a very faithful disposition," and also as "discreet and silent."

This was all to my liking and I at once began a conversation that went on in the dining room for hours, as Harker ate and then accepted a cigar. We discoursed mainly on the circumstances of his journey—I was particularly interested in trains, which at that time I had never seen, and I enjoyed our talk immensely.

Toward dawn a companionable silence fell between us, broken shortly by the howling, from down the valley, of many wolves.

"Listen to them," I said, for a moment unthinking. "The children of the night. What music they make!" A momentary look of consternation came into my guest's face; I had forgotten that only a few hours earlier, as I in my guise of coachman brought him up the winding mountain road, he had seen wolves at disturbingly close range.

I quickly added: "Ah, sir, you dwellers in the city cannot enter into the feelings of the hunter." And shortly we took our separate ways to rest.

Not having gone to bed till dawn, and being wearied from his journey, Harker naturally slept until late in the day, and as I thought would not have been surprised not to see or hear from me until after sunset. When I looked for him at that hour I was briefly alarmed at not finding him in his own rooms. I had not wished to shatter the spell of that first evening of human society by trying to explain to him how dangerous to him certain parts of the castle could be.

To my relief, he had strayed no farther than my nearby library, where to his "great delight," as he recorded in his journal, he discovered "a vast number of English books . . . magazines, and newspapers . . . the books were of the most varied kind—history, geography, politics, political economy, botany, geology, law—all relating to England and English life and customs and manners."

"I am glad you found your way in here," I said with honesty, "for I am sure there is much that will interest you. These companions"—I gestured at the books—"have been good friends to me, and for some years, ever since I had the idea of going to London, have given me many, many hours of pleasure. Through them I have come to know your great England; and to know her is to love her. I long to go through the crowded streets of your mighty London, to be in the midst of the rush and whirl of humanity, to share its life, its change, its death, and all that makes it what it is. But alas! as yet I know your tongue only through books. To you, my friend, I look that I know it to speak."

"But, Count," Harker expostulated, "you know and speak English thoroughly!"

"I thank you, my friend," I responded, "for your all too flattering estimate, but yet I fear that I am but a little way on the road I would travel. True, I know the grammar and the words, but yet I know not how to speak them."

"Indeed, sir, you speak excellently."

"Not so. Did I move and speak in your London, none there are who would not know me for a stranger. And that is not enough for me. Here I am noble; I am boyar; the common people know me and I am master. But a stranger in a strange land, he is no one: men know him not—and to know not is to care not for. I am content if I am like the rest, so that no man stops if he sees me, or pauses in his speaking if he hears my words, 'Ha ha! a stranger!' I have been so long master that I would be master still, or at least that none other should be master of me. You come to me not alone as agent of my friend Peter Hawkins of Exeter, to tell me all about my new estate in London. You shall, I trust, rest here with me awhile, so that by our talking I may learn the English intonation; and I would that you tell me when I make error, even of the smallest, in my speaking. I am sorry that I had to be away so long today, but you will, I know, forgive one who has so many important affairs in hand."

Harker pledged his willingness to help me with my English and then asked if he might use the library at will. This seemed like a good time to issue my warnings, so I said:

"Yes, certainly. You may go anywhere you wish in the castle, except where the doors are locked, where of course you will not wish to go. There is reason that all things are as they are, and did you see with my eyes and know with my knowledge you would perhaps better understand."

"I am sure I would, sir."

But I knew that he could not begin to understand, as yet, and I tried to press the point, still without giving away too much. "We are in Transylvania, and Transylvania is not England. Our ways are not your ways, and there shall be to you many strange things. Nay, from what you have told me of your experiences already, you know something of what strange things there may be."

Thus having led the conversation into the murky region of Strange Things, and seeing my guest nodding soberly in apparent agreement, I momentarily hesitated, on the brink of trying to Tell All; but no, I decided, I must first make Harker my good friend.

He now took the opportunity to ask what I could tell him of the mysterious blue flames that he had glimpsed on the night of his arrival, and about the odd behavior of the "coachman." In reply I told him a substantial portion of the truth.

"Transylvania is not England," I repeated, "and there are things here which reasonable men, men of business and science, may not be able to understand. On a certain night of the year—last night, in fact, when all evil spirits were supposed by the peasantry to rule unchecked—a blue flame is seen over any place where treasure has been concealed. That much treasure has been concealed in this region, there can be but little doubt; for this is ground fought over for centuries by the Walachian, the Saxon, and the Turk. Why, there is hardly a foot of soil hereabouts that has not been enriched by the blood of patriots and invaders." Speaking of the past began to bring it back to me, as it does now; again I felt the movement of the warhorse beneath me as his ears picked up the sounds of battle, the clash of metal and the cries of terror. Again I smell the stinks of war; and see the banners and the blood. I remem-

THE DRACULA TAPE

ber the treachery of the boyars, and recall the beautiful, beautiful loyalty to me, the *voivode*, warlord, of the men who worked the land and knew me to be fair. How good it was to breathe the air with them . . . but never mind.

To Harker I went on: "In old days there were stirring times, when the Austrian and the Hungarian came up in hordes, and the patriots went out to meet them—men and women, the aged and the children too—and awaited their coming on the rocks above the passes, that they might sweep destruction on them with artificial avalanches. When the invader was triumphant he found but little in the way of gold or precious stuff, for all had been sheltered in the friendly soil."

Harker was now at least halfway to believing the tiny marvel of the flames and treasure. "But how," he asked, "can treasure have remained so long undiscovered when there is a sure index to it if men will but take the trouble to look?"

I smiled. "Because your peasant is at heart a coward and a fool!" The villagers below in 1891, I had in mind. "These flames only appear on one night, and on that night no man of this land will, if he can help it, stir without his doors."

We drifted into other matters, and back at last to real estate.

"Come," I enjoined my guest, "tell me of London and the house which you have procured for me." Whilst Harker was getting his business papers together in another room I took the chance to clear the table of his latest meal, linen cloth and all in a bundle a-down the cliffside from a western window, where for a thousand feet the

21

soiled dishes sang in air before the garbage was knocked off them on the rocks. By the time he rejoined me I had lit the lamps and was lying on a sofa reading *Bradshaw's Guide.*

The paperwork connected with house buying was complex but Harker seemed competent to lead me through its mysteries. He remarked once on my knowledge of the estate's neighborhood— that of Purfleet, some fifteen miles east of the center of London, on the north bank of the Thames—which I had managed to gain even from my remote location, and I replied: "Well, but, my friend, is it not needful that I should? When I go there I shall be all alone, and my friend Harker Jonathan—nay, pardon me, I fall into my country's habit of putting your patronymic first— my friend Jonathan Harker will not be at my side to correct and aid me. He will be in Exeter, a hundred miles and more away, probably working at papers of the law with my other friend, Peter Hawkins. So!"

I signed what seemed innumerable papers, which were then wrapped for posting back to Hawkins. My gypsies, *Szgany* as I called them then, were at the castle frequently, and through both fear and loyalty they were, in what touched my own person, most dependable. They carried mail for me, as well as bringing me horses and caring for them. They brought me food sometimes—I will discourse of my eating habits later—and formed for a long time a useful although shaky bridge twixt me and other men.

When we were done with signing and mailing Harker read to me his notes describing my new estate and how he had located it. I remember the description well, as I remember the rest of my enemies' journals for that year. I am not likely to forget a word.

"At Purfleet, on a by-road, I came across just such a place as seemed to be required, and where was displayed a dilapidated notice that the place was for sale. It is surrounded by a high wall, of ancient structure, built of heavy stones, and has not been repaired for a large number of years. The closed gates are of heavy old oak and iron, all eaten with rust.

"The estate is called Carfax, no doubt a corruption of the old *Quatre Face*, as the house is four-sided, agreeing with the cardinal points of the compass. It contains in all some twenty acres, quite surrounded by the stone wall above mentioned. There are many trees on it, which make it in places gloomy, and there is a deep, dark-looking pond or small lake, evidently fed by some springs, as the water is clear and flows away in a fair-sized stream. The house is very large and of all periods back, I should say, to medieval times, for one part is of stone immensely thick, with only a few windows high up and heavily barred with iron. It looks like part of a keep, and is close to an old chapel or church. I could not enter it, as I had not the key of the door leading to it from the house, but I have taken with my Kodak views of it from various points. There are but few houses close at hand, one being a very large house only recently added to and formed into a private lunatic asylum. It is not, however, visible from the grounds." This last was not an accurate statement, as I later discovered; but of course I was ready to make a few allowances for salesmen's puffery.

"I am glad that it is old and big," I said when he

had finished his description. "I myself am of an old family, and to live in a new house would kill me. A house cannot be made habitable in a day; and, after all, how few days go to make up a century. I rejoice also that there is a chapel of old times. . . . I am no longer young and my heart, through weary years of mourning over the dead, is not attuned to mirth. . . . I love the shade and the shadow, and would be alone with my thoughts when I may."

We spent a long evening, similar to the last; and this, the night of May seventh to eighth, 1891, was the last for a long time, many months, when either of us felt that things were going well, indeed, when we were not pondering each other as enemies, at least in potential.

I had naturally taken the precaution of removing all mirrors from the rooms of the castle that I expected my guest to occupy or visit. On the third morning of Harker's stay, however, I entered his room early in the hours of daylight—an uncomfortable time for me—to find him shaving with the aid of his traveling mirror.

It had been a conceit of mine that when I began to be fully and unquestioningly accepted in the normal world as human, the psychology of most men and women would not permit them to credit the objective fact that I cast no reflection in a mirror, at least none ordinarily perceptible to the human eye. Let me say here parenthetically that film and the cathode ray tube are something else again. But whatever the outcome of research along this line is to be, on that morning I had deluded myself into thinking that this reasonable, unsuperstitious Englishman would not be allowed by his own psychology to perceive the exact truth: that when I entered the room behind him as he shaved, my figure cast no reflection in the glass.

I was wrong. When I said, "Good morning!" almost in his ear, he was so startled that he reacted physically and his straight razor made a slight cut on his chin. At the same time I was made aware that he had indeed noted my image's absence from the mirror, for he alternated his glance from me to it not once but several times whilst he struggled not to let his bafflement show on his face. This was a blow to me, the first indication that my plans were indeed impossible, and it hit me hard, though I struggled to maintain composure.

After a moment Harker gave up looking for me in his glass, returned my greeting in a flustered way, then put his razor down and began to look for some sticking plaster in his kit. His chin was beading blood.

Hemophile that I am known to be (in the true sense of the word), it is not true that the mere sight of blood under any and all circumstances is enough to trip me into a paroxysm of lust for the good red stuff. According to Harker's journal, which is unforgettable to me and from which I quote verbatim, my "eyes blazed with a sort of demoniac fury" as soon as I saw his blood, and I "suddenly made a grab" at his throat.

Now I ask you—you enjoy a good rare beefsteak, perhaps? Naturally. Now, suppose you stroll into the dining room where a guest of yours is finishing his lunch, and observe a morsel of meat left on his plate. Does the sight make your eyes blaze with demoniac fury? Or suppose that under circumstances of perfect propriety one guest in your house is a young lady, an attractive one, let us say. And suppose further that through some truly innocent mistake upon her part or yours you open a door and discover her unclad— are you so automatically provoked that you literally make a grab at her, without thought for the consequences? No more am I provoked in comparable situation. Great heaven, if male hemoglobin were all that I desired I should hardly have gone to all the trouble and expense of buying an estate in London so they should send me a ruddy young solicitor.

There was, as always—I admit it—a certain pang of longing at the sight of blood. But it was concern for Harker's welfare, nothing else, that prompted me to reach out a hand in the direction of the wound. The bitter shock of realization that he had noticed my absence from the mirror was augmented severely at the moment when my outstretched hand brushed the open collar of his shirt, and just beneath it touched the string of beads which an old woman in Bistrita had forced upon him when she learned his destination.

String of beads? Of course at the moment I discovered them I knew they were a rosary, and at its end I knew the cross was hung. And since I had already learned in one of our conversations that Harker was a staunch Protestant, an English Churchman as he put it, there was but one interpretation that I could put upon his wearing of a crucifix—he had acquired it, or at least it had been thrust upon him and accepted, as armor for his journey into a vampire's lair.

I, who had begun to think of myself as already accepted by society, had my fool's hopes dashed before they were well launched. In the moments before I could get them off the ground again, and counsel myself to patience, I behaved rashly. My first impulse was to tear the beads from around his neck but reverence held me back from that—I am a Catholic myself, you know, though born into the Orthodox faith, and in my days of breathing I endowed five monasteries. With a moment in which to reflect I realized the injustice of an assault upon the person of Harker, an ignorant, well-meaning youth who doubtless did not understand fully the implications of the good-luck charm he had been given to wear.

"Take care," said I, whilst struggling to master my anger and disappointment, "take care how you cut yourself, for it is more dangerous than you think in this country." I had in mind Anna, Wanda, and Melisse, whose reaction to the sight and scent of fresh young male blood was sure to be much less restrained than my own. "And this is the thing that has done the mischief!" I cried out, forced by the strains upon my soul to take *some* kind of violent action, and seizing on the symbol of my alienation as its object. "It is a foul bauble of man's vanity. Away with it!" I wrenched open the heavy window and threw out Harker's shaving glass, to be splintered by the fall to the courtyard.

Not trusting myself to say more at the moment, I left the room. My months and years of careful, meticulous preparation, had they all gone for nothing? Would Harker carry home the truth and the terrible lies about me, all mixed up, and find a way to make them all believed? Would I arrive on the quay at Whitby, or in Charing Cross station in London, and find exorcist priests and stinking garlic-mongers drawn up in a phalanx to repel me?

Whilst I, on that fateful morning, was trying to regain my composure and rethink my plans, Harker, as he records in his journal, began a rather panicky exploration of those parts of the castle not sealed off from him by locked doors: finding a great many of the latter, he at once adopted the idea that he was a prisoner.

Not that he ever told me so straight out, or plainly asked me if it were true. As he wrote: ". . . it is no use making my ideas known to the count. He knows well that I am imprisoned; and as he has done it himself, and has doubtless his own motives for it, he would only deceive me if I trusted him fully with the facts. . . . I am, I know, either being deceived, like a baby, by my own fears, or else I am in desperate straits."

A little later Harker returned to his room, as I was making his bed, and we exchanged a few polite words, neither of us alluding to the incident of the shaving mirror. Later, in the evening, my spirits rose again, for my young visitor sat down with me to chat as usual, and began to question me on the history of my land and of my family.

He understands, I thought, at least he begins to understand, and he does not prejudge me, but continues to greet me and speak to me as a friend. It was all true, then! True, what I had heard and read, of the noble English respect for the private affairs of every man! Though it had seemed to me earlier that Harker carried this tradition of respect too far, now I saw how valuable such an attitude could be for my purposes.

Pacing the floor and pulling my mustache in excitement, I spoke of the glorious history of my family and my race; of Viking ancestors come down from Iceland to mate and mingle with the Huns, whose warlike fury had swept the earth like a living flame "until," I cried, "the dying peoples held that in their veins ran the blood of those old witches, who, expelled from Scythia, had mated with the devils in the desert. Fools, fools! What devil or witch was ever so great as Attila, whose blood is in these veins?" And I held up my arms—like this.

"Is it a wonder," I went on, "that we were a conquering race; that we were proud; that when the Magyar, the Lombard, the Avar, the Bulgar, or the Turk poured his thousands on our frontiers, we drove them back?" I recounted with love and joy the feats of the decades of my own breathing life: "Who was it but one of my own race who crossed the Danube and beat the Turk on his own ground? This was a Dracula indeed! Who, when he was beaten back, came again, and again, and again, though he had to come alone from the bloody field where his troops were being slaughtered, since he knew that he alone could ultimately triumph! They said that he thought only of himself. Bah! What good are peasants without a leader? Where ends the war without a brain and heart to conduct it? Again, after the battle of Mohacs, we threw off the Hungarian yoke, and we of the Dracula blood were amongst the leaders, for our spirit would not brook that we were not free. Ah, young sir, the Szekelys—the very name means 'guardians of the frontier'—and the Dracula as their hearts' blood, their brains, and their swords—can boast a record that mushroom growths like the Hapsburgs and the Romanoffs can never reach. But now the warlike days are over. Blood is too precious a thing in these days of dishonorable peace; and the glories of the great races are as a tale that is told."

I raved and praised myself, as I say, and my little Englishman was tolerant of it all, but he was dull, dull, dull. A brooder, but no dreamer, he. There was no imagination in him to be fired. But then to be honest I must admit that with more imagination he might have fared even worse in Castle Dracula than he did.

On the next evening, that of May eleventh, I had a last lengthy discussion with Harker on the conduct of business affairs in England, which concluded by my asking him to write some letters home.

I inquired: "Have you written since your first letter to our friend Mr. Peter Hawkins, or to any other?"

"I have not," he answered, some bitterness audible in his voice, "as I have not yet had opportunity of sending letters to anybody."

"Then write now, my young friend," I said, putting a conciliatory hand on his shoulder. "Write to our friend Hawkins and to any other, and say, if it will please you, that you shall stay with me until a month from now."

"Do you wish me to stay so long?" His lack of enthusiasm at the prospect could not be concealed. He was obviously brooding upon some difficulties of his own, but I still had high hopes of being able to win him over.

"I desire it much," I said. "Nay, I will take no refusal. When your master, employer, what you will, engaged that someone should come on his behalf, it was understood that my needs only were to be consulted. I have not stinted. Is it not so?"

He acquiesced with a silent bow, but had on such a troubled face that I knew I had better take an interest in the contents of the letters he sent out. I therefore added: "I pray you, my good young friend, that you will not discourse of things other than business in your letters, except of course that it will doubtless please your friends to know that you are well, and that you look forward to getting home to them. Is it not so?"

On taking my leave of him that evening, with his letters in my hands along with some correspondence of my own relating to my projected trip, I paused at the door, my conscience somewhat troubled.

"I trust you will forgive me," I said—Harker only looked up, his face closed against me—and I went on, "but I have much work to do in private this evening." Our larder was depleted. "You will, I hope, find all things as you wish." He continued to be sulky, and I had a strong premonition of plans going wrong, trouble just ahead.

Before going out I added, "Let me advise you, my dear young friend—nay, let me warn you with all seriousness—that should you leave these rooms you will not by any chance go to sleep in any other part of the castle. It is old and has many memories, and there are bad dreams for those who sleep unwisely. Be warned! Should sleep ever be like to overcome you, then haste to your own chamber or to these rooms, for your rest will then be safe. But if you are not careful in this respect, then—" And I finished my speech with a hand-washing motion. Still he only continued to look at me, a dour and increasingly frightened man.

And that, of course, was the night on which he happened to see me leave the castle. Why, on that particular spring night, did I choose to crawl head first down the wall above the precipice, rather than fly out unnoticeably in the form of a bat, walk less terrifyingly on four legs, or even expectably on two? I can only answer that my various physical forms and modes of locomotion have each their own comforts and discomforts, their pleasures and predicaments; besides, if truth must be told—and that is why I am here, is it not, speaking into this machine?—I was trying to avoid Anna, with her ceaseless pleading to be allowed to sample Harker's blood, and thought a climbing egress from the castle best calculated to serve that end.

And so poor Jonathan, by chance gazing from a window out into the moonlight, observed me, as he wrote, "emerge from (another) window and begin to crawl down the castle wall over that dreadful abyss, *face down* with his cloak spreading out around him like great wings . . . it could be no delusion. I saw the fingers and toes grasp the corners of the stones"—my boots I had tied by their laces to my belt—"just as a lizard moves along a wall. What manner of man is this, or what manner of creature is it in the semblance of a man?"

Three nights later Harker saw me leave again by the same means, and when I was absent he attempted to get out of the castle by the main entrance. I had left the door securely locked, for his own good, and he turned away, baffled, to seek another exit.

A door that I had neglected to fasten quite securely led him into the west wing. This was, he surmised, "the portion of the castle occupied by the ladies in bygone days." He was led to this conclusion by the presence of "great windows . . . and consequently light and comfort" here where "sling, or bow, or culverin could not reach" because of the height and steepness of the cliffs below. Here he supposed that "of old, ladies had sat and sung and lived sweet lives whilst their gentle breasts were sad for their menfolk away in the midst of remorseless wars." Fortunately the ladies of old were, like those of his own time, somewhat tougher and more capable than he ever gave them credit for being. His understanding of this point would have made a great difference, not only in his life but in my own. But I am getting ahead of my story.

Having forced his way into these closed-off rooms, Harker for a while admired their spacious, moonlit windows, and the furniture, which had "more air of comfort" than any he had seen elsewhere in the castle. Although he found in the suite "a dread loneliness" which chilled his heart, "still it was better than living alone in the rooms which I had come to hate from the presence of Count Dracula, and after trying a little to school my nerves, I found a soft quietude come over me.''

Of course, notwithstanding my most solemn warnings, the clodpate schooled his nerves until he fell asleep. I returned in time to save him, though barely, and even I was struck speechless for a moment by the extent of his folly.

Without even putting down the burden with which I had reentered the castle, I listened for his breathing in his own rooms and heard it not; then I sped, faster and faster, through the dark corridors, looking and listening for my guest, with ever-growing concern. When I found the open door to the west wing, which I had thought securely locked, I could only pray that I was not too late.

Barely in time for him, I say, I came upon them, in a chamber thick with moonlight that laid enchantment upon the prosaic ruin wrought by time, Harker supine upon an ancient couch, where he had lain down oblivious to the dust. Wanda and Melisse stood at a little distance, biding their time, waiting their turns, whilst over him crouched fair Anna, who had actually laid the pinpoints of her canines upon his throat. I came in man-form up beside her and put my hand around that fair white neck of hers; raised her soft body that had in it the strength of ten good normal men and hurled her staggering back, halfway across the room.

I shot a glance down at Harker and saw that his vessels had not yet been tapped. He was nearly unconscious at the time, in sleep and trance commingled; lips half parted in a fatuous smile and a sliver of eyeball gleaming beneath each sagging lid. Hoping that he would not remember this scene upon the morrow, or would recall it only as a dream, I held my voice to a whisper despite my rage.

"How dare you touch him, any of you? How dare you cast eyes on him when I have forbidden it? Back, I tell you all! This man belongs to me! Beware how you meddle with him, or you'll have to deal with me."

Fair Anna, no doubt aching with frustration at being robbed of her delight when it had seemed so certain, let out a sick and bitter laugh and dared to answer back: "You yourself never loved; you never love!" And in her laughter the other women joined, when they saw I had not moved at once to punish her.

"Yes, I too can love," I answered softly. And in that moment my thoughts went back to a far different world, a world once sunlit and alive within that castle, within that very chamber that now held only dust and mold and ruin beneath the glamor of the moon.

But that world held in my memory was none of theirs, nor did I mean to give them material for mockery. "Yes, I can love," I said. "You yourselves can tell it from the past. Is it not so? Well, now I promise you that when I am done with him you shall kiss him at your will. Now go, go! I must awaken him, for there is work to be done." These lies I told to be rid of the women without punishing them. I had no real wish to punish them for Harker's stupidity. I dislike cruelty, and am not cruel unless it is quite justifiable.

"Are we to have nothing tonight?" Melisse

whined, pointing to the bag that I had brought, which now lay moving slightly on the floor. It contained the relatively poor results of my foraging expedition—a rather lean pig offered up to me by a peasant woman in hopes of my doing, in return, some damnable evil upon one of her rivals in love. I nodded, and the women sprang to surround the bag, and bore it away with them.

At this a faint gasp issued from Harker's recumbent form. I looked round sharply and could now be sure that he was quite dead to the world. What I did not then know was that he had witnessed the women pouncing upon my shopping bag, and had interpreted the porcine squealing therefrom, if his "ears did not deceive" him, as "a gasp and a low wail, as of a half-smothered child." My unimaginative solicitor had fainted.

Needless to say, there was no possibility of doing business with him that night, even if I had been so minded. I carried him, still oblivious to the world, back to his room and put him to bed; it was still my hope that he might interpret his evening with the girls as a mere nightmare if he remembered it at all. I also took the liberty of going through his pockets, and got my first look at his journal. But it was kept in shorthand, a code I did not understand until much later, and after pondering briefly I left the little book where I had found it.

"If I be sane," he wrote in it the next day, "then surely it is maddening to think that of the foul things that lurk in this hateful place the count is the least dreadful to me; that to him alone can I look for safety, even though this be only whilst I serve his purpose." And it had been my thought that, should he remember anything of the moon-lit horrors he had so narrowly escaped, he would upon waking bless me as his protector and friend. Alas, for my innocent and long-persisting faith in human nature.

I began to realize that my problem was no longer so much how to win Harker's friendship as it was what to do with him, or do about him. Were I to send him home at once, he must at the very least have some strange stories to tell about me when he got there. My own departure was scheduled for June thirtieth, still more than a month away, and Harker could easily be back in London within a week, there to prepare for me a reception of the most unpleasant kind. His knowledge of my business affairs in England was so great that I could not hope to avoid such an outcome if he left Castle Dracula as my enemy and were given a head start. At the same time, he was as yet my guest, my responsibility, and honor and justice alike forbade that I should do him any harm. I yearned that he would either come out with open accusations to which I might openly reply, and demand his freedom if he minded the locked doors, or else that he would show himself my enemy, in order that I could justly kill him.

We came near reaching the latter solution when I discovered that he was attempting to smuggle out a secret letter. It was addressed to his fiancée, Miss Mina Murray, to whom he had written openly at my request only the day before. Harker threw this clandestine letter, along with another one, addressed to Hawkins, out the window along with gold, to some of my gypsys, who of course brought the letters to my attention.

The secret letter to Hawkins was very brief, and merely asked him to communicate with Mina Murray; but the letter to her was written in code, the same shorthand as Harker's secret journal. When I had examined it I came near going to his rooms to do him violence. I had to remind myself forcibly that my guest was still my guest, that he was in strange circumstances for an ordinary, untraveled Englishman, and that I did not really know that the coded missive contained anything untruthful about me or meant to cause me harm.

Still, I was angry. Rarely had I been so angry since the day I nailed the Turkish envoys' turbans to their heads when they refused to doff them for me. Remind me to tell you about that later. But in my greatest angers I show outward calm. Taking the two letters, I went to Harker's room and sat down beside him. He looked up at me with the guilty, hopeless, haggard look that now grew worse upon his face with every day.

"The *Szgany* have given me these," I began steadily. "Of which, though I know not whence they come, I will of course take care. See!"—and I reopened one letter—"one is from you, and to my friend Peter Hawkins; the other"—and I pulled from its envelope the one in code—"is a vile thing, an outrage upon friendship and hospitality! It is not signed. Well! So it cannot matter to us." And then and there I burned it, in the flame of Harker's lamp . . . ah, I really do not care for electric light.

"The letter to Hawkins," I continued, "I shall of course send on, since it is yours. Your letters are sacred to me. Your pardon, my friend, that unknowingly I did break the seal." I handed Harker the letter and a fresh envelope, and watched him as he addressed and sealed the message anew. There was in his face such despair, with a nervous twitching at cheek and eye, there was such a tremor in the fingers with which he tried to write, that my sensibilities were touched and I was glad I had not been more severe.

I had at that time been a frequent observer of human beings under stress for more than four hundred years, and it was plain to me that Harker now teetered on the brink of mental breakdown. This was regrettable in itself, and also I felt at least some indirect responsibility; yet all the same I felt as if a weight had been lifted from my shoulders. With any luck he was going to be a couple of months in a sanatorium after he left my domain, and no one would believe vampire tales from the mouth of one whose mental scales so obviously had tipped.

Hawkins might call upon me at Purfleet, I supposed, and perhaps Harker's much beloved Miss Mina Murray, too—her name had something interesting about it for me, even then—to see what might have happened in the Carpathians to upset the poor boy so. And I would be concerned and gracious, and would entertain them, for which purpose I meant to have my estate in part at least, renovated according to modern standards of comfort. By the time Harker had managed to make his stories credible, if he did not prudently choose instead to alter or disavow them, I should have managed to establish new

English sanctuaries for myself, even to alter my appearance, and I might well be able to get beyond the reach of any investigation launched.

Meanwhile, there were the three predated letters I had wisely obtained from Harker a few days earlier, by making up some story for him about the uncertainty of posts. They were chatty, innocuous reports of good health and a pleasant journey, ostensibly written by him on the twelfth, the nineteenth, and the twenty-ninth of June, the third dated from Bistrita rather than from the castle. I had got these letters in anticipation of some unhappy ending to Harker's visit, and now my foresight was proven wise. If for some reason he failed to arrive home in good health, suspicion would be shifted from me.

When I took the readdressed—and now harmless—letter to Hawkins back to the gypsies to be posted, I informed the leader of their band that my guest was becoming *non compos mentis* and that we should all have to take good care of him. Tatra, a swarthy, compact man who could meld into a centaur with his horse, for some reason received this news with little surprise.

"On the day after I am gone, Tatra," I added, "I charge you to put on the coachman's uniform and drive him down to the Pass, so that he may in good time board there the diligence for Bistrita, where he may regain the railroad. Obey his orders or requests in any small matters that seem reasonable; nay, in anything that will not be dangerous for him. It is not his fault that he has suffered here, or at least not his alone."

Tatra bowed and swore that he would do as the master wished; I hoped silently that it was so.

My own mood was brighter than it had been for some days when I returned to Harker's rooms, unlocked his door—I had begun to fear he might do something truly rash—and went in, to find him asleep upon a sofa. He roused when I entered and looked up at me with haggard wariness. He looked almost too worn to be afraid.

"So, my friend, you are tired?" I asked, briskly rubbing my hands. "Get to bed. There is the surest rest. I may not have the pleasure to talk tonight, since there are many labors to me"—my stock of provisions for him was far depleted, he having consumed the greater part of the pig whose squeals had so alarmed him earlier—"but you will sleep, I pray."

He got up like a sleepwalker and went into his bedroom, where he threw himself face down upon the covers. Shortly he was indeed asleep again—as he wrote in his journal the next day, "despair has its own calms"—and I took the opportunity of removing his papers, money, and so on from his apartments for safekeeping. I also borrowed his best suit of clothes, so that some of the gypsy women might try their hand at preparing for me garments more in the English style, with Harker's as a pattern.

This task took them a couple of weeks, but I was able to wear the finished product when I left upon another provisioning errand on the night of June sixteenth. I wished to try my new clothes' fit and durability. Only much later, when the chance came for me to read Harker's journal in type-script, did I understand that he had spied on me again that night, and had imagined that I was wearing his own suit as I crawled down the wall—for the purpose, if you will believe it, of blackening his reputation; that "any wickedness" which I might do to the local people should be attributed to him. No, Mr. Harker, I assure you—can you hear me now, from your presumed post in heaven above?—other matters which I judged more important than besmirching your name were claiming all my energies. "Great God!" some yokel doubtless exclaimed upon that night, when he beheld my tall figure, white-haired, white-mustached, red-eyed, and decked out for Savile Row. "There goes the vampire in the clothes of the young Englishman. He must have eaten him."

Scarcely had I completed my night's labors and come back to Castle Dracula—lugging in my straining bag a newborn calf to give my girls some blood, and provide for my guest a taste of veal—when that poor woman from the nearest village came to the castle pleading for my help. That poor, brave woman whose face I never saw; not one in a thousand down there would have dared so much in bright sunshine, let alone the middle of the night. But the commands of motherhood give wonderous strength sometimes.

"Master, find for me my child!" the poor wretch called up to Harker, whose moonlit appearance at a high window she mistook for my own. Yes, I know, I know very well, that in his journal he sets down her words as: "Monster, give me my child!" But do you suppose that she spoke English? Or that he had ready his "polyglot dictionary" that he had needed in the coach from Bistrita, to talk with these same folk?

For my part, I knew perfectly well that the

woman was there, without sticking my head out a window to see her. And I understood her words. Nor did I need to raise my voice to summon up a few pretty children of my own—the wolves— from a kilometer or two around. These set to work at my command. They combed the forest quickly and in the space of an hour had found the straying child. They herded it with nips and tugs into the courtyard, where the stupid woman—I suppose it was through some negligence of hers that the child had gotten lost—still beat her flabby hands upon my door, until she saw her infant come amid the howling escort. At that point she grabbed it up and ran for home, and small thanks I or my four-pawed rangers ever got. And Harker's book implies that, having stolen the child for my own snack, I then called up the wolves to eat the mother. . . .

Now I see in your eyes that this time you do not believe my version of the event at all. Well, and why should I not have helped her, as I helped a thousand others when I ruled as Prince? She came to me in my capacity of lord, and asked for help, and I was duty-bound to render it. That actions so elementary and right, on her part and on mine, must be verified and spelled out shows how far the world has fallen . . . but there, I now sound like an old man.

Still you doubt. You will insist on believing that I would rather drink a baby's blood than dandle it on my knee. And you are right, or would be, were those the only two courses of behavior from which I had to choose.

Very well. Now is as good a time as any, and we will discuss the drinking of the blood. You eat flesh. Do you eat that of man and woman? Maybe a playful love bite now and then, but not beyond that, hey? So, very approximately, the matter rests with me. My only material sustenance is blood, warm and preferably mammalian, but I am indifferent as to what species I use for nourishment. For now, take that as given. Later, if we have time, we will discuss how, as I believe, most of my needful energy comes to me by an as-yet-unmeasured radiation from the sun.

Another peculiarity of the vampirish existence is that the reproductive organs, along with other systems of excretion, cease to function; the body throws off neither seed nor waste. This is not to say that we are passionless; far from it. But whereas in breathing men and women there are many raging lusts—go without food two weeks, water two days, air two minutes, and see if I am using the wrong words—besides the lust for mere sexual activity, for us the blood is the life, the blood is all.

The love of women I have known all my life and for me its essence does not change. But its mode of expression had changed when I awoke from my mortal wounds of 1476. Since then, for me, the blood is all. Oh, I can do without the blood of sweet young women for two months, two years, two centuries, I suppose, if there were reason for such abstinence. I have told you that I never forced Lucy, or Mina, or any of the others.

But never mind. It was on the day following the poor village woman's visit that Harker, maddened by fear, dared to climb down the outside of the castle wall from his window, far enough to enter my own rooms. Then following an interior passage down to a lower chapel, he came upon the boxes of earth which I and my friends had been preparing for my journey. And snooping into the boxes, he found in one of them your obedient servant, resting. He might have destroyed me on the spot, had he been clever and malign enough, had his wits matched his foolhardy courage that let him dare that wall. For I, of course, was not aware at the time of his investigation.

The trance of daylight, which we usually—but not always—undergo between sunrise and sunset, actually marks, as I believe, our dependence upon the sun. As breathing men cannot healthfully engage in heavy exercise while eating and digesting food, we of the vampire persuasion are at best somewhat lethargic when in the presence of the sun; nor can any of us bear its unshielded rays for very long.

At any rate, he found me there, within the wooden box half full of soft, moist earth, in trance. The grip of this day-trance is hard to rouse from, as we shall see, and it is apt to be more open-eyed than common human sleep. We do not grow fatigued in the same sense that breathing humans do, yet eventually we must rest, and rest is possible only in the raw earth of the homeland. Why this is so I do not know; time later, maybe, for a theory or two of mine.

Not knowing what to make of my state, unbreathing, motionless, but somehow still undead as well, Harker went back to his rooms; nor, of course, did he mention his intrusion to me later. Four days later, on June twenty-ninth, my plans, and the labors of my helpers, were alike complete. In the late evening I went to Harker and said:

"Tomorrow, my friend, we must part. You return to your beautiful England and I go to some work which may have such an end that we will never meet again. Your last letter home has been dispatched; tomorrow I shall not be here, but all shall be ready for your journey. In the morning come the *Szgany*, who have some labors of their own here, and also come some Slovaks. When they have gone, my carriage shall come for you and bear you to the Borgo Pass to meet the diligence from Bukovina to Bistrita. But I am in hopes that I shall see more of you at Castle Dracula." Need I add that I was sometimes more diplomatic than truthful in my conversations with Harker? I most heartily wished never to lay eyes on him again.

My unexpected statement came to him as a shock, beyond a mere surprise. It had a tonic effect; he started to his feet, and I could see his modest store of wits returning whilst he summoned up reserves of courage to confront me, evidently a harder feat than scaling a sheer stone wall.

In a firm voice he finally asked, straight out: "Why may I not go tonight?"

"Because, my dear sir, my coachman and horses are away on a mission." In bald fact, Tatra, the only one of the *Szgany* whom I would have considered entrusting with a delicate mission out of my presence, was at that moment in a village of Bukovina, negotiating for a new horse; the three dear ladies of my household had drained a black stallion of its life the night before, and I expected the Slovaks and their dogs to munch the stallion's flesh upon the morrow.

Harker actually smiled, as if he had trapped me now—it was a smooth, soft, diabolical smile, if I may say so—and I feared from what I saw in his eyes that he was a little mad already, an expectable outcome of his long brooding over fears and doubts rather than having them out with me in open argument. He said: "But I would walk with pleasure; I want to get away at once."

"And your baggage?"

"I do not care about it. I can send for it some other time." When he had written about it in his journal, though, he had cared, accusing me of stealing his good suit and his overcoat and rug, as well as threatening his life and sanity. But now he stood firmly on his feet, looking for the first time in weeks like the confident and capable young man who had come to Castle Dracula in early May.

I sighed inwardly. I did not completely trust the *Szgany*, even Tatra, to carry out to the letter my instructions regarding Harker, not once I myself was boxed and shipped. So, I thought, why not take him at his word and let him walk down to the pass? The only real danger I foresaw was from wolves, and a word from me to some of them before he started would provide him with such an escort that his safety would be assured at least until he reached the domain of ordinary men, after which he would have to take his chances like the rest of us.

So let him walk, I thought, it is only a few kilometers down to the pass; and though the road was poor it did not branch and it went downhill nearly all the way. I suppose I assumed without thinking about it that he still had some money of his own in his pockets, along with the diary he still retained. I suppose also I really should not complain about the gold coin he stole from me on his departure, as I, or rather my household, was at the same time left in possession of a letter of credit, his best suit of clothes—which I had got a gypsy wench to clean, with lamentable result—and the overcoat and traveling rug mentioned earlier, along with railroad timetables, et cetera, et cetera.

I stood aside from the door of his room, relieved that my guest had finally plainly expressed his obvious desire to leave, and that I could accede to it so quickly and directly that his opinion of me was bound to be improved. I intended to press into his hands at the last moment a few weighty pieces of antique gold, as mementos of his visit. My grand, elaborate scheme was all going to work out after all, I thought. Once Harker had won back to reasonable human surroundings he would change his mind about what had actually happened under my roof, or change his story about it anyway. And going home might do him so much good that any mental breakdown could be avoided after all.

As Harker notes in his journal, it was at this point that I said to him, with a "sweet courtesy" that made him rub his eyes because "it seemed so real":

"You English have a saying which is close to my heart, for its spirit is that which rules our boyars: 'Welcome the coming, speed the departing guest.' Come with me, my dear young friend. Not an hour shall you wait in my house against your will, though sad am I at your going, and that you so suddenly desire it. Come!"

I took up a lamp and went ahead of Harker down the stairs, he following hesitantly, testing every footstep as if suspicious of some trap. Meanwhile, using that inner utterance with which I converse with animals, I summoned up to the castle the three or four wolves presently lurking in the woods not far below, which I intended should provide my visitor with safe conduct on his way. I meant to bring them in and introduce them to my guest and let them lick his hands and learn that he was to be treated with good will. They were howling in the courtyard by the time we reached the front door from inside, and as I began to open it they threw themselves into the widening gap. I stood in their way till I could calm them enough to make my wishes clear.

Their noise, however, and the sight of those fanged muzzles, red-tongued and slavering, extending under my arm as I stood in the doorway holding my children back, were too much for Harker. In his diary he credits me with the "diabolical wickedness" of wanting him eaten alive by the wolves, as well as plotting to have him drained of blood by the three women; two mutually exclusive fates, as it seems to me, beyond even the power of Count Dracula to inflict on the same victim.

"Shut the door!" he cried out, and I turned my head with some surprise to behold him sagging in despair against the wall, hands covering his face. "I shall wait till morning!"

Obviously, he was after all in no state to be allowed to wander on the mountainside at night. I was bitterly disappointed—with some violence I threw the last howling child out into the darkness, and slammed the great door shut—but I said nothing more to Harker then. In silence I walked with him back to the library, where I bade him a very brief goodnight. I did not know until I read his journal that later those three damnable women came to whisper seductive invitations outside his door, taunt him with their lipsmackings and their laughter, and even imitate my whispered voice in pretended dialogue with them thus: "Back, back, to your own place! Your time is not yet come. Wait! Have patience! Tonight is mine. Tomorrow night is yours!"

No, Jonathan Harker, if you can hear me, I suppose that I can hardly blame you for what you later did to me. Nor did I feel much pity for Melisse, Wanda, and fair Anna when Van Helsing the sadist eventually came calling. . . .

But I must adhere to the order of my story. On my last night before leaving Castle Dracula I supped full well, on bright beef blood—not from mere appetite, though I had that, but with a view to acquiring a more youthful look. Of course I had not seen my own face in a mirror for some four hundred years—it may be evidence of some benign plan for the world, that neither do I have a regular need to shave—but from certain words dropped now and then by my occasional companions, I had gathered that my recent appearance was that of an old man, white of hair and mustache though quite hale, and on occasion red-eyed like some animal caught in a beam of one of the new electric lights. This aspect I could alter by regular heavy feeding, and meant to do so in case Harker should after all have the hue and cry out for me by the time I reached England.

I supped well, as I say, and expected to rest well too, trying out another of my stout new traveling beds. There is not much can rouse a vampire in bright day, when he has gone, fully sated, to his earth. One sure alarm clock of course is the sharp point of the wooden stake entering his rib cage, with a strong and determined arm hammering behind it. This I know, though of course not yet by direct experience. What is it about wood that makes the stuff, under the proper conditions, so utterly, no-nonsense lethal to my kind? That it itself was once alive but is no more? Metal, that hacks up in such fine style the flesh of breathing men and draws out the rich red streams of life from them, is alien to us and cannot find its way to kill. It bounces off, disperses through, and interpenetrates our peculiar flesh, but cannot transfer fatal force to us. Silver bullets? Their efficacy is mere superstition as far as vampires are concerned.

But metal hurt me in my box that day, a sharp-edged spade swung in the desperate grip of Harker, who once more had dared the castle's slippery outer wall to gain my rooms, who once more ransacked my chambers and my vaults in hopes of finding there a key or other means of getting out in daylight on his own. He found me in a box again, and, this time yielding to the impulse to do murder, snatched up the nearby digging implement.

Imagine the deepest sleep that you have ever

slept, the hardest to break free from, and multiply its inertia by tenfold. In dreamless near-oblivion I lay so, a leaden lethargy, a numbness, wound like chains on all my limbs. He might have found me, searched me, raped me, and I would neither have known nor cared until sundown. But when he took up the spade, the psychic blow, the impulse of wholehearted murder came singing through the vaulted air to rouse me, to begin my rousing, well before the whistling blade itself struck home.

"Bloody bastard." His voice was only a faint wheezing moan but yet I heard it clearly. "Monstrous bloody bloated leech."

My eyes were open, had been open all along, but only slowly, blurrily, did the blindness of trance clear from them. I realized that the lid of my box had been pulled open, for there was the groining of the stone above. There was light, faint daylight whispering down through many a room and passageway. And off in one corner of my vision, Harker's face, at first only a whitish oval blur, and then as my sight cleared and my eyes began to focus, a mask of madness, the face of breathing Man as he exists in all the vampire nightmares that ever were, mask of the hunter, persecutor, stake pounder, who would cleanse his world by making sacrificial goats of the undead.

Coming so very slowly and hopelessly up out of trance—I would not be in time, I knew, to act effectively in self-defense—I realized for the first time and with detachment that Harker had lost weight as my guest—his arms were thinner in their dirty sleeves—that his hair hung down disheveled around an evilly transformed face, that his shaving had been spotty at best during the weeks since he had lost his mirror.

"Bloody bastard!" he grated out again, and in the midst of that last word his voice broke on a sob. And with a little whining screech of indrawn breath he raised the spade, held it high in both hands for an edge-down swing straight at my face.

I am not boasting when I say I was not terrified. Later on I will discourse of fear. I say now only that I watched, unhappily, as that heavy blow came down. Impossible to do more than turn my head and try to glare at my attacker. The shovel struck in the middle of my forehead, and I took the shock and pain of it through my head, and tried to no avail to move my hands and feet, and thought that in a second more the blow would come again.

And Harker? What saw he? ". . . a mocking smile on the bloated face which seemed to drive me mad. This was the being I was helping to transfer to London, where, perhaps, for centuries to come he might, amongst its teeming millions, satiate his lust for blood, and create a new and ever-widening circle of semidemons to batten on the helpless. . . . I seized a shovel . . . and lifting it high, struck, with the edge downward, at the hateful face. But as I did so the head turned and the eyes fell full upon me with all their blaze of basilisk horror. The sight seemed to paralyze me, and the shovel turned in my hand and glanced from the face, merely making a deep gash above the forehead." In rebuttal I can only reiterate that the sight of Harker swinging a shovel at my head was somewhat perturbing to me as well.

Unnerved by my movement and by the failure of this first attack to destroy me, he let the shovel slip from his hands and it somehow brought the box lid slamming down, leaving me to wait in darkness for his next move. It is perhaps fortunate for those interested in this history that at this point our tête-à-tête was interrupted, by "a gypsy song sung in merry voices," offstage but approaching, and accompanied by other noises of the *Szgany* who were coming with heavy wagons into the courtyard to begin my move. Harker fled back upstairs to scribble more into his journal. As soon as the coast was clear of gypsies he took the daring chance of climbing down the whole surface of the castle wall, and shortly got clear away upon his own initiative. My carriage rested empty that day, and Tatra put on his coachman's livery for nothing.

Had my guest stayed with me a little longer and put his wits to work he might well have done me serious or even fatal damage. Of course a simple attack with a metal tool was doomed to fail, a point Harker might profitably have remembered later, when he and I resumed our social intercourse. By now the mark has entirely disappeared from my forehead—wouldn't you say?—or at least my fingers can no longer find the ridgelike scar, and no one has remarked upon it for some decades.

But I had been given a throbbing head, and some fresh food for thought, viaticum for my journey; I was in no state to communicate with the loyal *Szgany* as they nailed down my lid and began to roll me down the long road to the sea.

TRACK TWO

My overland journey, some five or six hundred kilometers across the Transylvanian Alps and eastward through the *banat*, the fertile plain, was uneventful. Once out of the mountains the roads were good, and my *Szgany* made good time with their wagons.

The sun of early July beat down upon my box as we passed through the city you call Bucharest— did you know I named it Cetatesa Bucurestilor, in 1459, when it was one of my important fortresses? For a time it was my capital. We crossed the Danube shortly thereafter, and by the evening of July fifth we were in Varna, on the Black Sea, from which port I would take ship for England.

Varna. I suppose the name means little or nothing to you now. In 1444, in a battle fought nearby, the young King Vladislav III of Poland died under Turkish swords, and Janos Hunyadi himself was lucky to escape the field of battle alive, with the aid of my Walachian kinsmen.

No, I was not there. I was thirteen years old in 1444, and already fighting battles of my own, without an army for support. When the Christians and the Turks fought near Varna I was away amid the mountains of Asia Minor, in Egrigoz, a hostage for my father's cooperation with the Turks; imprisoned with me was my brother Radu, the one they called the Handsome later, who then was only six. . . .

Can you picture me as a child? No more than Hitler, I suppose. But all who have at any time been human have traversed that phase, and I remember it. As the twig is bent . . . Great twig benders were those Turkish jailors of my youth. Never mind. They came to fear me ere I left their walls some four years later.

As I say, my journey to the Black Sea port was uneventful. My *Szgany* handed me over to my agent, Petrof Skinsky, and he in turn to the good Herr Leutner, with whom I had been in correspondence but who was too modern a man to ever have credited tales of *nosferatu* if they had reached his ears. Of Skinsky I was not so sure; and I will have a little more to tell you about him later.

So Leutner took faithful charge of my fifty large boxes of earth, and saw to it that they were loaded aboard ship, never dreaming that the consignor himself was voyaging along, his luggage of money and spare clothes packed in a sturdy traveling bag beneath him in the soil. I was shipped aboard the schooner *Demeter*, bound for Whitby, which is, as some of my hearers may not know, on the

Yorkshire coast about three hundred kilometers north of London.

I had ridden some river-going craft before but the *Demeter's* was my first sea voyage. Emerging from my box on the first night out—the box I happened to be in had been stowed beneath several others, but between sunset and dawn I can pass if I wish through a crack narrower than a knifeblade—I walked in man-shape up from the hold, and attained the deck by sliding through the watertight sealing of a hatch. In the comforting dark of night I could perceive a mass of land on the horizon to our starboard; the sea around was otherwise clear to the horizon, and a fresh east wind blew from astern. There were three other men on deck, and I did not long remain. By careful reconnoitering during those first nights of the voyage, I ascertained that there were nine men in all on board besides myself: five Russian sailors, a Russian captain and second mate, and the first mate and the cook, who were both Romanian.

Also I used my senses diligently, especially during the hours of darkness, to learn what I could of this new world of the sea. As you no doubt realize, I have some command of wind and weather, and had naturally considered using these powers to facilitate my journey. The difficulty, as I soon came to understand, was that although I was able to remember our course very well as we traversed each part of it in turn—we vampires having what I suppose would now be called an inertial guidance system, or something akin to one—I had not the slightest feel for where we should be going, which way to tell the wind to push. I had of course the pure intellectual knowledge that my destination's name was England, and that it was to be reached by a roundabout passage through the Black Sea, the Mediterranean, and the Atlantic. But this knowledge would be of small help in trying to speed the ship on its way, and so I was content to observe and try to learn.

Five days out of port we reached the Bosporus, and a day later we passed through the Dardanelles and entered the Mediterranean. It was at about this point, as I now suspect, that the first mate began to be aware of my nocturnal wanderings. I do not believe that he had actually seen me yet, but by means of the marginal perceptions that breathing humans sometimes have he came somehow to know that a tenth presence inhabited the ship after nightfall; that now a plank creaked slightly beneath an unfamiliar tread; that again there was no shadow on the moonlit deck just where a shadow should have lain, and that darkness lay instead just where the moonbeams should have fallen clear.

Sailors are a superstitious lot; I had not realized before how true this truism was. And the mate was a man, as I now suppose, abnormally sensitive to the abnormal; on July fourteenth, the eighth day of our voyage, the men having evidently caught the contagion of fear from the first mate, one of them disputed him about something and was struck. Whether the quarrel was about an apparition in the night or something totally unrelated I do not know, as it took place in daylight when I was snug below and my only knowledge of it is from my enemies' records.

These records also make the following night, that of July fifteenth to sixteenth, as the first on which I was actually seen by any of the crew. As the captain duly entered in his log, one of the seamen, "awestruck," reported watching "a tall thin man, who was not like any of the crew, come up the companionway, and go along the deck forward, and disappear." I had grown careless, and even a little carelessness is always bad.

On that night I still had no suspicion that my presence aboard was creating a stir, but when I roused at the following sunset I became aware that everything in the hold around me had been disarranged. My boxes were all moved at least slightly from their original positions, and the ballast of silver sand had been much trampled on.

There was no sign of any leak or other nautical emergency which would have required the crew to do so much labor in the hold, nor had I the feeling that a storm had come and gone. What then? The evidence suggested to me that the hold had been searched, though fortunately not with the thoroughness that would have been necessary to dig me from my earth.

The crew then, or some of them, probably suspected that something was amiss. But having searched around me once, they were not likely to search the hold again without good cause; so I thought, at any rate, and determined to lay low for a night or two. Thus I found out only later that one of the seamen had disappeared on the night of July fifteenth to sixteenth, an important fact which I would have learned sooner had I not stayed so prudently within my snug, attractive box.

Ah, my homes of earth! Good Transylvanian soil, consecrated by humble and worthy priests so long ago as my familial burying ground. Sometimes I wonder whether the strength I draw from my own earth is not purely a matter of psychology. But the fact is that nowhere else can I truly rest, and without true rest neither breathing man nor vampire can long survive. Bits of my ancestors' bones are in my earth, unrecognizable in their humility, along with an occasional patient worm or insect, timid creatures frightened alike of me or you, of anything that moves. Fragments of roots of sturdy trees, and compost of their leaves, and maybe here and there a particle of hidden Walachian gold, over which a pinhead of blue flame will burn whenever St. George's Eve comes round. Good black earth that yet does not unduly stain the clothes. It is only sliding about or rubbing in it that produces smudges, and my lying down to sleep is very still and my getting up is as a rule without the disturbing of a single clod. In England or anywhere else I would have been lost without the good earth of my homeland, as I knew and my enemies came to know full well. In time I hoped to make the native soil of England hospitable to me as well. . . .

But to the *Demeter* again. She went plowing into the rough weather she met in the western Mediterranean, her first mate gone violently but so far unobtrusively insane with brooding on his fears. And I was snugged down prudently—I have a quite irrational dislike of that virtuous word— in my coffin, where I could be of no help to my own cause.

How was that first sailor, that I have mentioned, lost? By some sheer accident, I would surmise. He had evidently been relieved on watch, during the night, then somehow had fallen overboard before he got back to his bunk. It happens. But there was the brooding mate, needing just this mysterious tragedy to send him over the rails of his own mind, into the vasty deep of lunacy. The mate went mad—as the captain himself later thought probable—and the mate was from somewhere about my own land, remember, and infected with its endemic terrors. He must have been mad enough to see *nosferatu* in every face, especially in the face of any man who approached him alone on deck at night. Then *whiss*! he would out with his knife and strike, and throw his victim overboard. It was all in an insane kind of self-defense, you understand. As if his knife could have done him much good against the real thing; but then I suppose the mate was a half-educated man at best, from the back country somewhere, and his fears were much greater than his knowledge of the subject.

During the remainder of July he disposed of four more of his shipmates in this wise, and the survivors of the now short-handed crew went staggering in fatigued despair about their duties, unable to imagine what evil fate had come upon their voyage. We had been at sea nearly a month before I again emerged from concealment. Though of course I did not at first realize the situation, there were by this time only the captain and the first mate and two sailors left to work the ship, the rest having died one by one in darkness.

The schooner had now passed Gibraltar, traversed the Bay of Biscay, and was nearing England.

On the night of August second I came on deck to find the foredeck deserted, and as a landlubber did not realize at first what a grave sign this was to meet upon a foggy night. I enjoy the fog and dark, and was in the bows drinking it in, lost in some fatuous dream of England as I imagined it: myself lord of some sunlit manor where no one minded that the lord did not go out by day, a pair of those great dogs that the English painters could execute so well sitting in attendance on me as I gazed into my fire . . . or squinted off across my meadows, perhaps . . . some buxom Saxon wench laboring there, gathering hay, the muscles showing rounded in her arms, and the veins in her throat beneath the suntanned skin. . . .

The mate was too near before I heard him, and his coming was too swift, for me to get out of his way entirely—small wonder that none of the breathing men he crept upon in the same way survived. His keen knife tore at my clothes, but passed through my flesh as through a shadow, leaving no damage behind but only searing pain. In a moment I had melded myself into the fog. Cursing my own innocent foolishness, I passed belowdecks, where I waited in bat-form for an outcry, for searchers bearing torches and weapons in their trembling fists. None came during the night.

At dawn I took to my earth in one of the lowest boxes, hoping that the unpiling of the others might give me warning enough to rouse myself for some defense if searchers came again by day.

All day I lay there undisturbed, and at sunset I was up betimes; but I waited for full dark, in fact for midnight, before emerging in mist-form from below. To my astonishment, I found the decks utterly empty of men. The wind was steady astern and the vessel moved on as if by her own will.

I was, and am, no sailor, but still presumed that such a state of affairs could not persist for long. Immediately I took what measures I could with the wind to prevent its shifting, and I listened intently for signs of life anywhere in the ship. The thought of being on an unmanned vessel, due for capsizing or wrecking on some unknown shore, and all my transported home-earth lost beneath the waves, was not one to give me pleasure.

Somewhere below me in the ship, two sets of lungs were laboring; and two hearts beat, though scarcely as one. No more than two. Great God, I thought, seven men dead, or at least gone. In the old days I would have suspected plague or pirates. In 1891 I did not know what to suspect.

I was about to shift to bat-form and go stealthily below, to find out what I could, when there came the sound of footsteps ascending the companionway, and the captain himself emerged. He was unshaven and worn-looking, like a man who has been in battle for days on end. He saw me not, though his tormented eyes darted this way and that about the otherwise deserted deck from which his crew had vanished one by one.

A moment later the captain had realized that the ship was unmanned, had thrown himself at the wheel, and was shouting for the mate. It was not long before the Romanian appeared, in his long underwear, disheveled and looking a very maniac. He at once went close to the captain at the wheel and spoke to him in a hoarse whisper, which I in the shadows not far off could plainly hear:

"*It* is here, I know it, now. On the watch last night I saw it, like a man, tall and thin and ghastly pale. It was in the bows, and looking out. I crept behind it, and gave it my knife; but the knife went through it, empty as the air." Even as the mate spoke he drew out the knife again to demonstrate; and my night-seeing eyes noted traces of fresh blood on the blade even as he flourished it. I realized that it must be the blood of the last helmsman, who must have been put over the side only minutes before.

I very nearly sprang forward and disarmed the first mate at this point, in my expectation that he was about to kill the only sane sailor left on board, the captain, who alone stood between myself and probable shipwreck and ruin.

But already the madman had sheathed his knife and was stepping back from the horrified captain, who maintained his grip upon the wheel.

The mate babbled on: "But it is here, and I'll find it. It is in the hold, perhaps in one of those boxes. I'll unscrew them one by one and see. You work the helm." And, holding a finger to his lips, enjoining silence, he went below. The captain stared after him, with pity, horror, and despair all struggling for expression amid the exhausted lines of his face.

The lunatic's assault upon my boxes I could not endure. If he armed himself with a few tools, he, laboring alone but with the fanaticism of madness, might in an hour or so have breached them

THE DRACULA TAPE

all, and their contents, so vital to my existence, would be mingled inextricably with the ballast and the bilge. Had I been certain that the captain unaided could steer the ship to some safe port I would have slain the mate there on the spot—but no, perhaps not even then would I have killed. As a soldier long ago I saw enough of killing, and as a prince more than enough to last a lifetime greater than my own.

Though I had no desire to encompass the mate's death I was forced to act to block him in his new plan. I altered wind just enough to keep, as I hoped, the captain occupied at the wheel, and stealthily followed the mate below. He was already in the hold, and in the act of raising a maul to strike at the lid of one of the boxes, when I confronted him.

He screamed, the maul flew from his hands, and he dashed for the companionway to reach the open air again. Let me say parenthetically that I find it strange how many people have inferred from the captain's scribbled record of these events that the mate actually opened one or more of the boxes and found me, somnolent, within. I would like to point out, first, that it was past midnight at the time, the hour when I am usually up and about; and secondly, that if he had found me in such a state, the man who had been trying for weeks to kill a vampire could hardly have failed to put me overboard at once, perhaps box and all; and thirdly, no one reported that any of the boxes were lidless or broken when they were finally received at Whitby. A small matter, perhaps, whether he found me in a box or active, but still indicative of how events are misinterpreted.

But to return. The mate shot up on deck again, by now, to use the captain's phrase, "a raging madman" beyond all doubt. He first cried out to be saved, and then fell into a despairing calm; evidently he realized that from the murderous phantom vampires of his disordered mind there could be no escape this side of death. Moving toward the rail, he said in a suddenly reasonable voice: "You had better come too, Captain, before it is too late. *He* is there. I know the secret now. The sea will save me from him, and it is all that is left!" And before the captain could move to interfere, the luckless mate had thrown himself into the sea.

I remained for some time concealed in the shadows on deck, steadying and moderating the wind and trying to think. Later in the night I tried to approach that brave man at the wheel; it was my wish to explain my position to him, at least partially, and to try to make him see that he and I shared a common interest in coming safe to port. The first grayness of dawn was on the sea when I walked toward him in man-form, boldly and matter-of-factly, with my approach in his full view.

His bloodshot eyes fixed on me after flickering once, almost longingly, toward the rail; he would not desert his post, and his fingers tightened convulsively upon the wheel's spokes.

I stopped when I was still some paces distant and tipped my hat. "Good morning, Captain."

"What—who are you?"

"A passenger who wishes only to reach port in safety."

"Begone from me, fiend out of hell."

"I understand your crew is gone now, Captain, but that is not of my doing. And I am ready to labor with you in our common cause of survival. I know nothing of sailing, but I can and will pull ropes, tie knots, whatever a sailor is supposed to do—and more." I deemed it inadvisable to propose at once that I could control the weather to his order. "You will find your new crew even stronger than the old, though the old had the advantage of numbers."

"Devil, begone!"

Alas, my Russian was imperfect. And the man at the wheel would not truly listen to me, but only muttered prayers and incantations and curses, and forgot to steer whilst I remained in sight. Shortly I thought, perhaps erroneously, that this neglect was like to wreck the ship at once, and I took myself out of his sight once more.

All the next day, whilst I rested uneasily below, he remained sleeplessly at his post. He took some time to scribble his continuation of the log on some papers which he then stuffed into a bottle and concealed in his clothing—this log I did not know of until much later, or I would have thrown it into the sea once he was dead.

When on the following night I came on deck again I saw that he had lashed himself to the wheel and was grown much weaker. Approaching as before, I again addressed him in soft words; but his terror grew, until I stopped out of compassion.

"Monster!" he shrieked. "Back to the depths from whence you came! I will yield to you neither my ship nor my immortal soul!"

"You may retain the captaincy of both," I

replied, trying to speak as soothingly as possible. "I ask this and no more, that you tell me which way lies Whitby. In what direction, England?" Ah! In the halls of my own castle, or amid other congenial surroundings, I flatter myself that I can indeed be soothing, charming. Whatever soft and summery impression you will have, that can I give. Aboard ship, though, I am outré, no matter what. I seized the poor wretch by the collar in my impatience and shook him roughly. "Tell me, you scoundrel, idiot, where lies the port of Whitby?"

By this stage, I think, he knew no more than I. Of course I was aware that by now we must have threaded through the channel, and be in the North Sea, somewhere in the region of my destination. The stars gave me rough directions whenever I blew a little hole in the fog to let them be seen. If the captain saw them too and used them to steer by I could not tell at the time; later I supposed that he somehow did.

Toward dawn the next morning he died; his body remained at the wheel, where he had contrived to bind himself, tightening the cord's last knots with his teeth. Of the rosary he had bound beneath his crossed hands I was ignorant, or I would have taken it from him as I would have taken his bottled writings—that neither might suggest the presence of a vampire aboard the schooner.

I considered untying his corpse from the wheel and letting him rejoin his crew in that great fellowship who sleep beneath the waves. But after reflection I left him where he had chosen to remain. The discovery of a ship at sea, completely abandoned by her crew, is a mystery more intriguing to the human mind than any mere wreck, and therefore more closely studied. I thought that when the *Demeter* came in one way or another to the land—I felt confident of accomplishing at least that much with my raw control of winds, though whether she would smash to bits or merely grate aground I could not guess—her crew would be believed to have simply perished in a storm. With this in mind I began to use my powers to raise such a storm as would make such a fate for them convincing.

The raising of the storm was a calculated risk; should the ship capsize or sink beneath me there would be nothing I could do but take flight in bat-form amid the gale. My boxes of home soil would be lost irretrievably and I would be a thousand miles as the bat flies from obtaining more. The chances of my survival under such conditions would not be great.

The storm brewed and grumbled for days out in the North Sea toward Scandinavia. I wanted it kept boiling, as it were, until I knew with some precision in just what direction its impetus should be applied against my drifting craft. It was with a surge of elation that I became aware one night of a headland to the northwest, and thought I recognized the towering cliffs of Flamborough Head from drawings and descriptions that I had pored over in my distant study. If this identification was correct, Whitby must lie no more than forty miles to the northwest, and with a little luck I should be able to blow the schooner right into the estuary of the Esk.

I called the storm on slowly, wanting only its

fringes to actually encompass the vessel in which I rode. The maneuvering proved not as easy as I had hoped, and all during the seventh of August I lay below decks in a box, rousing fitfully now and again from torpor, half expecting and hoping to hear at any time hail of English voices from another ship, and then their footfalls as men came aboard to see what ailed the derelict. Hoping, because to be boarded so near Whitby would, I supposed, get me an easy tow into the proper port. But no ship came close enough to take an interest in the *Demeter*, and when night fell again I judged that the time had come to get to land as best I could by my own actions.

The raising and ordering of a major storm is an exhausting business, and one not altogether pleasant. Even after I had identified the harbor that I sought and worked the ship 'round to it, great exertion was required to aim the schooner at last—"as if by a miracle," in the words of a newspaper account—between the piers that guarded the harbor mouth, so that she flew in to finally ground with little damage upon a shingle of dark stones just beneath the tall east cliff.

Electric lighting had then been in gradually increasing use in England for some ten years, but in my backwaters of Eastern Europe I had not yet seen it; and when the searchlight, quite powerful for its day, glared from one of the piers toward my fleeing ship I was startled and knew not what to expect next.

When the light struck I was directing the last necessary push of the wind in bat-form, so as to be ready to fly free, if need be, from a sudden grounding shock. My clawed feet were both snugly gripped about some rigging lines and my wings were furled close about me in the wind. Even in the searchlight's glare none of the onlookers thronging the piers and shore were able to make out my small brown form upon a mast. That so many folk were out to watch, at this hour of the night, was a surprise to me. I had not realized that Whitby was something of a resort town, full of folk not used to the ocean and its moods, and the storm itself had attracted hordes of sightseers to the shore.

Bat's eyes are bothered by electric glare, and as soon as I saw that the ship was inevitably going to ground in a few moments I dropped into the companionway and altered form to that of a wolf. As soon as the first thrill of grounding ran up through the schooner's bottom, the entertainment seekers on the cliffs were surprised to see an "immense dog"—as a reporter wrote—spring up on deck from below. It jumped ashore from the bow and at once vanished in the darkness beyond the searchlight's reach.

To run as a wolf is a powerful and easy mode of travel, less dreamlike and less dependent on the air than bat flight, faster and more effortless than running as a man. In less than a minute I had reached the darker, inland regions of the town, which seemed as still and deserted now as if the entire populace had gone to line the oceanside and watch the storm. After some little time spent waiting among the deeper shadows of a narrow street I felt sure that no one had pursued or followed me from the harbor, and let myself return to man-shape. This process excited a large mastiff that had been cringing, moaning its fear of the wolf, in a coalyard opposite. When wolf smell changed to something like man smell the brute was emboldened to attack, and came out after me.

Ordinarily I would probably have soothed the beast and sent it home again, but my nonphysical powers were greatly wearied by the raising and direction of the storm. Under the circumstances I thought the dog fair game, and drank its blood as a restorative. Its torn body was found the next day, but was not for a long time connected with the arrival in the harbor of fifty large boxes invoiced as clay.

Feeling stronger in the hours before dawn, I stalked the rain-wet streets of Whitby in search of a vantage point from which I might see the grounded schooner without coming too close to her. I was wearily reluctant to take on bat-form but still wanted to see what, if anything, was being done with her precious cargo.

For this purpose of observation the small churchyard on a cliff high above the town and harbor proved to be ideal. It was a wild, magnificent scene that I beheld from this clifftop before dawn; of course by now I had let go my reins on weather, and the storm was much abated. But the ocean was still sullen and unruly and the sky filled with low, scudding clouds. I was sated and revitalized with fresh blood and exalted in the grandeur of the scene and in what I took to be my victorious arrival against considerable odds. The small parish church near which I stood and the great ruined abbey above were both empty of human life, and I stood there watching until nearly dawn before taking my way on bat wings down to the ship again.

If I was roused from sleep at all by my box being unloaded with the others I have no recollection of the disturbance now. Mr. Billington, the good Whitby solicitor to whom the shipment had been consigned, had dutifully brought a crew of men aboard the *Demeter* with the morning tide, and when I woke once more at sunset I found myself still amid my fifty boxes of sweet earth, stacked now in a dry warehouse.

For the next few days I endured a rather passive though risky existence. Inquiries about the shipwreck were in the air. The admiralty, as I gathered from a few words overheard, were taking an interest; harbor dues were payable, and in the midst of these threatened complications Billington dawdled over completing the arrangements for my shipment by train to London.

Meanwhile I of course went out at night and despite these problems enjoyed myself enormously. Change and promise and success seemed to be in the air, along with the salt tang from the North Sea, which I began to practice breathing to enjoy. On my nocturnal ramblings I even caught myself looking for mirrors; I actually nursed stirrings of faint, unreasoned hope that at least the ghostly outline of my reflection would now be visible.

The mirrors were always disappointments but my existence otherwise had none. The life of the seaside town flowed on at night in the open air as well as behind doors, and no one's life seemed bound in secrecy or fear. I listened to band concerts on the piers. I heard much laughter in the streets. It seemed to me then that even the poor and wretched of this new country were conscious of all the possibilities of enjoyment in the world, and meant to have some for themselves. I marveled happily. After killing the dog I fed no more during those first few English nights. In fact I felt little craving for blood, a fact from which I drew hope for the fulfillment of my future plans; finer things than blood seemed stirring in the English air, and in my soul. I sublimated my fleshly cravings and platonically enjoyed the presence around me of all the women of the town.

Great heaven! If little Whitby were as full as this of life, promise, and humanity, then what, I thought, must London be? Surely in that vital metropolis I would not be able to remain a common vampire even if I tried. Not that I wished merely to be as one of the more ordinary inhabitants, lungs gasping perpetually in the sooted air for a lifespan of a few decades only. No, I saw myself as becoming a synthesis, the first of a new species, warmth-and light-loving as breathing men, and with as many lusts to satiate and enjoy: tough and enduring as the *nosferatu*, able to hold converse with animals if not necessarily to assume their shapes. With balmy thoughts like these I kept myself befuddled and bemused.

One of my favorite haunts during those first wildly hopeful English nights was the churchyard I have mentioned. It surrounded St. Mary's parish church, which clung on the east cliff high above the town, and was immediately below the ancient and ruined abbey. In this same Whitby Abbey, some twelve hundred years before I came to it, the plowboy poet Caedmon was the first in England to sing a hymn to the creative god of Christendom. I found the place to be invariably deserted after dark, and, like the poet of old, perhaps, I spent there many quiet hours in thought and dream. The harbor and the peaceful town alike were spread before me, as was the sea, to my sightseeing eyes, and the headland called Kettleness bulked low against the sky.

So I was, leaning against one of the abbey's remaining walls, and observing moonlit scenery in a euphoric mood, when sweet Lucy first came into my sight. It was close upon the hour of twelve, as I recall, some three nights after my tempestuous arrival. I was roused from contemplation of moon, earth, and sea by the appearance at one corner of my vision of a single figure in some kind of long, white dress, approaching the churchyard along the lengthy flight of steps that led up from the town. I turned to observe this figure more directly and made out that it was a young woman perhaps not yet turned twenty, and rather slight of build, with a diaphanous fall of hair about her shoulders. I did not move. Though with my night-tuned eyes I could see her at a good distance, I stood myself in partial shadow and thought it unlikely that she would become aware of me even if she should pass quite near, as she seemed like to do if she remained on the path that she had chosen.

She was sleepwalking, I realized as she drew within a few score yards, sleepwalking barefoot and in a thin, white nightgown. The gown shimmered about her with the vibration of her stride, calling to mind the blowing of pure snow, or moonlight of the rare Carpathian heights. Her eyes, the rare blue of sunlit English skies, were open, but even had she been fully dressed I would have known she slept—I have a knowing in such matters. Fair hair, to go with such eyes as those; wild heart, which though I heard it as she drew quite near I did not yet begin to understand.

She passed my place of shadow and I thought she was about to go on farther up, into the abbey or around it, but suddenly her footsteps slowed. She halted, and turned so that she seemed to be looking straight away from me, and out to sea; and at that moment, with a small and scarcely perceptible start, she came awake. You, watching from where I watched, could probably not have perceived the change, so easy was it. Nor did she herself know clearly if she woke or dreamt, as her first words showed.

I am not one to doubt the existence of a sixth, or even sixteenth, sense. Too often have the breathing members of humanity surprised me with the quickness and acuity of their perceptions. Even before she had fully awakened Lucy's face turned round in my direction, and my motionless form, in shadow some ten steps away, was the first object which her eyes found in their focus.

She looked at me as calmly as if it were midday, and I no more than some peculiar, quaint grave marker to be studied. She shifted her gaze to the fleeing clouds; the shattered pile of the abbey, whose tumbled stones may have witnessed sights stranger than a vampire in their time; she gazed upon the intermittent moon; then she looked back at me. You will remember that I had been at work to alter my appearance, and I suppose she saw my hair crisp curling brown instead of sere and white, my face perhaps almost unlined.

"Why, then, I am dreaming still," she murmured. "Good sir, what do you in my dreams? I have but lately had three men ask for my hand; am I to hear another wordy proposal of marriage still? But no, you have more the aspect of some old Viking, wrapped in his cape, come to ravish me away across the northern seas." And without her face showing any fear she gave a long shivering shudder, an altogether delicious movement that began somewhere about her throat and undulated down until one set of white toes went out of sight behind the other.

"Perhaps more Hun than Viking, my dear lady," I said, and left my shadow to walk a little closer. "As to the ravishing, that will be largely up to you. But it appears to me that you have already made up your mind in that regard."

She did not draw back as I approached, although she grew a little paler than before. Her eyes, lidding as if toward sleep again, were fixed on mine. "I ask only that you do not smother me with words," she murmured. "I am weary, oh God, so weary, with all the words of men in waking life."

My fangs were aching in my upper jaw. Without

another word she came into my arms, as smoothly and willingly as any wench that I have ever clasped to lips or loins. She trembled as I kissed her throat, and with my first touch above the jugular her knees were weakening. I led her to a bench nearby, and stood behind her as she sat, and bent to nuzzle at her neck.

A heavy clock somewhere below struck one in sullen tone. The warm salt richness of her life was trickling in its grateful radiance through my cold veins when I heard a name called: "Lucy! Lucy!" in a girl's voice that seemed to me far off, but was not so.

Lucy stirred beneath my mouth and hands, but when I would have raised my head to see who called her fingers knotted in my hair to clamp my parted lips against her skin. I raised my head anyway—drawing from Lucy a little disappointed moan—and saw and heard the other girl coming in our general direction from the head of the long stairs. Of course it was dear Mina, though I did not know her yet, and saw her only as a cursed interruption of my joy. She was hurrying forward purposefully, and had probably seen the two of us there on the bench; but her path led 'round St. Mary's church and for a few moments she would be out of sight again.

"Tomorrow night," I promised Lucy, holding her cheeks in my hands and looking down into her eyes, which were now almost closed. She was no more than half awake now—not from loss of blood, for the amount drained had been trivial to a healthy girl of nineteen. I saw unforced consent there in her eyes and heard it in her slowly calming breath. With women, of course, sex is far less localized anatomically than it is with most men.

By the time Mina came hurrying 'round the little church, and another racing cloud had fled to bare the moon, I was melted invisibly back into the shadows. Mina ran straight to where Lucy still half reclined upon the bench. Lucy's eyes were now fully closed in almost-self-convincing sleep, though her breathing was still heavy with the excitement of our embrace. Mina, murmuring maidenly endearments and expostulations, hastened to cover my erstwhile victim with a shawl, and stooped to put her own shoes protectively on Lucy's feet. I remarked to myself that this new girl, wearing a full robe over her own nightdress, was also attractive, though in a different way. Where Lucy was slight and dainty, the newcomer was sturdy, but yet graceful with her air of robust health.

As the girls left the churchyard, Mina leading her half-roused friend, I followed at some distance, wanting to discover where Lucy lived. I was somewhat puzzled to see Mina—whose name I still did not know—stop beside a puddle and daub each of her now-bare feet with mud; it came to me that she must be doing this in order that any chance passerby would think her shod. Why this should have been of any great importance I did not know; another vagary of the English mind for me to ponder.

After seeing the girls safely home and noting that they evidently dwelt in the same house I took me to an early rest and slept well through the day.

As for Lucy, Mina was relieved to note in the morning that she showed no ill effects from her night's adventure: ". . . on the contrary, it has benefitted her, for she looks better this morning than she has done for weeks. I was sorry to notice that my clumsiness with the safety pin hurt her. Indeed, it might have been serious, for the skin of her throat was pierced . . . there are two little red points like pin pricks, and on the band of her nightdress was a drop of blood. When I apologized and was concerned about it, she laughed and petted me, and said she did not even feel it. Fortunately it cannot leave a scar, as it is so tiny."

Lucy herself, as she later confided to me, was still uncertain as to whether her sleepwalking adventure had been a dream or not. She said no more about it as the girls went picnicking, accompanied by Lucy's widowed mother, who was with them on their seaside holiday as chaperone. It was probably fortunate for Mrs. Westenra that neither of the girls mentioned the nocturnal experience to her, for she was even then suffering from a severe form of heart disease; though Lucy, at that time, was as ignorant of her mother's illness as I was.

I had Lucy's name and knew the house in which she slept, and on the following night, true to my word, I called for her. Called silently, my mind to hers, as I was able to do since we had partially become one flesh. Wordlessly there came to Lucy the urgent fact of her lover's nearness and his desire for her; but she shared a room with Mina and could not readily get out. Lucy feigned walking in her sleep again but this ploy was foiled; her dependable and practical roommate, not wanting another midnight climb to the east cliff, had locked the bedroom door and tied the key to her own wrist. Lucy was led firmly back to bed and almost sat on till she was still. An hour or two later I called again, whilst perched in bat-form at the girls' window. This time Lucy was truly sleeping as she rose and tried the door. Mina was quickly wakened, and thwarted me as efficiently as before.

As you have doubtless read somewhere, it is one of the peculiarities of the vampire nature that we may enter into no house where we have never been invited. This being so, there was nothing more that I could do for the moment with regard to Lucy. Disappointed, I made a lonely tour of the town in bat-shape, and gained some additional evidence that when in their rooms and beds, and sure of being unobserved, the Englishman and the Central European were not very much different after all.

On the following evening, that of August fourteenth if I recall correctly, my persistence was rewarded. Mina was out for a stroll when I arrived at the girls' window. With a clear field it was no great trick to silently persuade the sleeping girl to open the window and lean out her head, stretching her white and slender throat in the moonlight upon the sill. With my small bat's mouth I tasted from first one wound and then the other of the two my man-sized canines had so delicately made. The dear girl moaned a bit and had a very pleasant dream.

Not enough blood could have been drawn into

FRED SABERHAGEN

my little bat belly, surely, to have made any real difference in Lucy's health. But she was not robust. Next day she pined and seemed fatigued, and had no explanation to offer to her dearest friend.

I called again the next night but Mina was home and once more kept Lucy from sticking her nose out of the room. I was taking a minor but definite delight in this young conquest of mine, and smiled to myself whenever in memory I heard her call me "Viking." As a matter of fact I took such interest in this dalliance that I almost forgot, for a time, that London was my goal.

Still, my attitude toward my affair with Lucy was casual, I confess, more suited to the late twentieth century, or to the mid fifteenth, my breathing days, than to the time and place when it occurred. Perhaps it was my attitude, more than my verifiable deeds of blood, that brought that pack of murderers down in full cry upon my trail at last. Really, it was my *fickleness*, I sometimes think, that they found unendurable. If I had restricted myself to only one of their sweet girls, and married her, and chewed her neck in private, I suppose I might, like an eccentric cousin, have been made almost welcome among family and friends in the circle of the hearth. But perhaps I misjudge what degree of eccentricity even an Englishman can tolerate.

Never mind. I came near to forgetting about London, as I say, and it was something of a shock when on the evening of August seventeenth I focused my well-rested eyes to find that the box in which I had slept away the day was being loaded aboard a train, along with its forty-nine fellows. I felt a little bit like one of those thieves who occupy the oil jars in *Ali Baba*.

That journey of some three hundred kilometers on the Great Northern Railway was my first train ride, and it was no joy. The stench of burning coal that wafted back from steam engine to goods carriages had something organic, almost food-like, in it that tried my endurance over the long hours.

When we had been chugging on our way some fifteen minutes, it being then practically dark, I oozed out through an imperfection in my crate and stood in man-form to reconnoiter. Swaying with the motion of the train in the long summer twilight, I tallied up my boxes, making sure that none had been left behind. With a roar of hollow, howling steel, a bridge passed under the wheels of the closed carriage in which I and my home-earth rode. Through a chink I caught the faint glimmer of a stream below, and I nodded in appreciation of how effortlessly the flying train could draw me over running water without a tug or pause, such as the strongest horses sometimes gave when freighted with a vampire.

Sliding the door of the goods carriage a trifle open, I peered awhile at the Yorkshire moors through which we were passing at such remarkable speed. Then, not wishing to precipitate anything remotely like the disaster of my first ocean voyage—I envisioned terrified train crewmen leaping off at sixty miles an hour, landing with fatal impact in pastures and manure heaps—I soon retired once more within my crate. Throughout the remainder of the night, and for most of the next day as I lay in my usual daylight stupor, we chugged and rolled into the south, with frequent stops for cargo, passengers, and fuel.

At what must have been nearly the scheduled time, half past four in the afternoon of Tuesday, August eighteenth, 1891, shouts dimly heard gave me to understand that we were arriving at King's Cross station, London. I roused somewhat with my inner excitement, and was awake as my box was slid among its fellows from the doors of the goods carriage directly onto a heavy wagon of some kind. With only the briefest of delays the carters took their seats and used their whips, the horses pulled, and we were off to my newly acquired estate, Carfax.

I listened to London on the way, although I could not see beyond my box. There were perhaps six million souls alive and breathing in the great metropolis through which I then moved for the first time; whistling, coughing, cursing, singing, praying, selling, calling to one another in joy and fury and fellowship, whilst their horse-drawn vehicles innumerable went past mine on all sides. I reveled in the symphony until at length it faded to inaudibility below the steady noise of my own wagon.

Purfleet, where my house Carfax stood, was, as I may have mentioned before, a semiurban district of Essex on the north bank of the Thames, some fifteen miles east of the heart of London. The teamsters grumbled and used good English words that I had never heard from Harker's lips, or read in books, as they heaved and pushed, and carried and slid the lord of the manor into his new home. My own delivery instructions, passed along through Dillington and Son, were followed faithfully enough, and by about eight-thirty in the evening my installation had been completed. The footsteps of the last laborer departed and there came to my glad ears the sound of the doors being pulled shut behind him. At about nine o'clock in the evening I emerged from my coffin, eager as a child to explore my new home.

I found myself standing in a ruined chapel, obviously built before my time, and giving evidence of having stood untenanted by breathing folk for perhaps as long as my own castle. Such remote, comforting privacy for my retreat, and London hardly more than walking distance off! I blessed Harker and Hawkins, stretched my arms high in my joy, and came near laughing for the first time since my first wife killed herself . . . a dear girl, but she became quite mad, and jumped from a castle parapet back near the middle of my breathing days. There was not much softness in me before that bitter day, but ever since there has been almost none at all. . . .

Where was I? Yes, describing my first evening at Carfax. A memorable night. Eagerly I toured the vast, deserted, crumbling house, talking now and then to rats, and then I explored the surrounding wooded acreage. Also I remembered to unpack from its nest of mold and earth my traveling bag with its freight of money and new clothes. The latter I hung up where they might stay free of damp and remain in a presentable condition until I should have occasion to try them in society. What foolish thoughts I doted on. . . .

During the centuries of my existence it has become my firm conviction that they are right who maintain the nonexistence, in a strict sense, of such a thing as sheer coincidence. Yes, I nursed foolish thoughts. How could I have known that Carfax, purchased by myself from a thousand miles away, adjoined a lunatic asylum governed by a man, Dr. John Seward, who had recently, though unsuccessfully, proposed marriage to my slender, passionate blonde of the churchyard and windowsill? And this fact is not the only, nor perhaps the most remarkable, link in the chain of "coincidence"—for want of a better term—that bound my fate so inextricably with those of Harker, Mina, Lucy, Van Helsing, and the rest. Who could have guessed that the sturdy young woman who had come to succor Lucy in the Whitby churchyard was in fact the fiancée, and would soon be the bride, of young Harker, whom I had left behind me in Castle Dracula? He at that very moment was tossing deliriously with what was then called brain fever, in a hospital bed in Budapest, unidentifiable by the good sisters who had him in their care. After climbing down the castle wall with a pocketful of stolen gold, he made his way somehow to the railway station at Klausenberg, where he had rushed in shouting incoherently for a ticket home. Employees in the station, "seeing from his violent demeanor that he was English," hastened to accept most of his money and put him on a train going in the proper direction. He got only to Budapest before he had to be hospitalized for what would now be called a nervous breakdown.

I can but relate these intertwined events as they occurred, or as they appeared from my own viewpoint as they were happening. Some intellect more powerful than my own may find a thread or threads of natural causation running through and uniting them all; I can find no sensible explanation for these wild chains of "coincidence" without appealing to causes that are above and beyond nature as she is commonly understood.

But to return again to Carfax, on my first night. I was not long in being disabused of the idea of the security, safety, and relative isolation of my new estate. Shortly after two in the morning, as I stood gazing fondly into the small lake that graced my grounds, the fun began. It started with a scrambling upon the western side of the high stone wall that completely surrounded Carfax, as of someone trying to climb over. What can this be? I thought, and hurried back inside my dusty, ruined chapel, where my precious boxes had been deposited and were yet in such vulnerable concentration. To guard them was imperative.

I heard a single breathing being climb the wall and drop onto my ground uninvited. The hesitant quickness of the intruder's movements made me think of a fugitive, seeking shelter; but I could not be sure.

The general silence of the night was helpful to my ears, this far from the bustle of the central city. Whilst my visitor was still a hundred paces off I could hear him well enough to be sure he was a man, and not a woman or a child. Motionless and noiseless as a basking lizard myself—more so, for lizards have lungs that work—I waited in the rat-trodden dust of my chapel, listening. The feet of the approaching man

FRED SABERHAGEN

seemed to be bare, and he wore some kind of a
loose garment that swished about him as he
walked. Now he was right outside the chapel
wall, and he suddenly threw himself down there
and began snuffling and groveling in the most
bestial style. With a feeling of sinking dismay it
came to me that he might be *nosferatu* himself.
Was England aswarm already with such as I, and
had Harker through some insane delicacy omitted to let me know? Then indeed were my hopes
likely to be doomed. It was with some relief I
noted that this man continually breathed.

Now the mysterious one had crept along to the
iron-bound oak doors that closed the chapel, and
now he strained what was evidently a powerful
pair of arms to open them, so that the hinges
creaked. But the doors held.

"Master, master!" he hissed then, lips close to
the door. It was a whispered entreaty that was
fierce and managed to be slavish at the same time.
"Master, grant me lives, many lives!"

What Anglo-Saxon idiom of speech is this? I
pondered, even as he went on: "Insects I have
now, master, to devour by the scores and hun-
dreds, and animals I may obtain . . . but I need
the lives of people, master! Men, and children,
and women, especially women. Women!" He
made a sound between a gurgle and a laugh. "I
must have them, master, and you must grant
them to me!"

He went on for what seemed like many minutes
in the same vein, whilst I stood just inside the
door, no more than an arm's length away, like a
priest in some mad confessional. With hands

pressed to my temples I tried to think. Of one thing only could I be sure: this man *knew that I was there*, knew at any rate that some being beyond the ordinary was inside the chapel, and he had come to offer me a kind of self-serving worship. My secure anonymity, upon which I had just been congratulating myself, and toward which I had spent so much coin and effort, was already nonexistent.

Even as I stood there at a loss I heard the footsteps of others, four or five more men, climbing the wall in the area where my first visitor had climbed. In something like despair I at first visualized a whole troop of worshipers, with this their gibbering high priest who had found the shrine and was going to lead them in their litanies: "Women . . . master . . . lives . . . master . . . women . . ."

But instead of the madman's acolytes it was of course his keepers who were coming after him, Seward and three or four burly attendants the doctor had wisely brought along. Only at this point did I remember Harker's casual mention of the asylum adjoining my grounds, and begin to grasp the true state of affairs.

Outside, the newcomers rapidly came closer. They fanned out into a semicircle centered on the man who knelt at my chapel door, and continued a methodical advance.

Meanwhile he continued to pour forth his pleas. "I am here to do your bidding, master. I am your slave, and you will reward me, for I shall be faithful. I have worshiped you long and afar off." To this day I am not certain whether this last statement was a lie meant to be ingratiating, a delusion generated in the sick man's brain, or actually the truth. Certainly Renfield—which was his name, as I later learned; a madman nearly sixty years of age, but of prodigious strength, and from a noble family—certainly, I say, Renfield was somehow aware of my presence as soon as I arrived at Carfax, and was subsequently able to detect my comings and goings there without leaving his own cell or room at the asylum.

He went on, almost slavering, in a repulsive hissing voice: "Now that you are here, I await your commands, and you will not pass me by, will you, in your distribution of good things?"

Behind and round him the other men were steadily closing in. Now I heard for the first time the voice of Seward, young, confident, and masterful: "Renfield, time to come back with us now, there's a good chap."

And another, wheedling, in accents of the lower class: "Come on now, ducky. Easy does it . . . *whup!*"

Masterful words or sweet ones would not do the trick for them that night. Though they were four or five to one, the struggle was not easy. Renfield's was no ordinary strength, as I discovered later for myself. Later also I read of how he had actually torn a window and its casing from the wall of his cell in making his escape that night. Seward and his men at length subdued him, and packed him away, bound like some wild animal to be bundled back over the wall; and stillness and the night were mine once more. But from the noise of that struggle I was well able to believe that, as Seward wrote of his patient on that very night: "He means murder in every turn and movement."

And my dreams of a new life had received another powerful blow.

TRACK THREE

I would have followed the keepers and their prisoner back to the asylum at once to learn if I could from what source Renfield derived his powers, but I expected that he would detect my presence there, and no doubt make such a fuss about it that those in charge of him, who so far seemed to think there was no point to his madness, would be impelled to further investigation.

Besides, there were my boxes, without which I would be homeless and soon doomed in this alien land. I saw now that I dared not leave them vulnerable to easy attack or even casual vandalism for so long as an hour, and I therefore spent the rest of the night making my position somewhat more secure, at least on my own grounds. It took me a few very worthwhile hours to replace the good Transylvanian earth in several of the boxes—even at this late date I am not going to tell you exactly how many—with English soil, equally good by most standards but not nearly as hospitable to me. One small portion of my home-land I transplanted into the ground within the Carfax chapel, and the contents of some other boxes I buried elsewhere on the grounds, in heavily thicketed places where no chance discovery of my digging work was likely.

Next day I could rest with some confidence through the hours of light, and by the following evening I had convinced myself that the madman's incursion was not so important after all. I did not want to spend the night lurking round an asylum, anyway; I wanted to see London, and I did.

Or I began to see her. There is of course no end to such an enterprise. Taking to my small leathery wings at dusk, I made short work of fifteen miles. Before I came within a mile of London's heart the roar of her never-quiet streets assaulted my ears and the glow of the metropolis dazzled my bat eyes. It was night, and summer, and many of the coal fires were out that on a winter's day would have quite blackened the sky about me.

There wound the Thames, girded by great bridges and giving back a million sparkling lights. There beyond the Green Park was the palace wherein Victoria herself graced the last years of her long reign; there sounded, close below me, the deep and solemn notes of Big Ben. The larger thoroughfares were all crowded, and my eye picked out here and there the unfamiliar, unnatural steadiness of electric light. The fronts of stores and restaurants glowed along Piccadilly and in the Strand; the Abbey, towering remnant of an age long gone, looked out and pondered on a changing world. A few lights burned in Parliament, where government of a far-flung empire no doubt could not afford to wait till morning.

Below me now St. Paul's Cathedral raised its dome; now passed the crooked streets and savage slums of Whitechapel and Bethnal Green. . . .

But I could talk for hours on London, and I must not. Let me now say only that night after night I came to her, and each night was more enraptured than the last.

Meanwhile . . .

I suppose it cannot be counted as remarkable coincidence that Lucy came down to London— or rather to its northern environs, where stood her family's house called Hillingham—some five days after I did. London was and is the Rome toward which all English roads must tend. It was at about this same time that she began to keep a diary, recording rather gloomy thoughts. It may be that after a few episodes of life lived keenly with her Viking she found the prospect of life with Arthur Holmwood no longer attractive.

Holmwood—shortly to become Lord Godal-ming, on the death of his father—was easily the wealthiest and most influential of Lucy's three breathing suitors, and he was the one she had accepted. I was to learn about him shortly. Dr. Seward, as I have said, was another. The third we will come to in a little while.

Since Lucy and I had come to be of one blood I vaguely sensed her geographic closeness when I awoke on the evening of August twenty-fourth. But I only smiled fondly to myself and went out to look at London once again, to taste the psychic nectar of her crowds, to mingle with her great masses of vital humanity, to study in her houses, streets, and monuments the records of her enormous past. Each hour I spent in these activities tempted me to spend two more, and it was only with difficulty that I could force myself to allot time for necessary business: the dispersal of my nests.

I now began to get about regularly during the daylight hours, and walked into the office of a carter's firm to arrange for the removal of some of the boxes from Carfax to secondary depots about the city. I was delighted to find that the proprietor and clerks, upright daytime citizens all of them, dealt with a vampire in a courteous and businesslike way: they observed my coin and paid little attention to my face. Meanwhile I also replaced the native earth in some more of my boxes with English soil. These refilled boxes I let sit in the Carfax chapel, whilst to hold the Transylvanian earth I employed some large boxes obtained at night, by stealth and strength, from a coffin monger's in Cheapside. I left some gold behind there, in payment more than adequate, but did not wish to attract attention by open purchase of such specialized items, when I was not an undertaker and had no stock of corpses to be exhibited on demand.

These modern double coffins I found to make delightful domiciles; with my native soil packed into the outer box, I could rest in perfectly clean comfort within the inner, leaden shell. One such double coffin I buried in the chapel, and another in the yard of a house at Mile End that I was already negotiating to acquire. A third box I kept in reserve, in a rented shed near Charing Cross. I tell you now quite freely where they were, for they are there no longer, though two of them are still in London.

It was not until the night of August twenty-sixth that I next saw Lucy, and then I came to her only in response to an appeal for help. Hers was a mental outcry of such vivid anguish that to refuse it lightly would have been cruel, and I think dishonorable as well. Therefore I found myself, late at night, waiting in man-shape outside the large suburban house called Hillingham, where Lucy lived with her ailing mother and a small squad of servants. I sent a mental message of reassurance in to the sleepless girl; she arose and managed to leave the house without disturbing any of the other occupants.

I smiled and stretched forth my hands as I saw her slight figure, in its dressing gown, coming through the garden under the trees.

"So, then," she murmured, coming near, eyes wide as they sought mine, "it was not dreams and nothing else." Somewhat hesitantly she took my outstretched hands; I believe she was at that moment almost afraid of me, though we were hardly strangers. I had given her much joy, and naught, so far as I knew, of any pain.

"My dear Lucy, lightbearer," I said. "Is that what so distresses you? That I am not a dream? You have but to wave your little hand, dismissing me, and never will your eyes rest on me again."

Her eyes were puzzled and full of pain. "You know, then, that I am distressed and afraid."

"Child, of course I know. I would not be here if you had not called to me, though only in your mind, for help."

"But how can such things be?" I was about to attempt an answer to this question when she presented me with another, that she evidently thought required answering more urgently. It came in the form of a bald statement: "I am to be married, you know."

"I had not known, but allow me now to extend such felicitations as may be welcome from a man in my position." I bowed.

"I really am going to marry Arthur, you know." Lucy blushed. "I love him—very much. And he loves me." She began telling me of Holmwood and his mannerisms and his prospects for wealth and position, till I began to feel rather disgustingly like a grim uncle or elder brother who had to be placated, his blessing sought. Of course at that moment Lucy had no other father figure in her life—Van Helsing had not yet come on the scene —and perhaps she did cast me most unsuitably in that role.

". . . so I do love Arthur, and am going to marry him. And you—you are still like a dream, or something out of one." Had she hoped to provoke me to a jealous declaration? Now the anguish in her face, as she gazed on me, was obviously that of longing, and her voice broke. "I don't even know your name!"

I was silent, not sure that I should tell it to her. Names have power, power that can cut both ways.

Nor was she quite sure, apparently, that she wanted to know more. "Hold me," was all she had left to say before coming with a slight tremble into my arms. Lucy understood only that what we did gave her supreme delight and that Arthur was not the only man she loved. We had held no theoretical discussions on vampirism, and I would wager that she had never even heard the word. It may be that I drank a bit too deeply on that night, for Lucy clung to me and would not let me go. . . .

Her wedding was scheduled for September seventeenth, a few weeks off. Whether Lucy would have wanted to continue her affair with me beyond that date is something I cannot tell, for women are unfathomable. What do they want? I ask, with Freud, in periods of bleak masculine despair.

Lucy pined during the next few days. Also some signs of her repeated nocturnal dissipations must have been apparent to Arthur Holmwood, who was seeing her frequently again now that she was back near London, for her fiancé a few days later called in Dr. Seward, his friend as well as Lucy's, to examine her. "She demurred at first," as Arthur complained in a letter. Well, perhaps she would have preferred a physician who was not a rejected suitor, or even more one whose specialty was not the study of mental illness. Though she had not Mina's capacity for sturdy independence, it is even possible that she resented not being able to decide such matters as the choice of a doctor for herself.

Seward interrupted his contemplation of his wealthy lunatics long enough to give her a cursory looking over and concluded that the basis of her—or rather, her fiancé's—complaint "must be something mental." That was true, so far as it went. Ah, Lucy, Lucy which means "lightbearer" —Lucy of the delicate and trustful nature. I suppose you were not a very good girl; but like so many women of your era, you deserved much better than fate gave you.

She tried to fob off Seward with some vague tales of sleepwalking, which of course were true enough as far as they went. But he was a pretty good doctor, for his time; at least he had an acute eye, or instinct, for the unusual. Not that he showed great judgment in knowing what to do about it. Seward's first act after he had caught a hint of something truly remarkable in the case— my shadow or my flavor on the girl—was to send to Amsterdam for his old teacher, Abraham Van Helsing, M.D., Ph.D., D.Lit., et cetera, et cetera, et cetera.

Van Helsing. . . .

Do any who hear my voice still fear my name? Is it believed by even my most timid hearers that I may represent a real danger? When I have made you understand the depths of the idiocy of that man, Van Helsing, and confess at the same time that he managed to hound me nearly to my death, you will be forced to agree that among all famous perils to the world I must be ranked as one of the least consequential.

Van Helsing tended to make a good impression, though, especially at first and with the young and inexperienced. Seward held, and stubbornly maintained, a very favorable opinion of this man, who he thought knew "as much about obscure diseases as anyone in the world." Well, perhaps. Medicine in the 1890s was in a miserable state. "He is a seemingly arbitrary man, but this is because he knows what he is talking about better than anyone else. He is a philosopher and a metaphysician"—right there, Arthur Holmwood, for whom this sales pitch was written, should have been warned—"and one of the most advanced scientists of his day; and he has, I believe, an absolutely open mind. This, with an iron nerve, a temper of the ice brook, an indomitable resolution, self-command, and toleration"—the latter not for vampires, of course—"exalted from virtues to blessings, and the kindliest and truest heart that beats. . . ."

And Mina, when she met him later, saw and described "a man of medium weight, strongly built, with his shoulders set back over a broad, deep chest and a neck well balanced on the trunk as the head is on the neck. The poise of the head strikes one at once as indicative of thought and power; the head is noble, well-sized, broad, and large behind the ears. The face, clean-shaven, shows a hard, square chin, a large, resolute, mobile mouth, a good-sized nose, rather straight. . . . The forehead is broad and fine . . . such a forehead that the reddish hair cannot possibly tumble over it, but falls naturally back and to the sides. Big dark blue eyes are set widely apart, and are quick and tender or stern with the man's moods."

Now let us see just what this paragon accomplished for us all. By the time he first examined Lucy, on September second, if I am not mistaken, she had recouped from our perhaps too-enthusiastic embraces of a few nights earlier, and was of course looking better. Van Helsing decided that "there has been much blood lost . . . but the conditions of her are in no way anemic." We must make allowance for the fact that English was not the professor's mother tongue. But neither was his knowledge of the blood and its disorders adequate, a circumstance we all had much cause to regret. After shaking his head over Lucy's case, but saying little, he went back to Amsterdam to think.

For several days I had remained away from

Lucy to allow her blood time to restore itself, and also to give serious consideration to the idea of breaking off with her permanently and at once. This I decided to do, and when I went back at night to Hillingham it was with the resolution that the time had come to say our last farewell. This decision was for her welfare as well as my own.

Firstly, I did not want to make her a vampire, when in her ignorance—a state I felt she preferred—she could give no informed consent, could not intelligently weigh the perils and pleasures attendant upon such a momentous transformation. And for us to have continued our intercourse at its then current frequency would shortly have brought her to the point where the possibility of her transformation into a vampire would have to be faced seriously.

Secondly, I argued with myself, that enjoyable as Lucy was, there was many a peasant wench simpering in my native land who was just as hot-blooded, heavy-breathing, and well-shaped, who might have afforded me the same joys at a small fraction of the expense and effort. Surely it was not for downy skin and tender veins that I had made my odyssey. Alas! how passion can make fools of us! On what was to have been my final visit, devoted to brief explanations and leave-taking, Lucy clung to me as before, and to my chagrin I once more left her noticeably weakened.

Nevertheless my basic decision was unshaken, and I brought away with me conviction that the assignation just concluded had been our last. The affair was over, I was certain, whether Lucy realized it or not. The chance of her becoming a vampire, which only a few hours earlier had still been relatively remote, had been brought by our most recent embrace to the status of a clear and present danger—or opportunity, depending upon one's point of view.

Of course on the next day, which I think was September sixth, Lucy looked somewhat wan and weak and strange again. Holmwood was off attending to his slowly dying father, but Seward looked in on her and did not like what he saw. Again he called in Van Helsing, who had requested that daily telegrams be sent to keep him informed of the patient's condition.

The professor hurried back to London, a gleam in his eye I have no doubt, and a bagful of his tools in hand. Before I could have the least inkling of what his intentions were, or even that he was attending Lucy—she had not mentioned to me his earlier visit—the fool had attempted to perform a blood transfusion, with Arthur Holmwood selected—for purely social reasons —as the donor.

Let us try to see this matter in historical perspective. Not until 1900, some nine years later, did Landsteiner discover the existence in man of the four basic blood groups, A, B, AB, and O, at which point in time the feasibility of transfusion without great peril for the patient may be said to have begun. Of course ever since antiquity some hardy folk have survived their enterprising physicians' attempts to transfuse blood from human to human, or even from animal to human; no doubt in many cases the survival of the patient has been due to failure of the transfusing technique to work, so that no appreciable fraction of inimical blood cells were introduced into his vascular system.

I was myself quiescent in my tomb in 1492, the year of the supposed transfusion of Pope Innocent VIII with the whole blood of three young men; therefore I cannot venture an opinion on the accuracy of that most shocking story. During a period of activity in the mid-seventeenth century I read with interest more than casual of Harvey's epochal discovery of the circulation of the blood. From time to time I continue to gather facts and learned opinions in the field. Although my own opportunities for actual research have been more circumscribed than you might think, and my natural bent is toward action rather more than intellectual affairs, still by 1891 I had accumulated some small knowledge of this subject of more than passing consequence in my own life. Had I known what Van Helsing was doing to treat a vampire's victim—as he saw the case—I would have stopped him. You may believe that I would not have callously left Lucy to her fate. But though I perceived through the continued communion of our minds that she was now definitely unwell, and suffering, I did not guess the cause.

Whether because of a fortunate compatibility between Holmwood's blood and her own, or because of some equally lucky failure of the technique to transfuse much of any blood at all, Lucy not only survived that first operation but by next day had regained something of the appearance of health. She had been narcotized during the operation, and on waking had no clear grasp of what had happened, although of course there was the small bandaged wound upon her arm to give her food for thought. When she questioned the men who had her in their charge they lovingly told her to lie back and rest.

On the night of September ninth she suffered a relapse; or it may have been a fresh illness, some bloodborne infection from her fiancé. Van Helsing's prescribed treatment for this setback was a second transfusion, this time with Seward as the donor, as the youngest and sturdiest male available at the moment. Those who wonder at the girl's surviving this second assault—and a third one, later on—at the hands of the indomitable scientist may ponder also Lower's similar operation, which was also successful or at least nonfatal, performed in London in 1667. And another in Paris in the same year, by Denis, who is documented as transfusing the blood of a lamb into the veins of a boy left anemic by conventional medical treatment—that is, bloodletting—of the time. The nineteenth century in England saw the obstetrician Blundell, and others, attempting the transfusion of blood between humans with increasing frequency, and often claiming favorable results.

But many unpublicized attempts must have been made that concluded more unhappily. And Lucy's second transfusion, from Seward—who wrote that he was much weakened by his donation—had a bad effect upon her.

As she languished in her bed—and I of course unknowingly pursued my own affairs—on September eleventh the house at Hillingham received from Holland the first of a number of shipments of garlic, including both flowers and whole plants. These of course were ordered especially by the philosopher and metaphysician, who

by this time knew—though he had told no one—
that a vampire was lurking about. Now, the
powerful smell of *Allium sativum* is at least as
discouraging to a suitor of my persuasion as to
one of the more common sort—nay, more so, for
even bland food can be disgusting to a vampire—
but it is not quite the impassable barrier Van
Helsing evidently hoped for. Still, had I really
been intent upon effecting the poor girl's ruin,
this new tactic would at least have been better
than injecting her with foreign proteins.

On the night of September twelfth Mrs.
Westenra, though herself semi-invalid, roused
sufficiently to throw the supposedly medicinal
flowers out of her daughter's room and leave the
window open. Perhaps her own life was somewhat prolonged by this removal of the irritating
stench of diallyl disulfide and trisulfide and the
rest, but Lucy's was thought—by the doctors, at
least—to suffer. One of the most advanced scientists of his day had of course omitted to tell Lucy's
mother of his theories that her daughter would be
better off with windows shut and stinking blooms
in place. Had he spelled out all his ideas for
Lucy's mother, I suppose she might have thrown
the flowers out anyway, and Van Helsing with
them, and we should all have been far better off.
However . . .

Naturally Lucy's vampire visitor was blamed,
by Van Helsing then, and by the whole crew later,
for the continued deterioration of her condition.
In fact, I was walking the streets of Whitechapel
on the night the flowers were thrown out, and far
into the morning; but I could have produced no
witnesses. On that night I spoke with and joked

with an eyewitness to one of the Ripper's shocking crimes of three years before. I believed her surprising version of that event, but I doubted that a jury would accept her word on my whereabouts or her testimony as a character witness for me.

She was welcome company, for during most of that night I walked alone and nursed a grim, post-midnight kind of thought. The first real doubts were rising in my mind as to the feasibility of my planned reunion with the mainstream of humanity. Much as I enjoyed being in London, I was being forced to the realization that my mere presence there was not changing me as rapidly as I had hoped.

On September thirteenth, as Seward recorded in his journal—which he kept, by the way, on an early variety of phonograph, nowhere near as efficient as this admirable machine into which I speak—"again the operation; again the narcotic; again some return of color to the ashy cheeks . . ."

This time Van Helsing himself was donor, whilst Seward, at the master's direction, operated. With such an agglomeration of cells in her poor veins, it is only a wonder that the poor girl lived as long as she did.

I must now recount the events of September seventeenth, which was a most fateful day for all of us.

Jonathan and Mina Harker, fresh from being married in Budapest, where he had long lain in hospital, were now prosperously installed in a house in Exeter. Mina had now read her bridegroom's somewhat feverish journal of his stay at my castle, but the subject of vampirism had never been discussed between them, and no doubt at this point neither thought such horrors would touch their lives again.

Arthur Holmwood still watched at his dying father's bedside in Ring, with moral support from a young American named Quincey Morris, Arthur's frequent companion on hunting trips round the world, and the third of Lucy's breathing suitors.

At the asylum on that evening, Renfield, loose again, came after Dr. Seward with a kitchen knife. Seward, fortunately for himself, managed to stun his powerful antagonist with a single punch, and the madman was soon disarmed and returned to confinement.

Van Helsing, back in Antwerp on one of his habitual commuting journeys, but still commendably concerned about his patient Lucy, telegraphed to Seward that it was vital for Seward to stand guard at Hillingham that night—to guard against exactly what, Van Helsing had yet to specify. Seward of course would have unquestioningly complied, but that telegram for some fateful reason was missent. It was not delivered until it was twenty-two hours overdue.

And I myself, on September seventeenth, was visiting Regents Park. My doubts were with me, and I was resolved to work harder at being human. I sat on a convenient bench and read the *Times* of London for the day:

CRYSTAL PALACE
Astounding Performance
TIGER DRIVING GOAT

. . . enough of that.

MASSAGE AND ELECTRICITY
(Weir Mitchell system) with
Swedish and German move-
ments combined. As each LES-
SON of two hours' duration is
given daily on a living subject,
pupils can be perfected in a fort-
night. No bruising; those who
bruise have been improperly
taught. . . .

Mary Jane Heathcote, 28, was
indicted for the willful murder of
Florence Heathcote . . . her little
girl . . . aged five years and six
months. . . .

At Clerkenwell, Henry Bazley,
29, bookbinder, was . . . charged
with having taken away out of the
possession and control of her
mother a girl named Elizabeth
Morey . . . aged 16 years 10
months. She was traced to
Highgate, where she lodged in a
room for which the prisoner was
found to be paying 5 shillings a
week, and where he visited her.
. . . Detective-sergeant Drew,
who had executed the warrant
for the prisoner's arrest, said that
he found him at home hiding in a
backyard. The prisoner was a

married man with four children.
When told the charge he said it
was a lie. On the application of
the prosecutor the prisoner was
remanded. . . .

. . . Do you doubt I can remember all these
items as they were? Well, I found them memorable. Check your library's microfilm files of the
Times if you doubt me.

(To the editor) Sir—Contrary to
my inclination, it has fallen to my
lot to refute the theory put forward by my friend Mr. Haliburton at the Oriental Congress
that a race of dwarfs exists between the Atlas and the
Sahara. . . .
            Jas. Ed. Budgett Meakin

Sir—The necessity for a ready
communication between the
front door and the upper floor of
a house in case of fire or other
urgent need . . . is so obvious as
to require no comment. . . . I
have thought of the following
simple contrivance: A loud-
ringing bell is hung in the upper
floor; the wire of this bell termi-
nates at its lower end on a chain
and hook in the basement of the
house. At night the hook is at-
tached to the crank of the ordi-

nary housebell and is detached in the morning . . . by this means also the filthy and insanitary practice of having a manservant sleeping in the pantry, that fertile source of much immorality, both in and out of doors, may be avoided.

Yours, & C. H.

PICCADILLY (Overlooking Green Park)—self-contained FLAT—four rooms, bath room, lift, etc., to be LET, on LEASE, and Furniture sold. Apply Housekeeper, 98, Piccadilly, W.

. . . That was interesting. But I would rather buy than rent, wanting nothing to do with nosy landlords.

Sir—If one of the delegates who spoke so strongly in favor of the eight-hours movement was, on his return home, seized with a sudden and dangerous illness; and if, on sending for his doctor, he got an answer to say that the latter had just finished eight hours of work, and that for the next sixteen hours he was going to rest and enjoy himself, what would he think of the new arrangement?

Yours truly, J.R.T.

... And back to the front page ...

MOULE'S PATENT EARTH-CLOSET COMPANY
(Limited)
Garrick-street   Covent-garden,
LONDON
MOULE'S   COMPANY   NOW
MAKES:
CLOSETS—for the garden
CLOSETS—for shooting boxes
CLOSETS—for cottages
CLOSETS—for anywhere
CLOSETS—Complete are now made, fitted with "pull out" apparatus
CLOSETS—fitted with "pull up" apparatus
CLOSETS—fitted with self-acting apparatus
CLOSETS—made of galvanized, corrugated iron
CLOSETS—to take to pieces, for easy transport
CLOSETS—can be put together in two hours.
CLOSETS—to work satisfactorily
CLOSETS—only require to be supplied
CLOSETS—with fine and dry mold
CLOSETS—on this principle never fail
CLOSETS—if supplied with dry earth ...

The litany went on, and I read it, eyes almost in hypnotic bondage. But my higher attention was still back with that manservant sleeping in the pantry. Why was his condition so "filthy and insanitary"? Had he his feet resting on the bacon, or was his foul breath contaminating bags of sugar? And where exactly in the "fertile source" did the noxious weeds of "immorality" sprout? Was I to read into the letter dark implications of the deadly sin of gluttony?

The London papers, that in my own homeland had seemed to promise marvels, seemed only to grow more bewildering the longer I dwelt amid the world which they described. It would take time, I comforted myself, and threw my paper into a dustbin nearby—the park was very neat. Getting to my feet, I strolled on to the zoo. The day was overcast, and, top-hatted like a proper gentleman, I found the sun scarcely bothersome at all.

It was a relief to reach the zoo and see more animals than people round me for a while. Great throngs of humanity, though I had sought them out and still found pleasure in them, still were wearying to one who like myself had been so long removed from crowds. A stranger in a strange land was I indeed, notwithstanding a reasonable facility in the English speech and an appearance acceptable in the metropolis.

Naturally enough I gravitated toward the cage of wolves, where three gray beauties suffered with innate dignity their ignominious confinement. Although I at first made no effort to converse, one wolf of them knew me; more accurately, he knew that I was not as common men, and that I was far closer kin to him than any

FRED SABERHAGEN

two-legged creature he had ever seen before. He knew that I knew what it was to run on four gray paws, and leap to the kill, and drink the raw red blood from flesh my teeth had torn. He knew, and could not decently contain his knowledge. While the other two in the cage, who may have known something too but did not care, lay drowsing and wondering at him, he bounded like a madwolf against the bars, and let his feelings out in the only kind of voice he had.

An elderly keeper came from somewhere and regarded me with suspicion. There was no one else about at the time and I was obviously at the focal point of lupine uproar.

I was not in London to be mysterious, but to bind myself more closely to the great mass of humanity. "Keeper," I said, to have something to say, "these wolves seem upset at something."

"Maybe it's you," the man retorted, and his gloomily surly manner reminded me of a Turkish jailer I once had, and the resemblance made me smile even as it aroused my further sympathy for the confined wolf.

"Oh, no, they wouldn't like me," I answered vaguely, distracted by a communication from another source. *Freedom*, the wolf was saying, looking out. It was not a question but a complete declarative sentence.

I cannot give you that. I answered him. *Take it for yourself and it is yours.*

"Ow yes they would," the old man answered me, impertinent with the privilege of crabbed and independent age. "They always like a bone or two t' clean their teeth on about teatime, of which you 'as a bagful."

Freedom! came from the gray iron cage.

114

Take it. Transcend. Do you want it more than food, more than retaining your own wolf nature? Will you put by your very body and its known comforts to have this thing you say you want? Simply to be free of your cage?

And the early years of Turkish imprisonment were once more very clear to me. Radu was then a mere child, a small child, too easily frightened to offer any sport at all to our inventive jailers. But I was fourteen years old when they began on me. . . .

The animal's brain was churning with unworded thoughts, but for the moment it quieted and lay down. The keeper looked at it in puzzlement, looked back to me, and then walked over to the cage and reached inside to stroke the ears of the panting beast. To startle the old man I did the same, and had my reward in his expression.

"Tyke care!" he said. "Berserker here is quick!"

"Never mind, I'm used to them." The wolf's eyes were not on me but fixed on distance now, as he thought of running in unbarred, unbounded space.

"Are you in the business yourself?" the keeper asked, his tone now friendlier. He took off his hat. Perhaps he hoped to buy another wolf or two from me.

"No, not exactly." And I tipped my own hat to him and to Berserker in farewell. "But I have made pets of several." And with that I turned and walked away. The wolf's wordless thought-voice was falling off in my mind to mere muted distant mumbling, but the infinitely more verbal noise of Lucy's thoughts was audible again and mounting higher. I did not wish to hear either of them.

115

Something was seriously wrong with Lucy, I could not help but know that much, but I closed off my mind against knowing more.

There was no possible way I could have guessed that after dark Berserker would break the railings of his cage, forcing iron bars loose from their fastenings, and come racing unerringly to find me in the night—at Hillingham.

I could not know what the night before me held. But still as I walked out of the park I was perturbed in spirit.

I said before that I would later speak of fear, and now the time has come. I will not say that I have experienced infinite fear, but I have known all fear that my mind and soul could ever bear, and more. The first time that my Turkish jailors stripped me naked in my cell and carried me, paralyzed with terror and dripping with my own excrement, out to the impalement stake, I had no doubt that I was going to die upon it. Some in my situation would have fainted, others would have gone mad. What I did . . . well, perhaps only a caged wolf could begin to understand.

Of course I did not die. If the guards had killed me they would have had no fun for the next day. I was not even really—or I should say "not permanently"—impaled. The end of the upright stake was blunt and drew no blood immediately when it was inserted into a natural orifice of the body; and by standing on tiptoe I could keep it from entering deeply enough to do serious damage. I could not stand on tiptoe indefinitely, but when my weight began to come down the men were quick to take me off the stake. They certainly did not want me to die on it then and there. Never before had they seen anyone who retained consciousness while being so deliciously, excruciatingly, helplessly frightened.

Next day they played a new game, showing me first what they claimed was a signed order for my execution. Again I believed them, for my susceptibility to terror gave me no choice. Perhaps I am not really exaggerating when I say that on each of these days I died of fright. The new game had to do with being burned alive, and I had blisters and scorched hair before they called a halt. And on a succeeding day there was a game involving voracious rats; and again, one with a Turkish woman whose husband, she said, had been tortured to death by Walachians; and after that . . . but I have no wish to disgust you with all details.

It was when the cycle came round to the stake again that I realized abruptly that I had nothing left to fear, that in fact I was afraid no longer. I had used up all the fear my soul could ever generate, were I to live to be a thousand. My life's ration of anxiety, dread, timorousness, and terror, all was consumed before I had a beard to shave. From those days to this, I have feared nothing. I am not brave and never was; that is a different matter entirely. . . .

It seems to me the most striking proof that this estimate of my condition is correct that I simultaneously lost all desire to be revenged upon my jailors. A high official of the sultan himself, happening to pass through Egrigoz, observed with astonishment how imperturbably I bore some of the fruitless later attempts of my enemies to frighten me. They were in fact applying torture at the time, but, do you know, it is the moment-to-moment *fear* of pain that is the worst part of pain itself? This high official, as I say, applauded what he took to be my fortitude, and took an interest in my case. In time he became my friend, to such an extent that, had I wanted revenge upon my low-ranking tormentors, I could probably have had it. And it was my refusal of revenge, not out of any heroic Christian virtue but rather because of sheer fearless indifference, that so frightened them in turn. Man fears that which he cannot understand, and I had gone far beyond the comprehension of those simple but evil men. . . .

So as I walked the London streets it was not with fear or hatred but in gloomy meditation that I thought back upon the Turks. Was I so sure that I *wanted* to rejoin the ranks of the mainstream of mankind? To shorten my life, possibly, in doing so? Not that I feared a shortened life, or aught else in the world or out of it.

Not even God, my friends, although I know him better than you do. . . .

An hour or so before the wolf escaped at midnight I had been standing in a Soho tavern, acutely conscious of the fact that there was no image of myself in the cracked and cloudy mirror behind the bar and that the fleshly girl clinging to my arm would be indeed surprised were she ever to note that fact. I was acutely conscious also of the warm fluid pulsing so rapidly within her *Vena jugularis*, and of the impossible odors of alcoholically fermented grain rising from the glass that waited untasted before me on the arm-smoothed wood. Conscious with all my soul of the gulf between me and those round me, all of them unarguably human, misshapen in mind and body and spirit though they were.

It was in this state that I felt Lucy call to me with a new urgency, cry with a terrible fervor across the four or five miles of the city that separated us. In her fear and sickness she was appealing for my help, calling on me as her protector and her lord, and so it was I answered her. From the shadows of a Soho alley I took flight, and came down to rest on earth again in the dark, timbered lawn of Hillingham.

From there I sent my wordless summons, as before. This time, however, I soon learned that she could not or would not try to come out. Nor could I simply enter the house upon my own initiative. Whether the reason is to be found in physics or in psychology I am not sure, but the fact is that I may enter no dwelling place of breathing folk unless I have been at least once invited to do so by one who dwells within.

I knew by this time which window of the upper floor was that of Lucy's room, and I quickly took wing again and perched outside it, on the ledge. The blind was drawn and at first I could not see into the room, but Lucy's voice was plain. She was engaged in a shrill argument with another, older woman who could only be her mother. The argument ended abruptly when Lucy fell back exhausted upon her bed, thus coming partially into the narrow range of vision into the room I had obtained by pressing my bat head as close as possible against the glass at one side, where a chink was open twixt blind and casement. Round Lucy's neck, I saw, were garlic flowers garlanded, together with the long green leaves, and the whole room was fetid with the plant.

Almost simultaneous with this shocking discovery—which meant of course that someone was attempting antivampire measures—I heard Berserker's first low howl below me in the shrubbery, and looked down over one batwing in absolute consternation. It might take long minutes to quiet the wolf and send it peaceably back to the cage from which it had so recently, obviously, broken free, and Lucy's mental anguish was too urgent for me to spare the time for that. Feeling like a general beset in camp by a series of sudden surprise attacks, I crouched there on the windowsill and tried to marshal my thoughts calmly. Could there be some reason for the garlic, other than the one with which I was most familiar? There were undoubtedly some English customs of which I had not yet heard; but I had little hope that this was one of them.

The women inside had not yet heard the wolf, or else they thought its howls were those of some dog in the neighborhood, for the noise made no impression upon them. Contorting my small, furred body, I made a greater effort to peer in beside the blind and got a better look at Lucy in her nightgown. It was something of a shock to see how ill she looked. I also saw Lucy's mother in her robe, looking tired and drawn herself—recall that even at this time neither Lucy nor myself had yet any inkling of the very grave condition of Mrs. Westenra's heart—just as she tottered from the room and closed the door behind her. This was my chance; I sent another mental summons and simultaneously flapped my bat wings at the panes. Lucy turned her head a little on the pillow, but no more. Her eyes were closed.

Clinging carefully to stone in the autumnal night, I altered back to man-form right on the windowsill. I drew mass and weight unto myself—from nothing? Say from the great reservoir in which God kept such things before deciding to enact Creation, and to which some of his creatures are allowed a limited access still. How do I do it? Let me ask how you sort out the myriad atoms in your lungs each time you draw a breath to oxygenate your blood.

Now I tapped at the window with a long fingernail and spoke aloud. Lucy rose up in bed, with a startled look that soon changed to joy. She got up as quickly as she could, and came to the window, and was about to speak the words that would have let me pass in to her; but on the instant the door of her room opened once more and Mrs. Westenra's figure was plain in my field of vision—and mine, alas, in hers.

Lucy had already drawn the blind full back. When the unsuspecting old woman looked over her daughter's shoulder into the night it was my visage that she saw peering in at both of them.

I expected shock, but not what happened. Mrs. Westenra extended her arm for a second or two, pointing at me in silence, her face contorted with her fright; and then there came from her throat a gurgling noise and she fell as if an ax had struck her down.

"Mother!" Lucy cried out, and hurried to try to lift her aged parent from the floor; but in Lucy's weakened condition the shock and the exertion were too much for her, and she crumpled over also, in a faint.

Mrs. Westenra's heart and lungs had already ceased their labors and I was not sure that Lucy's would not shortly do the same, so feebly and irregularly were they now working. She had called to me for help and I was anxious—nay, almost desperate—to fly to her aid, but I could not. I had not yet been bidden directly to enter the house wherein she lay. I, who might pass like smoke through barriers impossible for breathing men to penetrate, was held back by a law as inexorable to me as gravity.

Another low wolf howl rising from the shrubbery at last jogged my slow brain back into action. I dropped lightly to the ground, which was some twelve feet below the windowsill, and called Berserker to me. For a moment I held the big gray wolf tightly, one hand gripping his muzzle, my eyes locked on his, trying to force into his willing brain knowledge of the service that I required of him. I wanted him to force his way into that room above, and lick at Lucy's face to rouse her; failing that, to drag her by her nightdress or her hair to the window where she might come within my reach.

Why did I not go instead, in my most suave and reassuring style to knock at the front door? All this was in the middle of the night, remember, and the house was isolated. Lucy had once mentioned to me in passing that no male servants slept in the house—the pantry at Hillingham was evidently a place of impeccable morality. Were the women within likely to open a door for me, under whatever pretext I came? I thought not. My instincts argued for direct action, and I have learned to trust my instincts in emergencies.

It took me two, three, tosses to cast the heavy wolf up to the windowsill above. Its surface, though broad enough for a lean and rather acrobatic gentleman to sit on at his ease, offered but scanty purchase for Berserker's paws. He whimpered at the treatment I accorded him but seemed to realize that in adopting me as master he had acquired an obligation to carry out my orders. In a moment he had swung his heavy forequarters round and smashed the glass panes of the window in.

I was leaping up to catch the windowsill with both my hands just as the wolf fell back. As we passed I saw the red cuts on his muzzle and the small gleam from a bit of broken glass that had stuck in his fur. I meant to tend his wounds, who had served me faithfully, but I would see to Lucy first. I will be human, I will be, I kept repeating to myself.

I crouched on the sill again, my face framed in the broken-edged aperture of glass. "Lucy!" I called in, quietly but fiercely, using mind as well as voice.

On a carpet littered with broken glass and garlic flowers Lucy stirred and sat up slowly, not seeming to realize that she was half entangled with her mother's corpse.

"What . . . who . . . ?"

"Lucy, your Viking is here to aid you. Call me to come in. Call me to come to you."

Her eyes lifted slowly, puzzledly, to behold my face. Now belowstairs I could hear some of the housemaids stirring; no doubt they had been awakened by the crash of glass. Outside, the wolf howled once again, this time in pain. Lucy raised a hand to try to put back the blond hair from her face, but she was too weak and the gesture failed halfway through.

"Lucy, my name is Vlad. Bid me to come in, quick."

"Oh. Come, then, Vlad. I feel so sick, I am afraid that I am going to die." Then, when I had lifted her in my arms, she made a gesture toward the still form remaining on the floor. "Mother?"

"Your mother is not suffering," I said, and put down Lucy on the bed. Then, before I could do or say anything more, a multitudinous shuffle of feet in the carpeted hall outside the bedroom door announced the arrival of the housemaids in a frightened group.

"Miss Lucy? Are you all right?"

"Answer carefully!" I whispered, gripping Lucy's arms. My eyes burned into hers, my voice commanded, and she seemed to regain a little of her strength.

"I am all right," she called out weakly, "for the moment."

"Is your mother in there, Miss Lucy? May we come in?"

I nodded.

"Come!" she called out, and the handle of the door began to turn; before it had completed its motion I was under Lucy's bed, stretched out at full length and ready to melt to mist or shrink to bat-form in an instant.

Eight bare girlish feet paraded into the room and round the carpet near my head, accompanied by dancing nightgown hems, outcries, and lamentations. Mrs. Westenra's body was lifted to the bed, the broken window marveled at, and horror expressed at the continued howling of the wolf outside. Injured—and thinking himself betrayed, for he went home before I could get out to tend his wounds—he had better cause to howl than they did, and he made less noise.

And there were those garlic flowers on the bedroom floor, now crushed almost into my very nostrils. Vlad, I asked myself, reviewing the situation as I lay beneath the bed; what is the world, the great breathing human world which you expect to join, going to make of all this?

Lucy sat exhaustedly in a chair whilst the maids were laying out her mother's corpse. But despite her weakness and illness she retained presence of mind enough to realize that a man was in danger of being found concealed in her boudoir, a state of affairs less tolerable than death. And she retained the wit to do something about it. I saw her suddenly get up and leave the room, and heard her soft feet descend the stairs, whilst the maids remained gathered round the bed with the dead woman on it and the live vampire out of sight beneath. The maids did not note their young mistress's departure or her quiet return a minute later. During this minute I heard, faint but distinct, the sound of a brief trickle of liquid being poured somewhere downstairs.

Lucy was now standing upright, with an effort, just inside her bedroom door. "All of you," she commanded, having to raise her voice slightly to cut through the maids' continuing babble, "go down to the dining room and take each a glass of wine. Take only the sherry, mind. Then come back when I call."

There was no problem in obtaining prompt obedience to such an order. In a moment the whole moaning and cooing herd of them was gone, and Lucy had closed the door behind them and locked it. I wriggled out from concealment in a trice and found her once more on the point of swooning. She would have thrown herself upon the bed already but that her mother's clay lay there. I put her down there anyway, after moving the old lady next to the wall.

"Now the servants will leave us alone," Lucy said to me in a voice rapidly growing vague and distant. "For I have drugged the wine . . . oh, Vlad, are you my death? Your face is sometimes . . . if you are indeed death, then I must plead with you. Whoever you are . . . my mother's dead, but I'm too young. I'm to be married in September."

"Lie still now. I think that you are very ill." Giving Lucy a quick examination, I noted the bandaged incisions on the inside of each arm at the elbow. "Who is your doctor, and for what has he been treating you?"

"There are two: Dr. Van Helsing, of Amsterdam, and Dr. Seward."

I looked up sharply at that first name; I had heard it once before, from a vampire of my acquaintance. "And who is Dr. Seward?"

"He is about thirty, and very nice. In fact . . ." She paused. "He is superintendent of a lunatic asylum in Purfleet."

My mind raced, seeking understanding. But there is no understanding coincidence, or the imitation thereof by fate. "And their treatments? What are these little wounds? Surely they do not bleed you, in this day and age?"

"Ah, Vlad, I do not know. The doctors are kindly, and they mean well, I am sure. But they tell me nothing, and I am too ill to argue with them and insist on knowing." After a gasping pause, during which I tightened the bandage once more on her arm, she went on: "They bring me garlic flowers and bulbs. And three times now I have been drugged, and the doctor has performed some—some operation whose nature I do not fully understand."

"Three times. Damnable. Which doctor operates?"

"Dr. Van Helsing, I think. I feel so safe when he is with me. But still . . ." She had lost the strength for speech. I bent and laid my ear against her breast, and liked not the laborious pumping sounds of the machineries of her body. By modern standards I am certainly no qualified physician, but then neither would many of those be who earned their bread as such during the nineteenth century.

Her eyes were on mine, trusting, praying.

"Lucy. Be clear, lightbearing girl. Be clear now in your thoughts. There is a most momentous decision that we may have to make tonight." And I caressed the golden beauty of her hair. In four hundred years of war and peace I had seen death come to many, and I thought her unlikely to survive the night. Unless . . .

"Vlad, help me, save me. Arthur is not here, and I fear the others are killing me with what they do." A spasm of fear had temporarily renewed her energy. "Don't let me die." And Lucy was seized with sudden nausea, and retched feebly over the side of the bed. There was an acid smell but little vomitus. "Hold me, Vlad!"

Yet I did not pull her into an embrace, but straightened and stood upright beside the bed. Belowstairs, all sounds of the maids' movements had ceased, save for the stertorous breathing of their four pairs of lungs; for all intents and purposes, Lucy and I were in the house alone. There was a little time, at least, in which to plan and think. Perhaps no more than a little; she might well die, I thought, before a long discussion could be held.

"Lucy. Death will come soon or late to all of us. And it is not the worst thing in the world, though full well I know how frightening it can sometimes be."

"No, no!" Terror gave her a terrible, momentary energy, and her nails tried to bite at my arm. "Save me, Vlad! Do something. I see in your eyes that there is something you can do."

"Lucy, there is one way in which I can—not cancel your death, for I am not God—but put it off, for some indefinite time. But to take this road will mean a great change in your life. Greater than you can possibly imagine now."

"Only save me, Vlad, I beg of you. I do not want to die!" I cannot describe the emotion that was in her failing voice as she uttered these words.

I lifted her weightless-seeming body from the bed; in shifting her slightly in my arms, so that the whiteness of her throat where I had left my marks before was tautly exposed, I also turned my own body slightly. There was a mirror hung on the wall across the room, and inside its gilt frame Lucy's unsupported body hung, her nightdress gathered up at the knees and back by the pressure of invisible arms. Then I bent down my head. . . .

When I had taken something of her blood it was time to give her to drink deeply of mine. I undid the clothing over my own heart and tore the flesh there with one of my own talonlike fingernails—no other cutting tool can do the job so well—and quickly pressed Lucy's mouth against my breast as if she were a suckling babe and I a crooning nurse.

As soon as we were done with exchanging a considerable quantity of blood I wiped her pretty lips and put her back into bed, having done all that I could do. At the moment she was still nearly comatose, but I knew now that she would not die before the night was out, at least not of unmatched blood put straight into her veins. I thought she was no longer likely to die at all, in the near future. It was still quite probable that she would soon be put into her grave, but as we know, that is not quite the same.

"Lucy," I said softly, and extended my hand toward her still figure on the bed. She took it and arose, although her eyes stayed shut until she came gracefully to her feet. Then they opened. Ah, changed . . . Van Helsing would be sure to see it, and what might he do then?

But I had come to London on my own affairs, and not to fight him for this woman. She meant very little to me, except that she had called on me for help, which I had now given as best I could.

"Lucy, you will not die tonight. You may feel ill. But if they come to you tomorrow, to drug you and transfuse you once again, I would advise you to refuse them."

"But they never ask." Change in the voice, too, already; it was at once a little livelier, and more remote.

"Insist that this Arthur of yours be called, if he will help you take a stand against them. Do you understand? They are putting the blood of other people into your veins. I suppose they do mean well, but what they were doing had brought you to the point of death."

"But, Vlad . . . I feel stronger now. I believe that you have saved me."

"And so I have, my dear, for the present.

Snatched you from death, put back the Day of Judgment for you. Not many men can truthfully claim such power. It was what you wanted from me." I sighed. The warning I was about to attempt would not, in my opinion, do much good. New-made vampires must find their way at first by instinct, much as newborn children do.

I went on: "You may at some time soon fall into—another coma. If you allow them to give you another transfusion I would say this is quite likely. And if you fall into this coma you are going to wake from it in circumstances that will be at first quite hard to understand; but be of good cheer and understanding will come." The first emergence from one's grave is a unique experience indeed.

"I will be of good cheer, Vlad. Oh, Vlad, tell me again that I will not die."

"You will not die." It was a lie, such as one gives the wounded after battle sometimes. A lie, because I did not know what Van Helsing might decide to do with her now that she had changed; and all must die the true death sometime. Earlier, when the great decision had still been hers to make, I had been as truthful with her as I could be in the small time we had. Now there were only small but troublesome decisions left and I judged it better to be simply soothing.

"Now, my dear. Eventually the women you have so cleverly drugged below are going to awake, and also other people can be expected to enter this house when morning comes. There is much here that will require explaining." I sighed; there were my fresh fang marks on her throat, about which nothing could be done.

As I spoke I was stroking Lucy's bare arm, and her forehead, to strengthen her with suggestion for the tasks ahead. There was the broken window to be accounted for, and the wolf outside, whose howls the maids had heard and whose role in the night's events might, for all I knew, not yet be over. There was the mother, dead of heart failure as unexpected by Lucy as it was by me; and there were the maids, who would certainly tell any investigators of their drugged sleep, even if they should rouse from it before anyone else had entered the house.

Above all, there was the condition of the girl herself. Van Helsing could not now fail to detect her symptoms of incipient vampirism. Could he be moved to pity for her? I thought perhaps he might, if she could be made to appear a purely innocent victim of the evil count.

I had continued to stroke Lucy, and she had fallen by now into the beginnings of hypnotic trance. "Find us some paper and ink, little girl," I told her. "Before I leave you the two of us in collaboration are going to compose a short story. As wild, perhaps, as one of those of Mr. Poe."

It was about ten o'clock on the following morning when Drs. Seward and Van Helsing arrived, practically simultaneously and both in desperate haste, at Hillingham. The missent telegram I mentioned earlier had caused them to leave Lucy unguarded through the night. Both were distraught because of this. In Van Helsing's mind, of course, the peril from which she needed protection was vampires; Seward had not even this warped version of the truth, but he loved the girl, or thought he did, and knew she stood in danger; and, in his inexperience, he followed his former teacher blindly.

They found the house locked up and barred from the inside, and their increasingly urgent knockings went unanswered. At last they broke in through a kitchen window, to find in the dining room the four servant girls still lying unconscious on the floor. In Lucy's room, upstairs, they found the two women still on the bed, the younger still breathing but by now unconscious again.

Lucy had not even the chance to plead against a fourth transfusion, and that of course is what Van Helsing gave her. This time blood was drawn from the veins of the young American, Quincey Morris, who arrived innocently on the scene with a message of inquiry from Arthur Holmwood, and was thrown, so to speak, into the front lines at once.

"A brave man's blood is the best thing on this earth when a woman is in trouble," Van Helsing is quoted by Seward as saying whilst they got out the knives once more. I suppose his prescription for Lucy might be taken as closely resembling mine, though unfortunately his method of operation differed. So, sad to say, did the result.

It was noted in passing by the busy doctors that the decanter of sherry on the sideboard in the dining room had a peculiar odor, had in fact been doped with laudanum from a bottle kept nearby as medicine for Mrs. Westenra. And, when Lucy was lifted from her bed to be treated to a hot restorative bath, there "dropped from her breast" a sheet or two of notepaper. Van Helsing's brief perusal of these papers brought to his face "a look of grim satisfaction, as of one who has had a doubt resolved."

These papers bore, of course, our literary effort of the night before. It was a first attempt at fiction by a beleaguered vampire writing in a foreign tongue and a half-tranced girl who had just been shocked by the sudden demise of a parent. Seward's first comment after reading our creation was: "In God's name, what does it all mean? Was she, or is she, mad; or what sort of horrible danger is it?"

One might suppose that in response to such straightforward and heartfelt appeal Professor Van Helsing would have shouted: "Is a vampire, young man! One hell of a hideous monster that drinks your blood!" But that would not, maybe, have been quite philosophical or metaphysical enough. As matters actually went, "Van Helsing put out his hand and took the paper, saying: 'Do not trouble about it now. Forget it for the present. You shall know and understand it all in good time; but it will be later. . . .'"

When Lucy emerged from her coma she at first tried to tear up the story we had concocted, but then relented, evidently realizing that it was better than nothing to offer as some explanation for the weird events of the preceding night.

The story of course purported to be "an exact record" of those events, set down in her handwriting almost as they occurred. It related how Lucy had been awakened from peaceful sleep by "a flapping at the window," and shortly thereafter heard "a howl like a dog's, but more fierce and deeper." She had gone "to the window and looked out, but could see nothing, except a big bat, which had evidently been buffeting its wings against the window."

Unperturbed by this commonplace event of suburban London, Lucy in our fiction returned to her bed. Presently her mother looked in, spoke "even more sweetly and softly than her wont," and came to lie companionably at her daughter's side. But the "flapping and buffeting" returned to the window, quickly followed by "the low howl again out in the shrubbery, and shortly after there was a crash at the window and a lot of broken glass was hurled on the floor. . . . In the aperture of the broken panes there was the head of a great, gaunt gray wolf. Mother cried out in a fright . . . clutched the wreath of flowers that Dr. Van Helsing insisted on my wearing 'round my neck, and tore it away from me." I thought it best my enemies continue to believe in the efficacy of garlic.

"There was a strange and horrible gurgling in her throat; then she fell over . . . a whole myriad of little specks seemed to come blowing in through the broken window, and wheeling and circling around like the pillars of dust that travelers describe when there is a simoom in the desert. I tried to stir, but there was some spell upon me. . . ." Comparing the coy approach of the vampire to the simoom was, I confess, my own idea. Somehow at the time I thought that it created a vivid image.

Our story goes on to relate how Lucy recovered consciousness; how she called for the maids to come in and, after they had decently arranged her mother's corpse, sent them to take some sherry as a tranquilizer. When they failed to return betimes she pursued them to the dining room and found there on the floor "the sleeping servants, whom someone has drugged . . . The air seems full of specks, floating and circling in the draught from the window, and the lights burn blue and dim. . . . I shall hide this paper in my breast, where they shall find it when they come to lay me out. . . ."

The relation ends thus, save for a few stylized groans. I suppose I need make no apology for its inadequacies, since it served its intended purpose, viz., it was accepted by Van Helsing and the rest as a true account of the night's events, and got Lucy off the hook, as the slang expression has it, on any possible charges of collaboration.

But, by the beard of Allah, and all the relics of the Patriarchs! That such a farrago of falsehood could have passed successfully under the noses of even the most inept investigators is still a source of wonderment to me. Inspector Lestrade would not have wasted five minutes on it—I say nothing of Sherlock Holmes.

Consider the evidence of the drugged wine. Presumably, if the maids had not taken it Lucy would have escaped the full horrors of the night, as hinted at in the Dracula-Westenra manuscript. Some evil person, then, poured the laudanum into the decanter. It must have been the malign Count Dracula himself—wait, though, he could not have entered the house without an invitation, and had he been invited he would have had no need to employ a wolf as battering ram. And that the wolf had been so employed there is no doubt, for the poor beast was seen returning wearily to the zoo on the evening of the next day, with bits of window glass still in its bloodied fur.

Someone else, then, acting as Dracula's agent,

drugged the wine. But, given the existence of such an agent inside the house, that agent's most valuable function would have been to grant direct entree to her master, not to toxicate the wine on the sheer hope that enough people might chance to drink it to clear the field and give the count a clear shot at his goal.

Or is it reasonable to suppose that the four serving women, when Lucy sent them for a soothing draught, decided instead to render themselves completely insensible, as a defense against the dangers of the night? With a wolf prowling at large and evidently able to force its way into the house at will, this explanation would not have seemed likely to Lestrade, or even Dr. Watson. Either of those two relatively astute gentlemen would have bluntly demanded to know just who *did* let Count Dracula in. . . .

But let the story go. In passing, you think, I have let out the real truth, and it proves to be just what my enemies have claimed. I have now confessed that I deliberately made that girl into a vampire.

Is it not so? you ask. And I answer, jovially enough, in a phrase that men have used to excuse everything from genocide to sexual oddity: Yes, and what's wrong with that?

Will you tell me that the mere existence of a vampire creates a blot of unexampled evil upon the earth? You would be in danger of becoming insulting if you said that to Count Dracula. But never mind personal considerations for the moment. The fact is that you are arguing in a circle. It is evil to be a vampire because they sometimes make other vampires who are by definition evil.

Mere reproduction has not been thought a crime for human beings, at least not till very recently. Why may not I enjoy the rights of other men?

It is the *forcing* of death, or of a change in life, that's criminal, whether the force be applied by vampire fang, or wooden stake, or means more subtle used against a vulnerable mind or heart. And I say once more: my blood, and nothing else available in 1891, could save Lucy's life for her that night. Not that the saving was of much duration.

On September eighteenth and nineteenth Lucy languished, poisoned anew by Van Helsing's fourth transfusion; I sensed her pain, remotely, but I held aloof, having as I thought done all I could for her. On September twentieth she died, or so thought the grieving Arthur Holmwood, and Dr. Seward, who with Van Helsing were in attendance on her at the time. Though some miles away, I could feel, through our established mental contact, the moment when her breathing stopped, that once had blown so full and sweet across my cheek. . . .

On that same day laborers came to Carfax, to remove some of my boxes, in accordance with my plan of gradual dispersal. The madman Renfield once more broke out through the much-battered window of his room, to maul the workmen for having, as he thought, robbed him of his "lord and master." The lord and master, standing amid some trees behind the high wall of his estate—I was not resting in a box, for I could not be quite sure which ones the workmen might decide to take, or cast a look into—heard the row and resolved to speed up the dispersal process and to sell Carfax quickly thereafter, or simply abandon it if need be. The neighborhood seemed after all a little lively for my taste, with the irrepressible Renfield right next door, and his keeper consulting with Van Helsing, who, as I knew, had hunted vampires.

September twenty-second was in truth a day of mourning among my narrow circle of British acquaintances. On that day Lucy and her mother were both interred in a small cemetery near Hampstead Heath. And Jonathan Harker's former employer, more recently his partner, Mr. Peter Hawkins, was also buried on that day, he having perished almost immediately—of natural causes, so far as I know—upon the Harkers' return from abroad as man and wife.

Mr. Hawkins' place of burial was also near London, and it chanced that an hour or so after attending his last ceremonies Mina and Jonathan were strolling hand in hand down Piccadilly. Mina, in her account of the day's events, wrote that she was "looking at a very beautiful girl, in a big cartwheel hat, sitting in a Victoria outside Giuliano's, when I felt Jonathan clutch my arm so tight that he hurt me, and he said under his breath: 'My God!' I am always anxious about Jonathan, for I fear some nervous fit may upset him again . . . he was very pale, and his eyes seemed bulging out as, half in terror and half in amazement, he gazed at a tall, thin man with a beaky nose and black mustache and pointed beard"—these of course were the effects of a regular diet—"who was also observing the pretty girl. He was looking at her so hard that he did not see either of us"—ah, dearest Mina, Wilhelmina, how could I know that you were there?—"and so

I had a good view of him. His face was not a good face"—but one full of character, hey m'dear? "It was hard and cruel, and sensual, and his big white teeth, that looked all the whiter because his lips were so red, were pointed like an animal's."

The better to—but never mind. "Jonathan kept staring at him, till I was afraid he would notice. I feared he might take it ill, he looked so fierce and nasty. I asked Jonathan why he was disturbed, and he answered, evidently thinking that I knew as much about it as he did: 'Do you see who it is?' "

" 'No, dear, I don't know him. Who is it?' "

" 'It is the man himself!' "

When the lady drove off Mina noted that "the dark man kept his eyes fixed on her . . . he followed in the same direction, and hailed a hansom. Jonathan kept looking after him, and said, as if to himself: 'I believe it is the count, but he has grown young. My God, if this be so!' "

Poor Harker teetered for an hour or so on the brink of a relapse into the brain fever that had prostrated him for weeks after leaving my domain; but he had pulled himself together by the time the couple got home by train to Exeter. There a telegram from Van Helsing awaited them, informing them for the first time of Lucy's rapid decline and supposed death. The professor, empowered by the grieving Arthur to go through all of Lucy's effects, had found Mina's last unopened missives to her and had thus learned Mina's name and address. The professor soon invited himself to come to visit the Harkers in Exeter, and talk of vampires; or talk around them, rather. It would be some time yet before he spoke the horrid word aloud.

TRACK FOUR

Within a day after sending them his first telegram Van Helsing had conferred with both Mina and Jonathan, and had read a typescript, prepared by Mina, of her husband's Transylvanian journal; she herself had only been allowed to see this diary after Harker had with his own eyes beheld me walking the streets of London. Now Van Helsing not only had confirming evidence that there was at least one vampire active in the English capital, but knew my identity, and even the fact that my chief residence was likely to be at Carfax. Had our roles been reversed, that very afternoon would have seen me in the moldering chapel there, prizing off the lids of boxes whilst whatever brave friends I could muster stood by me, armed with wooden stakes and spears. But as matters stood my foe, the hunter, preferred more devious tactics.

FRED SABERHAGEN

At this time I knew of Van Helsing his name
and reputation, and that he had been one of
Lucy's physicians and therefore might now pose a
danger to me; but that is all I knew. I was not even
aware that the Harkers were in England, much
less that they had seen me in Piccadilly. I continued in the peaceful pursuit of my own affairs,
until on September twenty-fifth my attention was
caught by headlines in the *Westminster Gazette*:

EXTRA SPECIAL
THE HAMPSTEAD HORROR
ANOTHER CHILD INJURED
THE "BLOOFER LADY"

I hastened to read the article, and discovered
that the child mentioned was only the latest of a
series to have complained, within the past few
days, of being abducted and assaulted by a mysterious woman who roamed on Hampstead
Heath at twilight. Through some equally mysterious translation of children's jargon into that of
journalists, the unknown woman had acquired
the "bloofer" title. Wounds in the throat, no more
than pinpricks, were observed in every victim.

Whilst in a newspaper office, gathering what
additional facts I could from a study of recent
editions, I looked through columns of death
notices to find where Lucy had been interred. It
was too bad that since her rebirth she had taken
to molesting children; perhaps, I thought, her
brain as well as other organs had been damaged
by the transfusions. Although essentially I considered her depredations no more my affair than
those of Mary Jane Heathcote, alleged murderess

142

of her own child, or of a thousand other madfolk scattered about the metropolis, still I was forced to be concerned by her activities all the same. Van Helsing was very likely to notice the newspaper articles and to be visiting her tomb. This in turn might present me with an opportunity to meet my antagonist, take his measure, reason with him if reasoning was possible or, if it was not, adopt such other measures as might be necessary.

Of course I expected that any calls Van Helsing might make on Miss Westenra in her new residence would take place in daylight, when they would be safest. New-made vampires have this in common with infants newly born to breathing life: they are much more delicate than they will one day be and their powers are still largely undeveloped. *I* could walk through a field of garlic in full bloom and not be overcome, or even glare back briefly at the noonday sun, at least in the cool high latitudes. But Lucy in her tender, newborn state would be stunned even by garlic, and could not have long survived exposure to full daylight, even of the tempered English sort.

On the night of September twenty-fifth I located the Westenra family mausoleum, in the little cemetery near Hampstead Heath, surrounded then by nearly open countryside. Passing like smoke through the vault's locked doors, I stood on old stone floors strewn with dead and dying flowers from the double interment of three days before. Before me, raised on stone blocks and ornamented by iron and brass, was the coffin of Lucy's mother, with its freight of peaceful clay. And across the narrow interior aisle from it, similar in appearance, the vessel in which Lucy had been laid. I went to it and, placing my hands upon its oaken, outer lid, could feel the emptiness within its inner, leaden shell.

Where then was the girl whom I had once tried to help? Out prowling on the heath, most likely, if the newspaper stories gave true evidence. I had my doubts about them. But certainly the coffin was empty now.

I waited there an hour, rehearsing in my mind what I might try to say and do to help her when she appeared. The longer I waited the less certain I felt of what help I could now offer her, and the less certain also that I had been right in not allowing her to die in the first place. Yet still it seemed to me that it had been my duty to answer her cry for help at Hillingham.

Suddenly, with a force that keyed all my senses to full alert, the realization came to me that she might not be walking at all as I waited beside her coffin, but that her body might have been secretly removed from this place after being put to its true death by stake and blade. If Van Helsing was as dangerous an antagonist as I had heard, such might well be the case. If Lucy had been so disposed of, there was nothing I could do about it now. I waited half an hour more and then departed, yielding to my doubts, and still with no evidence of her whereabouts.

At midmorning on September twenty-sixth, and again in the afternoon, I returned to the cemetery in man-shape. In daylight I could not change my form at will nor melt smokelike into the tomb and out again. But I was still looking for my adversary and still thought that daylight was the only time to find him there.

Very few other people were about. At last, leaning against the outer wall of the Westenra tomb, I managed to pick up a faint radiance of Lucy's encomaed mind within. She was of course not breathing, but was fully as alive as me. The mysterious and powerful Van Helsing had not, after all, been competent enough to find and kill this baby vampire yet!

But scarcely had I allowed myself the relaxation of a smile when the thought hit home that Lucy might have been spared simply to bait a trap for me. What was Lucy to Van Helsing? By analogy, no more than a tiger cub tied mewling in the forest at night, whilst concealed men with electric lights and heavy weapons ready ring the spot about, waiting in silence for those great green glowing eyes to come, that bear a full hand's breadth of separating night between!

Yes, they might be willing to let her roam at night until I came to her. They might expect me there to teach her vampire lore, receive a pledge of fealty, or demand some other service from her. They might be cold and cruel enough to risk a breathing child or two . . . or had any children been attacked at all? Might the whole series of newspaper stories possibly be no more than a cunning fabrication, designed to draw me into the snare?

I looked round me swiftly. At the moment I could see no one; but inside one of those mausoleums eyes might be looking out and there might be a Kodak taking photographs, its operator protected by those walls and bars so strong that twenty men could not, bare-handed, tear them free.

It is well for the world's vampires that I am not the chief huntsman on their trail. Actually there was no effective plan against me at the time; in making the hasty retreat from the cemetery that I did I was an overcautious general for once. Meanwhile Van Helsing, on his part, was perhaps a little overconfident. He had been keeping a desultory eye on the cemetery, and had read the newspaper accounts of Lucy's activities, but that evening he did not approach her tomb until *after dark*. He brought with him a marveling and hesitant Dr. Seward, to whom he had begun to unfold the truth about Lucy's condition. The professor now intended to open Lucy's coffin and demonstrate to his younger colleague the incredible truth that he was trying to get across. Of course Van Helsing came well equipped with religious paraphernalia and garlic, expecting thus to be adequately protected, against Lucy at least; he had something of the mentality of his contemporaries, the American Indian Ghost Dancers, who earnestly believed that the signs and symbols of their faith would stop the bullets of the cavalry.

I was nowhere near Lucy's tomb that night, but only read of their expedition in Seward's journal later. Leading his skeptical friend along, parrying his whispered questions with mainly enigmatic and portentous words, Van Helsing entered the tomb—he had obtained the key at the funeral, under pretext of passing it on to Arthur—and opened the coffin. He cut through the sealed inner, leaden box, which was once more empty. The absence of a corpse was certainly startling to Seward, but not enough to convince him that dear Lucy prowled on Hampstead Heath with bloody fangs. Nor was he totally convinced of such an outrageous fact, even by a white figure that later in the night gave the doctors the slip amongst the trees and tombs, and from the path of which they recovered a small child, abducted but still fortunately unharmed.

And, whilst the doctors prowled and argued, where was the evil count? On September twenty-seventh I was engaged in moving some of my furniture—by which I mean of course nine boxes, the size of large coffins, each half filled with weighty earth—from Carfax to a house I had just bought in Piccadilly. With the idea of making things more difficult for potential hunters who might attempt to trace my movements, I chose on this occasion not to deal with a regular firm of carters and instead struck out on my own to make the acquaintance of a suitable laborer.

After several interesting experiences in the pubs of the East End I hired one Sam Bloxam, who had a cart and single horse at his disposal. With this equipage two trips were needed between Carfax and the heart of the city, and the entire day was occupied. I might have speeded up matters somewhat by loading and unloading the boxes myself, but did not want to lift them unaided in sight of Mr. Bloxam, who understood in his bones just how heavy they were. So we hoisted them on and off the wagon between us, he puffing and blowing with the forty percent or so of weight that I allowed him to feel at his end.

At length I grew impatient, and in Piccadilly enlisted three itinerant laborers off the street to help Bloxam bring the boxes up the high steps of the house. This created a new difficulty, for when I inadvertently overpaid the men, with shillings instead of pence, they grew surly rather than grateful, and demanded even more. Perhaps some instinct informed them that the job for which they had been hired was one that their employer desired should be kept as confidential as possible. Their self-appointed leader, the largest of them, actually grew blustery with me. I took him by the shoulder and looked close into his eyes, and counseled moderation; and then I heard no more from them till they were several houses down the street, when they gave vent to oaths.

So I was still going peaceably about my own affairs, not seeking conflict with those who were determined to be my enemies. I felt very domestic in my Piccadilly house and considered rigging up a night-bell, or a day-bell rather, with a wire, and rejoiced that there were no manservants in my pantry to give concern for immorality. On that same day, unknown to me of course, Van Helsing and Seward were back in the boneyard, where the professor intended to make another demonstration for his doubtful student. They mingled with the mourners at some stranger's funeral, then slipped away to an unpeopled corner of the cemetery where they laid low until the sexton had closed the gates. Then, using their key to enter the Westenra tomb for a second time, they naturally found Miss Westenra at home, though perhaps not in shape for receiving callers properly.

On this occasion Van Helsing had along his little black bag, with its cargo of hammer and stake and beheading knives, and he might have performed final surgery right then and there and discharged his patient. But once the doctors were in the tomb, and had opened the coffin to find the still-beautiful girl stretched out helpless and unconscious before them, it occurred to the professor, as he said to Seward: "How can I expect Arthur to believe? He doubted me when I took from him her kiss when she was dying . . . he may think that in some mistaken idea this woman was buried alive . . . that we, mistaken ones, have killed her by our ideas and so he will be much unhappy always. Yet he never can be sure, and that is the worst of all . . . again, he will think that we may be right, and that his so-beloved was, after all, an Un-Dead. . . ."

Van Helsing, of course had a prescription to save Arthur from this dilemma. "He must pass through the bitter waters to reach the sweet. He, poor fellow, must have one hour that will make the very face of heaven grow black to him. . . ."

In short, the old sadist wanted to get Arthur himself to do the killing, or be a witness at the very least.

After sending Seward home to his madhouse, and dining alone in Piccadilly—perhaps not far from where I was at my domestic tasks—Van Helsing returned to the Berkeley Hotel, where he was staying. He girded himself for a night-long vigil, and wrote out an impressive farewell note to Dr. John Seward, just in case. He left it in his portmanteau, and it was never delivered.

27 September

Friend John—

I write this in case anything should happen. I go alone to watch in that churchyard. It pleases me that the Un-Dead, Miss Lucy, shall not leave tonight, so that on the morrow night she may be more eager. Therefore I shall fix up some things she likes not—garlic and a crucifix—and so seal up the door of the tomb. She is young as Un-Dead, and will heed. Moreover, these are only to prevent her coming out; they may not prevail on her wanting to get in; for then the Un-Dead is desperate, and must find the line of least resistance, whatsoever it may be. I shall be at hand all the night from sunset till after the sunrise, and if there is aught that may be learned I shall learn it. For Miss Lucy or from her, I have no fear; but that other to whom is there that she is Un-Dead, he now have the power to seek her tomb and find shelter. He is cunning, as I know from Mr. Jonathan and from the way that all along he have fooled us when he played with us for Miss Lucy's life, and we lost; and in many ways the Un-Dead are strong. He have always the strength in his hand of twenty men; even we four who gave our strength to Miss Lucy it is all to him. Besides, he can summon his wolf and I know not what. So if it be that he come hither on this night he shall find me; but none other shall—until it be too late. But it may be that

150

he will not attempt the place. There is no reason why he should; his hunting ground is more full of game than the churchyard where the Un-Dead woman sleep and the one old man watch.

Therefore I write this in case. . . . Take the papers that are with this, the diaries of Harker and the rest, and read them, and then find this great Un-Dead, and cut off his head and burn his heart or drive a stake through it, so that the world may rest from him.

If it be so, farewell.

Van Helsing

And neither, perhaps, will I be greatly saddened when the time comes that I rest from the world, forever. But Count Dracula is not yet ready to be killed, nor was I then.

Though I wished nothing more than to be let alone, yet I could not forget that Van Helsing must know of me and that he was a killer. I avoided Carfax during the day, and at night, like my enemy, I took my way once more to the cemetery, to find out what I could.

The night of the twenty-seventh was warm and fair, and would have disappointed those cinematographers who deal much with vampires and such other improbable creatures as are thought to frequent graveyards. And this time I was in luck. Even from a considerable distance I could see that something new had been added to the Westenra mausoleum: from a chain looped over a roof ornament there dangled a small crucifix of wood, just opposite the middle of the doors.

Resuming the mist-form in which I had crossed

the cemetery wall, I drifted closer. But progress in that mode is very slow and it is hard to see or hear very much en route. In the deep shadow of some trees I resumed the form of man and was at once rewarded with the soft sounds of a single human heart and pair of lungs at work not far away. With his broad back set against a cross that served as headstone on a neighboring grave, a man who could be none other than Van Helsing watched with sleepless eyes the quiet exterior of Lucy's tomb. Inside, I felt her mind, not quite awake, but fretful.

Wishing to achieve some rational discourse with Van Helsing rather than put him to flight or come to grips with him, I circled to approach him from his front. In a few moments he looked up with a start at the sight of my figure walking toward him through the night along the grassy, seldom-used road.

"In nomine Dei, retro, Satana!" His hands were clenched, and he got his feet beneath him, ready to spring up.

"Pax vobiscum," I replied, but in such low voice that he may not have heard. "Dr. Van Helsing, I presume," I added, louder, as I drew near, in unconscious parody of Stanley's Ujiji words of twenty years before.

As I approached Van Helsing got to his feet, an obstinate bull digging in his heels to launch a charge at a locomotive. Despite his gloomy note left for Seward, he really thought himself protected. The great stone cross was still at his back; in his left hand I saw a small golden crucifix, and in his right, only partially visible, the whiteness of some folded paper.

He raised both hands and held them forward as I drew near. Let him think his toys would stop me, if he really believed such rot. I wanted the chance to talk. We eyed each other for some moments above the little crucifix.

"Count Dracula." He made a tiny bow. His nerve was high, his mouth smiling a little now.

"At your service," I replied, and gave him back his bow.

He tipped his head in the briefest nod toward the silent tomb. "You may not have her longer," he said, continuing to smile. "She is no longer yours."

"My dear young sir, she never was." Van Helsing's face at that time bore more agelines than my own, but he understood. "Not in the way you seem to think."

"You lie, king-devil Dracula. Ve know you, better than you realize."

"Very well, Van Helsing, we will have bluntness. I know your name, but nothing good of it. What are your intentions now?"

"That the so-young Miss Lucy shall have rest, and peace."

"And as regards me?"

"If it so may be," he said with a grim, measured determination, "that you shall trouble none other as you have troubled her."

I turned away and strolled about a little among the tombs, my hands behind my back and beneath my cloak, somewhat in the way that I have seen Napoleon walk when deep in thought. "Why?" I asked, stopping to face my antagonist once more.

And then I saw in his face, in his eyes, that he probably really did not understand my question.

"I mean why, Professor, do you persecute and torment us? I know of one vampire that you have slain near Brussels, and two more, a man and wife, near Paris. . . ."

"Man and wife!" He was outraged. "If there are marriages not in heaven, as the Scripture say, then surely not in hell either!"

"And we are hellish, of course; more so than other folk, I mean. Tell me, Van Helsing, if I took that cross from out of your grasp and hung it 'round my own neck, would you still be so certain that I came from hell?"

His pudgy fingers tightened on the gold. "By your works I know you, Dracula. I fear there is much power to you, and that you may play tricks with crosses, and the other things of holiness. In Brussels where I did my work of mercy I heard your name, and in Paris too; and I have read the journal of young Harker, from his stay at your damned castle, from which the powers of heaven so blessedly delivered him."

"Ah! And is Jonathan well, and back in London now?" As I spoke I recalled the notebook with Harker's ciphers in it. "I would be pleased to know that he is well, but saddened if he found my hospitality so hard to bear as your grim tones and looks imply."

Van Helsing now held silent, regretting perhaps that he might have given something away by mentioning Harker at all. Utter loathing was in his eyes, which remained fixed on me, but also the beginning of something like triumph as he saw that my renewed pacing brought me never any nearer to his crosses, nor to the white envelope in his right hand, whose contents I thought I had already guessed. He put this hand back into his pocket now whilst he swiveled the little gold crucifix to keep it facing squarely toward me as if it were a loaded gun.

Three quick strides, a twisting of my arms, and he would have been a vastly surprised corpse. But others—Harker, Dr. Seward, I could not guess who else—were certain to know of Van Helsing's vigil here tonight. They might even be watching us at the moment from somewhere nearby. Was I then to kill them too? The more I killed, the more the ranks of my enemies must grow, fed from the ocean of unbelievers in which both hunters and vampires were now no more than vastly scattered drops.

What should I do, then? Kneel down and pray a rosary? I might have done so, but never to placate a foe, and least of all a smirking, self-righteous enemy like this one.

I tried fair, honest words again. "I have not come to London to make war, Van Helsing, but to make peace with all mankind—"

"Then, monster, what of the girl? This so sweet young miss who was put in those walls of cold stone; and, worse, who do not stay—"

"Van Helsing, you may believe if you wish that being a vampire is worse than being dead; I see I am not likely to sway you by any argument. But forcing the consequences of this belief upon others is something else again."

"*You* dare to speak of forcings, monster!" His courage continued to grow as he saw that I continued to keep my distance. "You who forced that girl to yield to you her very blood and life—"

"Not so, murderer!" Now I did move closer to

him by a step. "You who drove those splintered stakes into the living breasts of my three friends in Brussels and in Paris! And as for Lucy, it was to save her life that I drank deep enough of her sweet blood to make her what she is—it was really *you* who sent her to the tomb!"

He gave his massive head a little shake, smiling all the while, not so much denying the accusation as failing even to understand it yet.

I leaned toward him. "You stopped her breath with the pouring of the alien blood into her veins."

"No!" Now understanding came.

"Yes." He started further protest, which I overrode: *"Now shall I call her forth to testify?"*

There was silence in the graveyard, save for a restless owl, and far away the rumbling of a wagonload of freight, and under that the polyphonic voice of distant London, that for a thousand years had not been truly quiet.

Van Helsing stood much as before, still holding me—as he thought—at a safe distance with his golden cross; but, reading his face through the dark night, I saw that my shot had told.

"You have done it before, butcher," I pressed on, guessing, and seeing that my guess was accurate as his face registered yet another inner blow. "And with some similar result. Is it not so? Has any victim of your blood-exchanging surgery yet lived?"

His smile was gone, his hands and jaw were trembling as he again brought out the small white folded envelope and raised it toward me with the cross. "Begone! To hell!" The words exploded from his mouth.

"Nothing wiser than that to say to me, Professor?"

"It shall be—" His voice cracked and he had to begin again. "It shall be war between us, vampire. War to the death."

"Let it be peace, *I say*. Or rather, tolerance. But remember that I have overcome in war a hundred stronger men than you." And with sad and angry heart I turned my back on that bad man and walked away, half expecting to feel the painful though harmless flick of a silver bullet between my ribs. If he does that, I thought, I shall turn back and insert his bullet, if I can recover it, into his own anatomy at some painful and inconvenient place. But he did nothing, and I betook myself to my newly acquired house to gaze over the moonlit trees of the Green Park toward Victoria's palace and think my foolish thoughts. A war, then, was inevitable. But how was I to fight it?

When Van Helsing rejoined his companions on the following day he told them that he had seen nothing during his dangerous vigil, and let it go at that. Free as he was with words, he was a close-mouthed scoundrel whenever it came to giving out hard facts to people who worked with him or tried to do so. But he must have been wondering how much I actually knew about those failed operations of his on the Continent and in what way I might use my knowledge to embarrass him. Needless to say, I would have done so if I could, but had no specifics to make known nor any way of quickly finding them out.

What Van Helsing did do on that day was

gather his troops for another expedition to the
Westenra tomb. This time he enlisted not only
Seward, but Arthur Holmwood—who had now
become Lord Godalming, by reason of his father's recent death—and the American, Quincey
Morris. In a pep talk the professor assured them
all—I am not making this up, you will find it in
Seward's diary!—that there was a "grave duty" to
be done. And some have called Van Helsing a
humorless man! Well, he was, but only when he
tried to joke.

Naturally they all agreed to accompany him,
though so far only Seward could have had any
inkling of just what the "grave duty" was likely to
involve. As far as the others knew, Lucy was
simply though unhappily dead.

"I have been curious," Arthur protested after
some discussion in Van Helsing's hotel room, "as
to what you mean. Quincey and I have talked it
over; but the more we talked the more puzzled we
got, till now I can say for myself that I'm up a tree
as to any meaning about anything."

Nor was he to be rapidly enlightened. The
professor strung them all along with earnest
pleas for their continued trust, enlivened with
hints that Lucy might stand in some vague danger
of hell-fire—I think Arthur almost hit him at one
point—or that she might not have been dead—
exactly—when she was buried. It was a masterly
performance by a compelling personality, and
Van Helsing not only avoided being punched but
in a little while had reduced the three younger
men to a state that I can only describe as quietly
submissive hysteria. Thus he got them out to the

graveyard once again, on the night of September twenty-eighth.

After finding Lucy's ravaged coffin empty—again—the four men left what Seward called "the terror of that vault" for the fresh air outside. There Van Helsing got down to business. As Seward's diary has it:

First he took from his bag a mass of what looked like thin, waferlike biscuit, which were carefully rolled up in a white napkin; next he took out a double handful of some whitish stuff, like dough or putty. He crumbled the wafer up fine and worked it into the mass between his hands . . . rolling it into thin strips, he began to lay them into the crevices between the door and its setting in the tomb. I asked him . . . what he was doing.

He answered: "I am closing the tomb so that the Un-Dead may not enter."

"And is that stuff you have got there going to do it?" asked Quincey. "Great Scott! Is this a game?"

"It is."

"What is that which you are using?" This time the question was by Arthur.

Van Helsing reverently lifted his hat as he answered: "The host. I brought it from Amsterdam. I have an indulgence." It was an answer that appalled the most skeptical of us.

And should have had a similar effect on the most knowledgeable and reverent. The scoundrel! An indulgence, indeed! As if any worthy priest would have pretended to be able to give him such to carry on his superstitious nonsense. At any rate, after an aching wait the men saw amid the gloom of distant trees "a white figure" carrying a small child. This form at last came close enough to be recognized as:

Lucy Westenra, but how changed. The sweetness was turned to adamantine, heartless cruelty, and the purity to voluptuous wantonness. Van Helsing stepped out . . . the four of us ranged in a line before the door of the tomb. Van Helsing raised his lantern and drew the slide: by the concentrated light that fell on Lucy's face we could see that the lips were crimson with fresh blood.

Although the child, as Van Helsing later admitted, was "not much harm."

When Lucy—I call the thing that was before us Lucy because it bore her shape— saw us she drew back with an angry snarl, such as a cat gives when taken unawares; then her eyes ranged over us. Lucy's eyes in form and color, but Lucy's eyes unclean and full of hell-fire, instead of the pure, gentle orbs we knew. At that moment the remnant of my love passed into hate and loathing: had she then to be killed, I could have done it with savage delight.

Lucy flung down her victim—her plaything, rather, that she had grabbed up in her addled state—and gazed on Arthur, the lover she still tenderly remembered. Then "with outstretched arms and a wanton smile" she advanced on him, whereupon "he fell back and hid his face in his hands."

She still came forward, however, saying in "diabolically sweet" tones: "Come to me, Arthur. Leave these others and come to me. My arms are hungry for you. Come, and we can rest together. Come, my husband, come!"

On hearing this appeal Arthur "seemed under a spell; moving his hands from his face, he opened wide his arms. She was leaping for them when Van Helsing sprang forward and held between them his little golden crucifix." Angered by this meddling which followed her beyond the grave, and I suppose utterly dismayed by Arthur's meek submission to it, Lucy "recoiled, and with a suddenly distorted face, full of rage, dashed past him as if to enter the tomb." But her wish to gain that shelter was thwarted by Van Helsing's putty, which doubtless contained an admixture of garlic.

She turned, and her face was shown in the clear burst of moonlight and by the lamp, which now had no quiver from Van Helsing's iron nerves . . . the beautiful color became livid, the eyes seemed to throw out sparks of hell-fire, the brows were wrinkled as though the folds of the flesh were the coils of Medusa's snakes, and the lovely, bloodstained mouth grew to an open square, as in the passion masks of the Greeks and Japanese. If ever a face meant death—if looks could kill—we saw it at that moment.

Van Helsing broke the silence by asking Arthur: "Answer me, oh my friend! Am I to proceed in my work?"

Arthur threw himself on his knees and hid his face in his hands as he answered: "Do as you will . . . there can be no horror like this ever anymore."

This agreement extracted, Van Helsing took some of his paste from the tomb's door.

We all looked on in horrified amazement as we saw, when he stood back, the woman, with a corporeal body as real at that moment as our own, pass in through the interstice where scarce a knifeblade could have gone. We all felt a glad sense of relief when we saw the professor calmly restoring the strings of putty to the edges of the door.

The professor and his acolytes went home then for a much-needed rest. But next afternoon all were back, and when the churchyard was otherwise deserted they went into the busy tomb— "Arthur trembling like an aspen"—and opened Lucy's coffin for the fifth time since her interment.

Van Helsing, with his usual methodicalness, began taking the various contents from his bag and placing them ready for use. First he took out a soldering iron and some plumbing solder, and then a small oil lamp, which . . . burned at fierce heat with a blue flame; then his operating knives, which he placed to hand; and last a wooden stake, some two and a half or three inches thick and about three feet long. One end of it was hardened by charring in the fire and was sharpened to a fine point. With this stake came a heavy hammer, such as in households is used in the coal cellar for breaking the lumps. To me, a doctor's preparations for work of any kind are stimulating and bracing, but the effect of these things on both Arthur and Quincey was to cause them a sort of consternation.

His bracing preparations finished, Van Helsing found time for another speech, leading to the conclusion that Lucy's forthcoming impalement was bound to make her ultimately happy, as it meant the termination of her hellish vampire life and it would be most intensely joyful for her if accomplished by "the hand of him that loved her best; the hand of all she would herself have chosen, had it been to her to choose . . . tell me if there be such a one among us."

All looked at Arthur, who, now thoroughly brainwashed by the old sadist, stepped forward bravely. Van Helsing quickly gave directions.

Arthur placed the point over the heart, and as I looked I could see its dint in the white flesh. Then he struck with all his might.

The thing in the coffin writhed, and a hideous, blood-curdling screech came from the opened red lips. The body shook and quivered and twisted in wild contortions; the sharp white teeth champed together until the lips were cut, and the mouth was smeared with a crimson foam. But Arthur never faltered . . . his untrembling arm rose and fell, driving deeper and deeper the mercy-bearing stake whilst the blood from the pierced heart welled and spurted up around it. His face was set, and high duty seemed to shine through it; the sight of it gave us courage so that our voices, reading a prayer for the dead, seemed to ring through the little vault. And then the writhing and quivering of the body became less, and the teeth ceased to chomp, and the face to quiver. Finally it lay still. The terrible task was over.

The hammer fell from Arthur's hand. He reeled and would have fallen had we not caught him.

The men now all perceived, in the face of the dead girl before them, the "unequaled sweetness and purity" that they remembered as having been Lucy's during her breathing days. It has long been my observation that nothing so improves a human being's character in the eyes of the world as death, final and irreversible. As when Lucy had "died" before, they marveled at her now unthreatening beauty, which Seward took as "earthly token and symbol of that calm that was to reign forever."

This was to have been the day she married Arthur; and now that she was dead beyond a doubt, Van Helsing gave his blessing to such union as could reasonably be achieved between the couple: "And now, my child, you may kiss her. Kiss her dead lips if you will . . . for she is not a grinning devil now—not anymore a foul Thing for all eternity. "

Arthur gave her his kiss and left the tomb; whereupon the doctors "sawed off the top of the stake, leaving the point of it in the body. Then we cut off the head and filled the mouth with garlic. . . ."

Cutting off the head with a metal blade, which is practicable once wood has shattered the vampire heart, serves to interrupt the nervous system, thus preventing the still-active brain from orchestrating a regeneration of damaged heart tissue, which would otherwise be quite possible. Another safety measure for the vampire hunter is to leave the point of the stake in place, at least until the vampire's body as a whole has reached an advanced stage of decomposition. This requires a period of time which varies with the individual, and is usually longest for those who like Lucy have not been long in vampire life. The old, old *nosteratu* like myself may disintegrate, like Poe's M. Valdemar, almost at once when we are staked.

As for the garlic stuffing, I can only guess that it is used in some confusion of this butchery with culinary art. Though I have never heard of any of the breathing actually trying to eat vampire flesh, I am sufficiently well acquainted with their other habits that I should not be too much surprised.

So, they took away such life as God had given Lucy, and I in my poor, well-meaning way had tried to help her to retain. When they were done they soldered up her mangled body in its coffin and then went outside and sealed the tomb, and looked about to find "the air was sweet, the sun shone, and the birds sang, and it seemed as if all nature were tuned to a different pitch. There was gladness and mirth and peace everywhere. . . ." And Arthur bestowed on Van Helsing his profuse thanks.

One bat in the ointment remained, however, and the professor would not let the others leave the graveyard before he had them all formally enlisted in "a greater task: to find the author of all this our sorrow and to stamp him out . . . do we not promise to go on to the bitter end?"

TRACK FIVE

Of these events surrounding Lucy's murder, as I say, I knew nothing at the time. When I left her alone with Van Helsing in the graveyard I considered that it was beyond my power to protect her further, and so turned all my thoughts toward the problem of my own survival.

Lucy had told me that one of her physicians was a Dr. Seward, director of an asylum in Purflect; and unless that whole neighborhood were given over to madhouses, I judged it likely that Seward was my own next-door neighbor as well as a consultant of Van Helsing. Then there was Harker, whose journal at least Van Helsing had somehow read; and Harker, who had arranged so much for me, knew that I was likely to be found at Carfax.

I did not know if Harker himself was back in England, or even if he was still alive, or sane. Nor did I know where in England Van Helsing might be staying. Dr. Seward was of course another matter, and I judged his asylum the best place to start in keeping an eye upon my enemies. It was a very old stone house—though not quite as ancient as Carfax—of many rooms, on two floors, much of the ground floor being given over to the rooms or cells for lunatics. The clientele came from the upper classes, and some of the best families of England were represented—Renfield himself was an example.

On the night of September twenty-ninth I ghosted in bat-form around this converted mansion, observing what I could wherever blinds were open. The first figure that I recognized was that of my erstwhile visitor Renfield, sitting placidly, with folded hands, in a ground-floor room whose window had been lately reinforced with heavy metal bars and fresh timbers. As I flew past I saw a sort of inner light come over the madman's face, and he started up from his poor chair—that with a simple cot made the chief furnishing of his room—and began to approach the window; but I flapped on my way, not wishing to provoke any sort of outburst from him.

In other ground-floor rooms the handful of other patients then in residence rocked ceaselessly upon their beds, or stared at their contorted fingers, or paced the floor. And from behind the half-closed blind of one such room came utterance in tones of such dismal, groaning sorrow that even I must draw near to see whose voice it was. I caught a glimpse of book shelves, paneled walls, and then . . .

It was Dr. Seward's study, and in fact his voice,

although it did not issue from his throat. Seated at a desk with her back to me was a sturdy, brown-haired young woman, her fingers poised above the keys of a strange machine that clacked rhythmically and printed words upon a sheet of paper that wound itself spasmodically through it on a roller. Upon the young woman's curly head rested a device of forked metal whose cupped ends managed to embrace both her ears, and from these ear cups issued Seward's voice—though of course I did not recognize it then—tuned to a groaning slowness that enabled the typist to keep up. From the headset a wire ran to a nearby table, where a cabinet contained a spring-driven mechanism that made things turn, and a needle rode lightly in the groove that wound about a waxen cylinder.

It was a simple type of early phonograph, of course—how far from that to this small wonder that I hold in my hand!—on which Seward was wont to keep his journal, which his new ally Mina had just volunteered to transcribe. I recognized her almost at first sight as Lucy's friend, the girl who had come to lead Lucy home from the Whitby churchyard at midnight.

On Mina's finger a wedding ring now gleamed, where none had been before; but I had no doubt of my identification. A female servant chanced to enter the room and Mina's voice, coming out faintly through the leaded glass when she spoke briefly to the girl, was the same that had called out "Lucy! Lucy!" on Whitby's tall cast cliff, that August night that already seemed so long ago.

The servant went out and a few moments later a stalwart man of about thirty entered. He had a rather stern, commanding look, though his voice when he spoke was mild enough: "And how is the work progressing?"

Mina's machine ceased clacking and she removed her headset. "Slowly but surely, Dr. Seward."

"I expect it will be a great help to have it all in typescript, Mrs. Harker."

What Mina replied, I do not know. I sat there on the windowsill for a full two minutes, blinking my little bat eyes, stunned by the club of coincidence once again. When at last I rose and flew, I was already over the wall and into Carfax before I remembered that it could no longer offer me safety for my rest. I flew on to one of my new lairs, in Bermondsey, thankful that my plan of dispersing boxes was already so far advanced, and pondered what new snares Fate might have laid in my path. That Harker and his wife should now know Seward came as no surprise; but that the wife of the guest I left in Transylvania should chance to be the second girl I saw in England was a staggering concurrence of events.

Harker himself was at that time in Whitby, trying to pick up my trail there. He had been galvanized into becoming one of my most enthusiastic persecutors by his recent meeting with Van Helsing. As it turned out, however, there was not a great deal for him to learn in Whitby, beyond confirming that my boxes had been sent on to London; and on the next day, September thirtieth, Harker was back in Purfleet, at the asylum, where his wife was already established in guest quarters. They were joined there on the same day by Van Helsing, Arthur, and Quincey Morris.

When I came to reconnoiter the asylum again that night I at once perched on a high windowsill of Seward's study; and it was with a sense of fortune at last deciding to smile upon me that I saw the blinds were partially open and a strategy meeting was in progress before my eyes.

There was Van Helsing at the head of a large table, with Mina, notebook open on her lap, sitting at his right hand as secretary. Her husband sat beside her, looking fully restored to health. Flanking Dr. Seward on the table's other side were a tall young Englishman, obviously of the upper classes—this was Arthur, as I soon understood—and a fresh-faced young American, Quincey Morris, who sat closest to the table's foot.

Van Helsing, as usual, was speaking whilst his disciples listened. Their expressions were varied, ranging from horror, through incredulity, to a sort of numbness that still was not exactly boredom; the subject matter of the address was of a kind to transcend deficiencies of treatment.

"He is of cunning more than mortal," were the first words I heard as I began to eavesdrop. "For his cunning be the growth of ages; he have still the aids of necromancy . . . and all the dead that he can come nigh to are for him at command; he is brute, and more than brute . . . he can, within limitations, appear at will when and where, and in any of the forms that are to him; he can, within his range, direct the elements; the storm, the fog, the thunder; he can command all the meaner things; the rat, and the owl, and the bat—the moth, and the fox, and the wolf. . . .''

Could I have commanded the pinworm and the body louse I would have sent a plague of them upon him. Apart from the superstitious rubbish about necromancy, though, he was doing a reasonably good job of describing the wanted man, of whose identity not one of his hearers was in doubt. The spellbinder's words went on and on. Something of the same dazedness that I observed upon the patrician features of Lord Godalming no doubt began to glaze my own mean little bat eyes as we both listened to this litany.

"For if we fail in this fight he must surely win, and then where end we? Life is nothing; I heed him not. But to fail here is not mere life or death; it is that we become as him . . . foul things of the night. . . ."

Harker had taken his wife's hand, which action interfered with her shorthand stenography; not that she seemed to mind the interference a great deal. I was surprised to feel something like a pang of jealousy, which I sternly put down. When the professor paused for breath the newlyweds exchanged a loving glance.

"I accept the challenge, for Mina and myself," Harker said then, resolutely. He had evidently been listening after all. And Mina, who had just opened her own mouth, thought better of expressing her opinions, and held her peace.

"Count me in, Professor," the young American declared in drawling Texas accents that were then quite strange to my ears.

"I am with you," Lord Godalming said. "For Lucy's sake, if for no other reason."

All stood up then and clasped their hands together above the table; their deadly purpose toward me was being sealed in a most solemn compact, and with a tiny sigh I realized that I might have to kill, and kill again, to thwart it.

But how then was I to resume my pursuit of peace?

They all sat down again and Van Helsing launched into a fresh harangue. I must have been near dozing at the window, for somehow I missed Morris's keen glance in my direction; and when from the corner of my myopic bat vision I saw him rise and leave the room, I thought only that nature must have called him, or some innate intelligence forbade him to hear more.

There was a little pause, in which others observed his exit, some not without envy, but said nothing. Then the professor resumed: "We know that from the castle to Whitby came fifty boxes of earth, all of which were delivered at Carfax; we also know, from seeing wagons and workmen there, that at least some of these boxes have been removed. It seems to me that our first step should be to ascertain whether all the rest remain in the house, or whether any more have been removed. If the latter, we must trace—"

The bullet from Morris's pistol came at me from behind and traversed the upper part of my right wing and then the right front quadrant of my tiny skull; had I been bat in truth, my small, furred body would have convulsed and fallen dead without managing a single wing flap toward escape. As matters stood I felt the pain and shock of the leaden bullet's supersonic passage as it interpenetrated the alien matter of my flesh and then passed on without spilling blood or breaking skin. Glass shattered in the window and the bullet whanged off the top of the embrasure and ricocheted inside the room, where Mina screamed in startled fright.

Mastering an impulse to descend in man-form to the ground and mangle the author of the agony that still reverberated through me, I took to my wings instead. Off into the wooded portion of the grounds I flew, there to change to man-form, lean against a tree, and try to think. The pain of being shot ebbed but slowly, like some molten silver tide, through all my throbbing nerves. The effect was worse than if I had been full size when I was hit.

"Sorry!" came Morris's voice, from the direction of the house. But it was not to me he spoke. "I fear I have alarmed you. I shall come in and tell you about it." And I heard the opening and closing of a door. Later I learned that Morris had not really identified me on the window-sill; it was just that in recent days he had taken to shooting casually at every bat he saw. He had nursed a dislike for the creatures ever since my breathing, winged South American namesakes had drained a favorite horse of its blood.

At any rate, it had been time for me to leave my observation post, for I had learned enough. The opposing forces were going to come, belatedly but with determination and ruthlessness, to Carfax. What should I do? Defend my property forcefully against intrusion? But the old objection remained in full force: the more successfully I used violence against my enemies the greater public belief in me would grow. Against Van Helsing I might logically hope to win a war but against England I could not. No, stealth and cunning were still going to be my most effective weapons, and with that fact in mind I held my own solitary council and made my plans. . . .

They were brave enough, or foolhardy enough perhaps, to launch their attack that very night. Mina of course was left back in the Harkers' cozy guest rooms. The men had decided that from this point on she was to be told only so much of their desperate adventures as would be good for her delicate female nature to know; and though she recorded in her diary that this chivalrous treatment was "a bitter pill" for her to swallow, she decided that she "could say nothing" against it, and went off obediently to her bed.

I was spending the remainder of the night on watch in my woods and of course was not surprised by the five men coming somewhat clumsily over my wall, their burglars' bags in hand. They approached my house with what stealth they could manage, sticking mainly to the shadows, as if they felt more comfortable there, where only God and Dracula could watch their slightest move.

At my front porch they stopped, and Van Helsing issued garlic to them all, and crucifixes, and—for "enemies more mundane," as he expressed it in a whisper—knives and revolvers. The well-equipped if somewhat tardy adventurers received also small portable electric lamps that could be clipped onto their clothing; and last, but scarcely least, each was given a small envelope like that I had seen Van Helsing clutching in Lucy's churchyard, containing a portion of the sacred wafer.

It was a tempting thought that I might quietly join their party whilst they milled around in the darkness of the porch, perhaps receive an issue of weapons from Van Helsing's bag, and later whisper a few words softly in his ear if I could get him alone in some dark inner chamber of the house. But I had no time for recreation, and contented myself with watching their preparations from the shadows of some trees. I wanted to make sure that they were in the house and fully occupied before I set forth on an expedition of my own.

All in readiness at last, the trespassers opened my front door with a skeleton key and turned it back on screaming hinges. They paused to invoke the blessing of the Lord on their endeavors, and then passed in over my threshold. All in all, they found their visit not enjoyable from that time on. Harker in his journal complains of a "nauseous stench" and of the dust they were forced to endure whilst in that "loathsome place," where they could observe to their further dissatisfaction that only twenty-nine of my fifty boxes now remained.

In order to entertain my guests whilst urgent business compelled me to be elsewhere I had called up from surrounding fields and farms a hundred or so rats—Harker records "thousands," a pardonable exaggeration under the circumstances—and enjoined them to mingle with the visiting men on terms of as close an intimacy as possible. The men took a dislike to this and managed to disperse my auxiliaries with a trio of terriers, which Arthur through foresight or by some accident had brought along to the asylum.

But I had not waited to watch the battle of the rats. At about the same moment that Lord Godalming was whistling up his dogs, and the other invaders coughed in dust and brushed at cobwebs, I was approaching the madman Renfield's window on the ground floor of the asylum.

Whatever the nature of his peculiar perceptions, he was aware of my approach and even of my wish for silence; for though his joy at the event seemed almost beyond bearing, yet he controlled any physical demonstration of it. Eyes popping wide, gray hair falling wildly around a gray-stubbled, broad face contorted with the effort of suppressing mad excitement, he was waiting for me amid the shabby respectability of his room. From outside the bars of his newly fortified window I let him see my face and I expressed with a gesture my desire to be admitted.

I had to wait a moment before he could control himself enough to speak the invitation that I required: "C-come in, Lord and Master!" And as I oozed between the window bars he bowed himself away as he might have done in the presence of an emperor. Later on, in a dying statement made to the doctors, Renfield was to claim that to obtain entry I had promised him the lives of rats and flies, which he had long found agreeable to his palate. But it was not so. Certainly I would have done as much, and more, to be able to get in, but no promises or gifts were necessary to win Renfield to my cause. He was my worshiper already, though on a false premise, which I did not fully understand until a later meeting.

It was not rats and bugs he wanted from me; that sort of life he could get on his own or with some cooperation from his keepers. In fact it was women that he craved, whose lives and bodies alike he wanted to consume. This truth was never quite made plain in the prim journals of my enemies, but truth it was. And, since Renfield had first seen her on the day of her arrival at the asylum, it was Mina in particular he wanted. She was the boon he desired from me, the goal of all his prayers.

These entreaties, in a low, reasonable, and terribly earnest voice, began the moment I first stood inside his room. Even in the brief space of time before I could cross his worn rug to reach the door he managed to inform me, in several disgusting variations, of his plans for that fresh young girl when she should fall into his power.

He was a madman, certainly, and I paid these mouthings little heed just then, but gave him a smile and nod in passing. No more did I think the doctors would heed him if he spoke of my visit.

I laid my ear to the crack of his room's massive, locked, and bolted door, then passed on through when I was satisfied that the hallway outside was untenanted. Now I found myself in a passage that ran nearly the whole length of the house. In other rooms nearby, servants and inmates were making their several kinds of moderate noises but at the moment no one was in sight.

Renfield was quiet behind me, whether in disappointment or satisfaction I did not care. I ghosted in mist-form to find a set of stairs, ascended them, and passed almost invisibly along another hall. Now, if my estimates were accurate regarding the configuration of the house and the distances I had traversed, I must be outside the door of the rooms occupied by the Harkers. The upper hallway was, at the moment, as deserted as the lower had been, and quieter. I resumed man-form, took off my hat, and tapped prosaically on Mina's door.

"Yes?" The answer in her familiar voice came through the door at once. She evidently had not been asleep.

"Mrs. Harker?" I called softly. "I am a neighbor of Dr. Seward's, and I bear a message concerning your husband."

There were quick footsteps inside the room, the shuffle of a robe being put on, and a moment later the door opened, to reveal a kind of small sitting room, comfortably furnished, with another door beyond that must lead to a bed chamber. Mina's face, rather broad but attractive, firm and intelligent, looked out at me framed by her brown curls. "Has something happened to Jonathan?" She seemed capable of bearing bad news if it had come.

"No, no." I hastened to be reassuring now that my foot, so to speak, was in the door. "At least he was in good health and reasonably good spirits but a short time ago." As I answered I marked that her concern for her husband, though genuine, did not seem at all exaggerated, or even quite as deep as might have been expected, given the circumstances. I saw also in her eyes that she recognized me, or was at least on the point of doing so. How this could be I did not know, being

then ignorant of her observation of me in Piccadilly, but I saw that the situation required the
finest handling.

"You will understand," I pressed on, in as
matter-of-fact a voice as some four centuries of
practice could give me, "that circumstances of
some urgency compel me to perform my own
introduction. I am Count Dracula."

She completed a movement already begun, a
half step backward from the door. She had been
on the point of trying to slam it in my face. But
there I stood in the attitude of a distinguished
male visitor in upper-class dress. Not trying to
force my way in, not menacing at all but very
formidable; I doubt that any Victorian girl could
have mustered up the nerve to slam that door.
And I was smiling, as I know how to smile at
women, with four centuries of practice in that art
also. My eyes were fixed on hers. . . .

I cast no hypnotic spell upon her then; I can
never do so against the firm will of the person
being hypnotized. But it seemed almost that such
was her state, as she half unwillingly remained
before me, one hand, still somewhat sun-
browned from her summer holiday, holding the
door open, the other raised to clutch her dressing
gown tight at the throat. She had started to open
her sweet mouth as if to scream for help, but then
was still.

She shook her head then, whilst her most
beautiful eyes clung to me and drank me in, till I
began to feel almost like a hypnotic subject
myself.

"May I come in, madam? There are some
vitally important matters I must discuss with

some representative of this household, and I suspect you are its most intelligent member. Pray let me reassure you that you have not the slightest cause for concern over your own safety." When Mina still made no move I added—very calmly, though now I could hear a servant moving on the stairs: "My visit really does concern the future safety of your husband."

Being thus provided with an acceptable reason for letting me in, Mina backed away and I entered the sitting room and closed the door behind me.

Almost as if in a daze, she gestured to a chair. "Will you sit down?" As I accepted she seated herself most decorously and then said in halting words: "Count . . . you . . . if I understood your words correctly through the door, you described yourself as a neighbor?"

"I have that honor, madam!" I held my tall hat straight upon my knee. "My estate, Carfax, is just behind the high stone wall you may have noticed that abuts upon these premises to the east." She was nodding, still dazedly. "Your husband, I regret to say, is over there in my house now, together with Lord Godalming, Drs. Seward and Van Helsing, and an American gentleman, if that is the proper word, who fired a shot at me last night."

"Quincey Morris," Mina breathed.

I acknowledged the information with a small seated bow. "Tonight they are trying to find me. If they should be successful they would do their best to run me through with a wooden stake and then cut off my head." I smiled slightly, inviting her to acknowledge just how ridiculous the whole business sounded.

"As they did with Lucy," Mina murmured softly, and in the midst of her words I could hear her fear beginning, just beginning, to rise up again.

"A very shocking business, that, involving Miss Westenra." I nodded, letting my own face show distress. "Dear Mrs. Harker, you see before you a man who is—*most* horribly misunderstood." I let my eyes fall, as if they had suddenly gone shy, away from hers. "Let me reassure you again, if there is still any need to do so, that you yourself have not the slightest cause for concern that *I* will ever do aught to c-cause *you* harm." Note that single deliberate stutter there. Gets 'em every time, as the Americans might say.

"Why should I wish you harm, dear lady?" I pressed on. "It is not you who trespasses on my land, breaks into my house, destroys my property, bears lethal weapons against me through the night." I looked up again. "Your husband, it gives me great pain to say, does all these things, persists in doing them, and because of unfortunate mis-understandings he seems likely to persevere in this mad course until he comes to grief. Yes, grief! And what am I to do? How can I possibly prevent it, without help? The men have come one and all under the influence of that fanatic Van Helsing, and their eyes and ears are closed to any entreaty of mine. It is my humble hope that with your help and guidance I may find a way to enlighten them, to turn their feet back to the paths of sanity and safety, before it is too late!"

Mina had not yet recovered enough from my introduction to be her true, quick-witted self. "Too late for what, Count Dracula?"

I leaned toward her and spoke slowly. "Too late for their own good, dear Mrs. Harker. I am not going to let myself be killed. What they did to Lucy they shall not do to me."

"I don't understand this," the lady murmured, and started to her feet and then sat down again, continuing to gaze at me. "I fear I do not understand this, at all. I think perhaps I'm dreaming."

I shook my head and remained sitting in a dignified position, top hat held resting on my knee.

"Count—did none of the servants offer to take your hat?"

"The servants are not aware that I am here, madam. I judged it wiser to speak to you in secrecy."

"Count Dracula—for so you seem to be in truth—how can you explain the fearful things that happened to my husband whilst he was visiting your castle?"

"Madam, I myself left the castle before he did. As to precisely how long he remained after my departure, or what may have happened to him in the interval, I cannot say, although of course some ultimate responsibility may be mine. As for what may have happened to him at Castle Dracula before I left, I am willing to offer an explanation on any point where you desire to have one."

"My dear Count . . ."

I braced myself.

". . . who were those three women?"

Within half an hour we were chatting more or less at our ease. Sweet Mina was perturbed at being able to offer me nothing in the way of hospitality, but I assured her that I did not eat or drink. "With one exception, of course, and even that is not really as you must suppose."

"No? Then you must tell me how it is."

I spoke to Mina on that night almost as I might have spoken to an intelligent and sympathetic breathing man, had there been any such creature in my universe. I touched only briefly upon the uncommon aspects of my life, and stressed my yearnings for a free and open life, my sore need for someone in whom I might sometimes trust and confide, and above all the absence from my existence of any gleam of true affection. Not that I rawly enumerated all these needs, but rather I gradually let their existence swim into her ken. Strange to say, or perhaps not so strange, the lady seemed to see into my heart of hearts right from the first.

Somewhat belatedly I steered the conversation back to the problem of how we might save Jonathan and the others from the dangers of their headstrong course. But before Mina and I could reach any constructive agreement on action to be taken, my keen ears brought me the sounds of the weary hunting party's shuffle-footed return across the grounds of the asylum.

When I announced her husband's imminent arrival Mina started up. "Oh! If you should be discovered here, what will happen?"

"Good Madam Mina, they shall not discover me: that is, they shall not if you and I can quickly reach agreement that I may call on you again tomorrow night? Or whenever your husband next absents himself. We have yet to decide upon a course of action."

"Oh." She listened to the opening of a door

belowstairs, to the hunters coming in with earnest, tired voices that must have been almost
inaudible to her. "Yes, yes, you may come. I see
we must consult, for Jonathan's own good."

I bowed and kissed her hand, turned to the
window, and in a moment I was gone.

Shortly her husband tiptoed into the room to
find her somewhat paler than usual, and, as he
thought, asleep. He sat down and wrote in his
journal, mentioning among other things his concern for his wife, and a decision the men had
arrived at, regarding Mina, on their inglorious
way home.

I hope that the meeting tonight has not upset
her. I am truly thankful that she is to be left
out of our future work, and even of our
deliberations. It is too great a strain for a
woman to bear . . . henceforth our work is to
be a sealed book to her, till at least such time
as we can tell her that all is finished, and the
earth free from a monster of the nether
world. I daresay it will be difficult to begin to
keep silence after such confidence as ours;
but I must be resolute, and tomorrow I shall
keep dark over tonight's doings, and shall
refuse to speak of anything that has happened. I rest on the sofa, so as not to disturb
her.

Much later in the morning, when the sun was
high and all the rest of the household up and
about, Jonathan "had to call two or three times
before Mina awoke." She did not even seem to
recognize her husband immediately, but looked

at him at first "with a sort of blank terror." Her life had been changed during the night, and for the moment neither she nor her husband had any inkling of how great a change had been wrought. Nor, in fact, had I any real idea of how my own life would be transformed from that point on.

Mina as usual wrote in her journal on this day, the first of October. But this time she wrote not of what had really happened on the night before. Rather it was an oblique and coded kind of entry, relating an experience of a dream, or dreamlike state, in which she had beheld mist creeping across the lawn and pouring in 'round her bedroom door, and a vague vision of red eyes. Rather diffidently she showed it to me, as a sort of maiden literary effort, when I came back the next evening.

My enemies were busy that October first, trying to trace the dispersal of my boxes from Carfax. Engaged in this task, Jonathan was out again, this time in Walworth, toward the south of London, when I arrived.

On this visit I found an attendant posted, evidently as a guard or lookout, in the corridor outside Renfield's room. The madman had suddenly become so cheerful, "singing gaily" and snapping up houseflies as of old, that Seward was made suspicious. It was Renfield himself, with many winks and grimaces and pointings of his thumb, who notified me of the presence of this lookout as soon as I came in through his window. Of course I was not required to pass through Renfield's room at all after once gaining admission to the house, but I had already begun to feel somewhat uneasy about Mina, lodged as she was in rooms directly above that of this inhumanly powerful man who yearned to rape and torture her. I thought I would try to soothe the lunatic with a few soft, calming words, as from his lord and master.

But first of all there was the attendant in the hallway to be dealt with. It was no great trick to send this sentry, who already nodded on its brink, toppling safely into the abyss of sleep. I did it by creating a certain electrical resonance between my brain and that of the subject, a means that your science is now beginning to discover.

Then I put my hands on Renfield's shoulders and gave him a few soft words. He took them rather sulkily, I thought. It was not peace and calm he wanted. But I tried. . . .

I left him quiet, if not pacified. Then, wraith-like, I went out of his room and past the guard who nodded in his chair, and up the stairs again. Listening outside the door of the Harkers' apartment, I could hear only one set of lungs at work within—Mina's, that I had already come to be able to recognize. And there came also to my sensitive ears the soft, thick murmur of her heart, so tender a pump that pushed such pure elixir through her veins. The fang roots in my upper jaw were aching as I tapped lightly at her door. And at my tapping her breath inside, that had already been quick with anticipation, quickened more. . . .

If chastity can be defined as that which is protected by a chastity belt, then Mina, like Lucy before her, was always chaste with me. But as I am concerned to speak the truth I must relate that Mina gave herself to me as fully as she could, as early as that night, our second meeting. Very little in the way of making plans did we accomplish then, for ourselves even, let alone for her husband's future welfare . . . ah, Mina! My true, enduring love! Dear one, heart of my heart. . . .

Harker on his tardy return home—to the asylum, that is—on that night of first October found Mina fast asleep, and thought her:

> a little too pale; her eyes look as though she has been crying. Poor dear, I've no doubt it frets her to be kept in the dark, and it may make her doubly anxious about me and the others. But . . . it is better to be disappointed and worried in such a way now than to have her nerve broken. The doctors were quite right to insist on her being kept out of this dreadful business . . . indeed, it may not be a hard task after all, for she herself has become reticent on the subject, and has not spoken of the count and his doings ever since we told her of our decision.

The next day, October second, I rested, glassy-eyed, in trance. That day saw Arthur and Quincey out looking at horses, with a view to purchasing some in case any sort of cavalry action should be required; they were basically men of action, chafed by Van Helsing's deviousness and delays. Harker continued his interviews with teamsters, by which he was methodically tracking down my boxes—though of course he had not discovered that several of them no longer contained their original soil. Seward had enough work of his own about the asylum to keep him out of mischief;

and one of the most advanced scientists of his day was reportedly at the British Museum's reading room, "searching for witch and demon cures" that he had told Seward "might be useful later."

Mina got some rest during the day, but the mental strain of her ambiguous new position was affecting her, and Harker on rejoining her in the afternoon thought she still looked wan.

She made a gallant effort to be bright and cheerful . . . it took all my courage to hold to the wise resolution of keeping her out of our grim task. She seemed somehow more reconciled; or else the very subject seems to have become repugnant to her, for when any accidental allusion is made she actually shudders. . . .

He had just found my house in Piccadilly, ripe for plundering; but had to record regretfully that he could not tell the other men of the day's great discovery whilst his wife was hanging about.

So after dinner—followed by a little music to save appearances even amongst ourselves—I took Mina to her room and left her to go to bed. The dear girl was more affectionate with me than ever, and clung to me as though she would detain me; but there was much to be talked of and I came away. Thank God, the ceasing of telling things has made no difference between us.

So many a cuckolded husband has comforted himself, I should imagine, as his last chance to retain first place in his girl's heart slips through his hands, unnoticed by himself.

Now come we to a night that formed another major turning point for all of us. When after dark I slipped into Renfield's room I found him seated moodily on a stool in the middle of his small floor. All day he had evidently been brooding, and had convinced himself that I had deliberately tricked and misled him, promised him Mina and then snatched her away for my own enjoyment. He looked sidelong at me as I came in and for the first time did not rush to fawn over me and protest his loyalty. His very stillness made me slow my passage through his chamber and look at him well, and mark the cunning of violent madness that gleamed so in his eyes.

He addressed me then in a most soft and beseeching voice, and wearing the face of perfect sanity that he put on periodically in his discussions with Seward and the rest; but Seward had never been taken in by this appearance, and no more was I.

Renfield pressed me again to grant him Mina for his obscene delight, as if she were some slave or chattel, whose favors and very flesh and blood were mine to do with as I chose. When I would hear no more, and made to walk past him in man-form to reach the door, he at last exploded in frustrated wrath.

"God! God! God!" he screamed. "Then I shall take her for myself. Twice before I have escaped and fled to plead my cause with you; the next time I go straight to her and do with her what I will!" He had a little more to say, namely some details of his plans, that I shall not repeat. And with that he hurled himself upon me, maniacal fingers reaching for my throat.

In all the years since I first rose from the grave I have never felt a stronger human grip; but if Renfield's strength in his full fit of madness was that of four stout men or five, why mine is normally that of four or five such robust raving madmen as himself; and when I heard his threats against Mina my sinews too were amplified by rage.

It gave me savage satisfaction to come to honest grips with a foeman at last. I lifted him like a scarecrow and slammed him to the floor, once, again, how many times I do not know. I heard bones grind and break, and when I let him go I marked the twisted way in which he lay. His blood, his life, poured freely out from several lacerations on his head and face. The last I saw of Renfield was that spreading scarlet pool, which I disdained as carrion as I turned my back on him and hastened to where my beloved waited in her rooms.

The struggle made noise enough to rouse the dozing attendant in the hallway. He, after a quick look in through the door's observation panel, hurried to tell Seward of the "accident." I had made myself nearly invisible before the man looked in at the door, and by the time Seward had got himself down to Renfield's room I was up above in Mina's, where Harker snored in bed, with honest oafish weariness, and where my lady sat in her nightdress gazing out the window, as if she sought the solace of the moon, or mayhap a pair of flapping wings.

My entry was utterly silent, but in a moment

she was somehow aware of my tall presence near the door, and looked around with an intake of breath.

"What are you doing?" she cried to me in a fierce whisper, her gaze meanwhile darting to her husband's sleeping form and back to mine.

I glanced at him and listened to his breath, and marked the rhythms of his heart and sleeping brain.

"Jonathan will not heed us," I remarked, and went on: "There is some news. The madman Renfield downstairs was utterly determined to supplant your husband and myself as well; I cooled his ardor as I passed, so you may still sleep easily tonight."

"Sleep easily?" she cried. "God, Vlad, how may that be?" Mina stared a long moment at me as if she had never truly seen me before. "Is Renfield dead, then?"

I bowed slightly. "It was done to protect your life, my lady, which is dearer to me now than my own."

"Oh, Vlad." Her voice lowered briefly to a whisper of pure horror. "And you and Jonathan stalking each other like—like—"

"*I* am not stalking *him*, dear heart." A blasé snore came from the bed. I went on: "I now have relatively secure lodgings available elsewhere, away from Carfax, and I am going to abandon my estate. We shall be neighbors no longer."

Mina came to my arms, moaned softly as I nuzzled her, and then stood back, raising her head proudly to look me in the eye. "Take me with you," she demanded.

There was a brief silence, in which I could find

nothing soft or smooth to say. Again, a faint and flaccid snore came from the bed. Downstairs, feet ran, and an attendant's footsteps climbed rapidly to our level but did not approach our door. I could hear the man tapping at another door, probably Van Helsing's, and then talking in low, urgent tones.

"You do not know what you are asking me," I said at last.

"You do not want me with you, then? But I cannot enduring this—this tension—anymore."

Our voices were both near breaking and I could resist no longer. Mina raised her arms and I caught up and crushed her soft body—ah, so tenderly, gently, my hands of twentyfold strength held in such exquisiteness of control—crushed her against me, and my lips sought hers before they moved on down to worship at her throat. . . .

Passion blinded and deafened both of us for a while. Mina, drained and white, but shuddering with the aftermath of ecstasy, clung close against my chest when I at last released her. "Now I am yours entirely," she sighed. "And you must take me with you."

"Yes, yes, my darling. But first I must think, and find a way." I had capitulated; but in point of fact she was not fully mine as yet, not in the physically irreversible way she seemed to think. And therefore to take her with me would be a hare-brained plan, as she herself must realize soon enough, if the attempt were made. Though she could in time become a vampire—nay, must become one if things went on as they were—she was not a vampire yet. She could not give up normal food, or be immune to cold or heat, or sleep on mold and dust in airless places, or pass as I do through a hair's breadth chink.

Nor would my enemies ever be persuaded to leave my trail, once I had taken her. Most important of all, once she became a vampire our love, though it went on, would be platonic, almost incapable of physical expression. T'would then be like incest, and worse, for us to try to suck each other's veins, and she would seek out breathing lovers, as would I. . . . I did not want that, not for a long, long time to come.

Mina, in her temporarily weakened state, had turned back to the bed, and Harker's breathing altered slightly as she sank down beside him. I deepened his slumber somewhat, as I had done for the attendant outside Renfield's door.

And still I wanted with all my soul to carry Mina away with me, although I knew the plan was sheer romantic foolishness.

"Mina," I whispered, "in the eyes of the world you are my enemy's wife. But in both our hearts we know that you are mine."

"Yes, Vlad." Her whisper was small and frightened now.

"And we shall find a way to be together. Come, I will bind us with a further tie." And, pulling open my clothing above my heart, I drew the sharp nail of my left forefinger across my flesh, deep enough to let the blood well out. "Drink."

Before she drank she murmured that her hands were cold, and I clasped both of them in one of mine—did you think that vampire flesh is always chill? Not so; it can be warming, too. And with my right hand I fondled the back of her strong neck as I raised her to a kneeling position on the bed. She stood higher for a moment, to kiss the scar her husband's shovel stroke had left upon my forehead. And then her lips came down to the level of my heart, and came tenderly against my bleeding wound, and she drank into herself some portion of my life. . . .

Thus you, Mina, my best-beloved one, became flesh of my flesh; blood of my blood; kin of my kin; my bountiful winepress. . . .

In that position were we, heedless of all the world, when the door leading from the bedroom to the hall burst in with a sudden crash and Van Helsing, Seward, Morris, and Arthur nearly fell into the room. The professor actually did fall, and so impeded the first onrush of the others.

The two doctors had spent some time in attendance upon Renfield, since the noise of our brawl had drawn attention to his room. Van Helsing and Seward had performed on the spot a hasty trephining operation, which the patient did not long survive—not that the best of surgeons could have saved him then—and from his dying words they learned that I was his killer and had gained access to the house.

The doctors soon roused their male companions in the hunt, and all—except for Harker—quickly armed themselves with the same collection of symbols and rubbish that they had carried on their invasion of my house. They understood in just what room I was likely to be found, and with Renfield's battered corpse before them still chose not to be headlong in their pursuit.

Eventually, no doubt eyeing one another and

trying to think of alternative plans, they climbed the stairs.

Outside the Harkers' door we paused. Art and Quincey held back and the latter said:

"Should we disturb her?"

"We must," said Van Helsing grimly. "If the door be locked I shall break it in."

"May it not frighten her terribly? It is unusual to break into a lady's room."

Regardless of who might have been terribly frightened, they finally brought themselves to the unusual act. When they hurled their bodies at the door it crashed in quite satisfactorily, and there I was, clasping Mina on the bed.

Taken unawares and at a peak of passion, I was prepared to react in a most uncivilized way to this intrusion. Pushing Mina back on the bed, out of harm's way, I turned on them with a loud snarl. The professor, who had just started to regain his feet, fell down again and all the others cowered back.

A whiff of stale garlic came from the crowd of them, standing there in their garlands, foreshadowing malodorous flower children of a much later age. In trembling hands they waved at me their small white envelopes, like suppliants before St. Peter at the gates who think they have the proper admission tickets in their hands but are still a little doubtful all the same.

I admit, this time it was those envelopes that tipped the scales and held me back. If I had followed my first impulse, and ground their bones to bits within their well-fed skins, or left them lying like so many Renfields in a bright lake of their own blood, it would have been impossible to avoid some further, grievous desecration of the Sacred Host. What else could it be they waved at me?

Infirm though my own faith may often be, and reprehensible my behavior on occasion, I draw the line at desecration of the Sacrament. And, when this reluctance on my part had given me a moment in which to take thought, I found my old objections to mass violence as valid as they had ever been. It must eventually array the over-whelming force of multitudes against me and bring down great sorrow and travail on Mina's head as well. That quick-witted girl was lying back now on the bed, with eyes closed as if she had been stunned. . . .

Seward records that at this point he and his friends advanced, lifting their crucifixes, whilst it was the evil count who cowered back. To one unacquainted with mirrors it is always helpful to have the objective evaluation of others regarding little details of personal appearance, for example:

The hellish look that I had heard described seemed to leap into his face. His eyes flamed red with devilish passion; the great nostrils of his white aquiline nose opened wide and quivered at the edge; and the white sharp teeth, behind the full lips of the blood-dripping mouth, clamped together like those of a wild beast.

A moon-covering cloud momentarily plunged the room into full darkness and I bent down to whisper into Mina's ear: "Say that I took you by force; adieu for now." And before the moon had brightened again I was gone, unseen out into the hall. Scarcely had I left the room before she emitted the most bloodcurdling scream, so that even in mist-form I started with alarm, and came near going back to rescue her, should Van Helsing have his stake point already at her breast. I realized in time, however, that the outcry had been calculated for effect, and hurried on my way.

My path led down to Seward's study. Mina had mentioned to me in an earlier talk that the hunters' records of their search—diaries, journals, and so on—were now kept mostly in that room, and it seemed to me wise to stop there and feed the fireplace such of their papers as I could quickly find. This I did, piling on also in the flames as many of the wax cylinders from Seward's phonograph as came to hand. All burned, but it was largely wasted effort on my part, for by this time most of their records existed elsewhere in duplicate, ironically as a consequence of Mina's stenographic service.

I was not interrupted in the study nor confronted by my foe on my way out of the house afterward. Arthur and Quincey were the first to come downstairs in pursuit, and even they were not all that quick about it. Whilst making my departure in bat-form I observed young Quincey in the shadow of a yew tree, observing me; this time he did not shoot. Turning my back on Carfax, I flapped on toward the city to the west, hurrying from the first presagings of the dawn that marked the sky behind me.

I could not win a war against all England but neither did I intend to give up, now that I had found her, the woman for whom my heart had yearned for centuries. Subterfuge, and not brute strength, must carry the day if Mina and I were to survive and continue to enjoy each other's love.

TRACK SIX

Mina of course was hounded for hours with questions, and although—or because—they were agonizingly sympathetic questions they were excruciatingly hard for her to face. She of course continued in her role of helpless victim of a vampire, I believe as much as to spare her husband as to save herself. As she told me later, the men all regarded even the victim's situation as such a horrible one that she dared not try to imagine their reaction if her true position as my lover were made known to them.

The men came and went from her side, making preparations to carry on the hunt, but at first Jonathan was with her continually, seeming to turn old and gray before her eyes. Also steadily at her side was Van Helsing, his usual domineering self, although more silent and watchful of her than was his wont. She sat or reclined—if she tried to get up and walk about one of the men would make her sit again—and told and retold her story.

She told them of waking from deep sleep to find beside her connubial bed "a tall, thin man, dressed all in black." She was quick to recognize:

the waxen face . . . the parted red lips, with the white teeth showing between . . . I knew, too, the red scar on his forehead where Jonathan had struck him. . . . I would have screamed out, only that I was paralyzed. In the pause he spoke in a sort of keen, cutting whisper, pointing to Jonathan: "Silence! If you make a sound I shall take him and dash out his brains before your very eyes." I was appalled and too bewildered to do or say anything. With a mocking smile he placed one hand upon my shoulder and, holding me tight, bared my throat with the other, saying as he did so, "First, a little refreshment to reward my exertions. You may as well be quiet; it is not the first time, or the second, that your veins have appeased my thirst!" I was bewildered, and, strangely enough, I did not want to hinder him. I suppose it is part of the horrible curse that such is, when his touch is on his victim . . . it seemed that a long time must have passed before he took his foul, awful, sneering mouth away. I saw it drip with the fresh blood!

To drink fresh blood from two small punctures on a living throat is difficult enough without trying to sneer at the same time; but Mina was giving her audience precisely what they wanted to hear, and none raised an awkward question. In her romance the evil count, once having imbibed his fill, announced that his fair victim was to be punished for what she had done to aid his enemies. To this end he forced her to taste his own blood; this was the tableau the men had witnessed on breaking down the bedroom door, and an explanation of it was naturally required.

After they had spent a good part of the morning with their questions, and with exchanging over her head silent looks of horror that she found harder to bear even than the questioning, they left her alone in her bedroom for a little time, to rest, as they said, and to ponder what might be her fate. She could already picture Van Helsing coming in with his black bag, which was long enough to carry a yard-long wooden stake.

Gray, trembling Jonathan soon looked in on her, but he could scarcely find a word of comfort for her. And sometimes he looked at his wife as if she were a stranger on that terrible morning. And soon he was gone again, to sit in on the councils of the other men.

And then my darling Mina, to whom I now seemed at moments no more than the phantasm produced by a fevered brain, was left alone in truth. Throughout the long, slow hours, marked by the heavy ticking of a clock that seemed to signal some approaching doom, Van Helsing would look in on her at intervals and murmur something that he no doubt meant to be soothing and probe her eyes with his that seemed so bright and wise.

Poor child! She told me later, sobbing, how during that endless day she became more than half convinced, in a way at once delicious and terrible, that she was damned, as are those who frequent the Black Mass and the Coven.

It seemed to her late in the day, but was really no more than normal breakfast-time when they came to call her to join their conferences—for some reason the men had decided that now nothing, "no matter how painful," must be kept from her.

Harker, when this formal council got underway, urged an immediate raid upon my house in Piccadilly, where, as they had learned, nine of my earth boxes had recently been transferred. Others agreed with Jonathan; it seemed to all that this house, because of its central location in the metropolis, was the most probable site for my new headquarters.

"We are losing time," Jonathan urged. "The count may come to Piccadilly sooner than we think."

"Not so," said Van Helsing, holding up his hands. "But why?"

"Do you forget," he said, with actually a smile, "that last night he banqueted heavily, and will sleep late?"

Mina, as she later told me, was left totally at a loss for enacting an innocent maiden's proper response to a remark so supremely churlish. She came near speaking out after all, to defend me as an honorable gentleman; but wisely settled for covering her face with her hands, shuddering and moaning in a style that could not fail to draw sympathy.

Seward records of Van Helsing that "when it struck him what he had said, he was horrified at his thoughtlessness and tried to comfort her." But it is my opinion that the remark was a test, uttered callously and deliberately by the professor, that he might discover from her reaction whether her association with me had been in any way voluntary.

He may have had a similar test in mind a short time later, when in a purported effort to "guard" Mina against further evil influences he approached her solemnly and touched to her forehead a "piece of sacred wafer in the name of the Father, and the Son, and—"

She screamed, this time in authentic pain. Harker records that the host "had burned into the flesh as though it had been a piece of white-hot metal."

I have in my time seen the effects on human flesh of divers metal objects at a wide range of temperatures, and I count this claim as something of an exaggeration. Still, I am sure that Mina felt real pain, and certainly a blistered and unhealing wound. Today I suppose it would be called a psychosomatic effect. Any good hypnotist working with a good subject can achieve a similar result. Van Helsing certainly had the forceful personality required to hypnotize; and his questioning and that of the other men must have brought forward all the subconscious guilt and fear that Mina was experiencing as a result of passionate embraces with a man who was not her husband.

FRED SABERHAGEN

In fact I had not "banqueted heavily"—the
bliss between lovers has little to do with fluid
volumes—nor was I sleeping late. Dimly and at a
distance I felt Mina's pain as she was scarred, and
raised my head and growled, earth crumbling
from my fingernails, but there was nothing I
could do to help her then. At that moment I was
in my Piccadilly house, even as Harker had surmised. Frozen in man-form for the hours of
daylight, I was at work in the backyard, prizing up
some of the flagstone pavement with my fingers,
and exchanging good London earth for Transylvanian so as to make myself another secret resting place. I could work in daylight as the yard was
quite secure from observation, there being only
windowless walls in sight except for the rear of
my own house. Ah, it grieved me to give up that
dwelling! From its upper windows I loved to look
over the trees of Green Park, to Buckingham
Palace less than half a mile away—and I did not
mean to give it up entirely.

The men who were gathered round Mina when
she was branded looked on with a mixture of pity,
horror, and disbelief. But I am compelled to give
Jonathan Harker his due. It was on this day that
he wrote:

To one thing I have made up my mind. If we
find out that Mina must be a vampire in the
end, then she shall not go into that unknown
and terrible land alone. I suppose it is thus
that in old times one vampire meant many;
just as their hideous bodies could only rest
in sacred earth, so the holiest love was
the recruiting sergeant for their ghastly
ranks.

206

Of course if the semantic bludgeons *hideous* and *ghastly* are omitted from this passage it may provoke the thoughtful hearer to a quite different evaluation of the matter.

Up to this point Carfax had still been available for my use, though my enemies had actually known for three days that it was my base and believed they had the means at hand to deny it to me—God send my foe such generalship in every war. But on the morning of October third, only an hour or so after Mina's forehead received its mark, Van Helsing acted at last, leading his troops in another invasion of my lands and house. To their disappointment they once more "found no papers, or any signs of use in the house; the great boxes looked just as we had seen them last." Their leader set about to distribute fragments of the Host in all the boxes; in order to deny the vampire his base of operations, he judged it necessary to:

sterilize this earth, so sacred of holy memo-ries, that he has brought from a far distant land for such fell use. He has chosen this earth because it has been holy. Thus we defeat him with his own weapon, for we make it more holy still.

Faith and reason are whipped together from the temple.

My own business in Piccadilly was finished before midday, and I came back by train and cab to Purfleet, walking the last half mile home to Carfax. In a lair lined with my native earth deep-hidden in a thicket on my grounds I rested, needing rest yet still wanting to be near Mina should she suddenly and urgently need help. I rested in the gloom of heavy undergrowth but did not truly sleep; and I heard the hunters when they came to bang about inside my house once more. If I listened attentively I could tell when they opened a box and when they closed its lid down tight again and could pick out their individual coughs and curses as they choked on dust. It was an opportunity to seek the further confrontation with them required by the plan that I had formed; but Mina did not know that plan as yet and I considered that her full cooperation would be vital.

After a while I heard the vandals leave, driving away on the road that fronted Carfax rather than going back to the asylum. I rested a little more, then walked out onto my overgrown lawn before my house, from which vantage point the upper front of the asylum, where Mina's windows were, was visible. In the hazy autumn daylight of England, mild and cloudy to the eyes of breathing men but enervating desert glare to me, I sought, as some weary traveler might seek the sight of an oasis, a glimpse of my beloved—and behold! To my great joy I saw her come and stand there in a window, waving, beckoning to me.

In one moment I was running toward the wall that separated our grounds, and in another I had leapt lithely up and over it. Intervening trees on the asylum grounds now kept me from seeing Mina's window. I was working my way toward the building, taking care not to be seen by others, when with a leap of my heart I beheld Mina's sturdy figure come running gracefully toward me through the trees. It might have been impossible for me to have entered the asylum in the daylight, forbidden to change forms, without some servant observing me. But Mina could stroll out into the grounds without attracting any particular attention, and she had done so.

After our first quick, tight embrace I held her at arm's length. "Mina, my dear one, it is a joy unutterable to see you . . . how is it with you now?" I was gazing with concern at the cruel mark that marred the whiteness of her forehead.

"You may see how I am," she replied, taking note of the direction of my gaze. There was a tremor in her voice but yet the words were clear and brave. "I have looked in the glass at the scar you wonder at, and have seen that it is nearly a mirror image of your own. For good or ill, it seems that I have in truth been delivered into your possession. Oh, Vlad, what is my life to be?"

"This," I answered, and gathered her, as willing as ever before, into my arms. Again we exchanged blood, there in the deep shadows underneath the trees. This time I took but little, so as not to weaken her.

"But," I added firmly, holding her at arm's length once again, "because I truly love you, I do not want to take you into my land now."

"To your land? You are going to leave England?" I thought I detected the smallest undercurrent of relief in her demeanor.

"Mina, my princess, my land is the country of the vampire. It exists here in England as well as abroad, but it is different from any country you have ever known. And were I to bring you there, those men would inevitably pursue us, and never

209

rest until they had destroyed us both. Do you think you would be spared because they love you now, or say they do? Remember Lucy's fate."

Mina shuddered, and raised one hand so that its fingers almost touched her scar. "I know I would not be spared." And suddenly she poured out in some detail the story of her terrible morning: the questions and the isolation, Van Helsing's suddenly pressing the Host against her skin, the conviction that followed at once amongst them all, that she had been contaminated. "Vlad, does this mark truly mean that you are a fiend from hell, and I am damned? When you hold me I feel no sense of evil force, but rather joy."

I shook my head. "You are not evil, love." I had seen something of mesmerism before, had seen folk paralyzed or blinded, and blisters raised on unharmed skin, by nothing but the power of the mind. "Have you a crucifix about your neck, or anywhere upon your person?"

She recoiled slightly. "Oh, no. After this branding I would not dare to try to touch one."

I looked about me, found a dry branch on the ground, picked it up, and snapped it into two pieces, one a little longer than the other. These I held up in the form of the *crux immissa*, the fingers of my right hand clenched about the joining. "Touch it," I urged her.

Mina put forth her hand, then hesitated. "I . . . I dare not try," she breathed. "The pain was terrible."

"Touch it! If *I* can hold a cross, what have you to fear?"

"I—I have not your strength." She dropped her eyes and turned away.

"Vile men," I muttered, and let the cross fall into its components on the sward. "Perhaps for the present, though, it is better that your brand remain. Van Helsing might take its sudden disappearance, whilst I still live, as a bad sign." I had in mind his reaction to the disappearance of Lucy's throat marks shortly before that poor girl breathed her last; Mina had said the record showed the professor to have been very much shocked by that, and convinced from that moment that Lucy would inevitably walk as a vampire.

I put my hands on Mina's quivering shoulders and turned her round to face me. "But all is far from lost," I went on. "Tell me, am I right in thinking that life with your husband, though having its drawbacks for an intelligent woman like yourself, is not without its compensations also? In short, that for Jonathan's good as well as your own—I can see how he must need you— you are not prepared to give him up entirely?"

She looked up; it was as if my understanding had lifted at least a part of the crushing burden of worry from her breast. "You are right, Vlad! Oh, how good and wise and kind of you! I love you, as you know. And yet I find I have not ceased to love Jonathan. The poor dear needs me now . . . you would hardly recognize him, he is so changed today."

"How so?"

"He is gray and haggard, and looks at me strangely sometimes, though he speaks as lovingly as before. And I have seen him sitting alone, mumbling to himself, and whetting an enormous knife that I think Lord Godalming or Quincey

Morris must have given him. I feel it would be too terrible to leave him now; but still, however am I to stay when he is whetting that knife for your heart and praying for a chance to plunge it in?"

"Dear lady, I have conceived a strategy that, if all goes well, will resolve this painful dilemma for you. If the future can be fitted to my design, you will be able to stay safely with a contented husband, yet you and I need never be more than a few hours apart, and we can continue to see each other frequently."

Mina seized my hand and covered it with kisses. "Dear Vlad! How can I thank you? What is this plan and what may I do to further it?"

I began to explain to her my scheme. It turned on my being able to convince the men that I had fled from England, with no intention of returning. Within a month or two after I was supposedly gone—actually I would be lying very low in London, in one of my still-secret lairs—Van Helsing would presumably have gone back to the Continent, perhaps hoping to pick up my trail there, and the rest of the vigilantes would have relaxed their vigilance. Mina and I would then be able to resume the enjoyment of each other's company on an occasional basis, which was all that would really be good for her, husband or not.

To set the scheme in motion required one more confrontation between me and my hunters. I pledged to Mina to do all in my power to assure that this encounter was nonviolent, and she in turn agreed to do what she could to arrange it for me. Therefore as soon as I took leave of her, at about one o'clock in the afternoon, she sent a telegram to Van Helsing at my Piccadilly house, where we knew he was likely to be at that hour. I wanted the gang to wait for me there, whilst I visited Bermondsey and Mile End, checking some hidden caches of home-earth to make sure they were still usable.

The message, composed at my direction, advised the professor to "look out for D. He has just now, 12:45, come from Carfax hurriedly and hastened toward the south. He seems to be going the round and may want to see you." It was signed of course by Mina.

Leaving her to see the telegram dispatched, I sent out toward the south just as it said. In going the round of my other houses known to the enemy, in Bermondsey and Mile End, I found to my satisfaction that the Eucharist had been placed in all of the boxes that I had left, so to speak, on display for visitors. The hunters would feel certain that these places were denied to me as refuges, and if necessary I could use them with impunity.

It was a little after two when I reached number 347, Piccadilly, and although the old house appeared from the outside to be untenanted I felt confident that my uninvited guests were still within. On reaching the front door I noted a few fine scratches around the lock, where their hired locksmith had been at work to open the house for them and provide a key. Who would question His Lordship Arthur in such a matter? Not the tradesmen, surely, and apparently not the policemen on the beat.

I opened the door with my own key and entered, moving at a casual pace but with great care. To underestimate the enemy is the surest prescription for disaster in any war. If they should be waiting in ambush with wooden spears or lances, in some room filled with numbing daylight, then I could be killed or seriously hurt. Still I thought that I should probably have to face, at worst, nothing more dangerous than silver bullets. Van Helsing had shown me that he did not really know his game.

Once I had got inside the house I could quite plainly hear their ten taut lungs like so many boilers working under pressure whilst their owners strove for calm and silence after hearing my key turn in the door. I could hear that the men were gathered behind the closed doors of the dining room; in the silent, dusty hall outside I paused, making certain of the number of my enemies and estimating their several positions within. There was Harker's familiar breath, that I had heard for two months in my castle; and over there was Van Helsing's slightly aging wheeze.

I drew a deep breath of my own—not from necessity, of course, but by a habit that still clings from days of old—and threw the dining-room door open as suddenly as I could. Bounding forward with the same motion, I leaped into the room, confronting them.

My leap carried me a little beyond the center of the room, so if any ambush had been planned for me at the door I was past it before it could be sprung; but I saw at once that nothing of the sort was being attempted. The men were in scattered positions about the room, a couple near the door by which I had just entered, others near the windows, and Harker alone before another door, which led into the front room of the house. Their plan, insofar as they had one, was evidently to bar my egress now that I had come. So far no one had spoken. I glared about at them in silence and saw unhappily that this time no one was cowering back from me.

Of my entry Seward wrote a little later:

> There was something so pantherlike, something so inhuman, that it seemed to sober us all . . . it was a pity that we had not some organized plan of attack, for even at the moment I wondered what we were to do. I did not myself know whether our lethal weapons would avail us anything. Harker evidently meant to try the matter, for he had ready his great Kukri knife and made a fierce and sudden cut. . . .

I got out of the knife's way, wishing of course to avoid its pain and also to give the impression that I was not immune to being slain by such weapons. One might have thought that Harker, who had seen what small effect was had on me by a full swing with a metal shovel, might not have placed his chief reliance on a knife; but sound judgment, when away from the law courts, was not the bulwark of his character.

The blade came close enough to cut open a pocket of my coat, from which spilled coins and banknotes in a jumbled stream; I cursed the inconvenience as they tumbled to the floor. A good part of my wealth was there. While avarice is probably not my greatest fault, money in this war as in any other was a vital resource, and its loss was to be mourned. Yes, damned inconvenient; but I hardly felt like stopping to pick it up whilst they belabored me from all sides with painful steel and lead.

My enemies, too, ignored the dropped money for the moment; evidently they had plenty of their own. While Harker still brandished his knife, Seward and the others moved to the attack with crucifixes and envelopes held aloft. "It was without surprise," as Seward wrote, that they:

> saw the monster cower back . . . it would be impossible to describe the expression of hate and baffled malignity—of anger and hellish rage—

of extreme annoyance, not to be redundant,

> which came over the count's face. His waxen hue became greenish-yellow by the contrast of his burning eyes, and the red scar on the forehead showed on the pallid skin like a palpitating wound. The next instant, with a sinuous dive he swept under Harker's arm and, grasping a handful of the money from the floor, dashed across the room and threw himself at the window. Amid the crash and glitter of the falling glass he tumbled into the flagged area below.

I saw no reason for leaving all my treasure to those thieves and it gave me some satisfaction that whilst running to the window I managed to knock Van Helsing off his feet once more. My plunge through the glass and fall onto stone caused me no noticeable damage and I sprang up immediately and rushed across the paved rearyard to make my "escape" through the stable. At its door I paused, having reached a place where I could deliver my message hinting at retreat without Harker's antics with his knife distracting the rest of my listeners.

"You think to baffle me, you bastards!" I called back to them. "With your pale faces all there in a row, like sheep in a butcher's! You shall be sorry yet, each one of you. You think you have left me without a place to rest, but I have more." To date, you see, they had found forty-nine of my fifty boxes, and desecrated Hosts within them; my idea was to keep them thinking about the one box they had not found, and turn their minds away from speculation on whether some of the forty-nine might be fakes, or might still be quite comfortable to me despite the sacrilegious treatment to which they had been subjected.

"My revenge has just begun!" I raved on, waving my fist, shouting with what I hoped would sound like the bravado often used to cover a forced retreat. "I spread it over centuries, for time is on my side, and I can afford to wait. Your girls that you all love are mine already, and through them you and others shall yet be mine— my creatures, to do my bidding and to be my jackals when I want to feed. Bah!"

With a final threatening wave I turned and fled. Of course I wanted to leave the impression that I was getting out of the country, but it would hardly have done to come right out and say so, and expect to be believed. I retired a short distance beyond Piccadilly Circus, into Soho, where I paused in a secret place to make sure that my

FRED SABERHAGEN

fiftieth original box was still secure, then went to
hire a cart to transport it to the docks.

Van Helsing and his crew meanwhile returned
to the asylum. Mina naturally heard of the day's
exploits with breathless interest. Seward records
in his diary that "she grew snowy white at times
when danger had seemed to threaten her husband, and red at others when his devotion to her
was manifest."

She also tried, in accordance with my plan, to
encourage an end to hostilities. She hardly dared
speak openly in my favor, of course, but attempted to at least plant some seed of sympathy:

"Jonathan . . . and you, all my true, true
friends . . . I know that you must fight, that you
must destroy even as you destroyed the false Lucy
so that the true Lucy might live hereafter; but it is
not a work of hate. The poor soul who has
wrought all this misery is the saddest case of
all . . . you must be pitiful to him too, though it
may not hold your hands from his destruction."

Harker leapt to his feet for his reply: "May God
give him into my hand just long enough to destroy
that earthly life of him which we are aiming at. If
beyond it I could send his soul forever and ever to
burning hell I would do it!"

And Mina: "Oh, hush! . . . you will crush me
with fear and horror. . . . I have been thinking all
this long, long day of it—that perhaps . . .
someday . . . I too may need such pity. And that
some other like you—and with equal cause for
anger—may deny it to me!"

According to Seward this appeal left the "men
all in tears," and Mina "wept too, to see that her
sweeter counsels had prevailed." Alas for her

218

hopes, that gang of scoundrels was as determined as ever to impale me one day on a stake: that they might now be willing to murmur a prayer or shed a tear whilst murdering me was not, from my point of view, such a very great improvement.

Meanwhile I had got my fiftieth box hauled to Doolittle's Wharf, where I was pleased to locate the *Czarina Catherine*, a Russian ship bound for the Black Sea and thence on up the Danube. Visiting the docks, I wore a straw hat so that I could hardly fail to be noticed and engaged *Czarina's* captain in a rather conspicuous argument, even summoning up some fog to shroud his ship until I should have my box safely on board; subtlety of an order to challenge Sherlock Holmes was hardly in order against my present foe. The box I had conspicuously addressed to Count Dracula, Galatz, via Varna; and before leaving London I wrote to my agent Hildesheim in Galatz with instructions for its reception.

I of course booked no passage for myself, the idea being that my hunters were to think I was in the box, even as I had made the outward trip. But at the turn of the tide I boarded the ship, ostensibly to see to the box's storage. This was after sunset, and none of the crew saw me again. They cast off, thinking I had gone ashore. Soon they were right, for when the tide next turned—to transport myself over flowing water is much easier at the turning—I flew in bat-shape back to Southend-on-Sea, and thence made my way back to Purfleet before dawn, to obtain some much-needed rest in my hidden lair on the overgrown grounds of Carfax. I had taken care to bring with me from the ship some small splinters from her

main mast and planks, and a little soil and mold from crevices below. With these materials at hand I could from afar keep track of *Czarina Catherine's* movements, and even provide her with my choice of winds.

Before sinking into a stupor at dawn I managed to transfer from my mind to Mina's, in her bedroom only a few yards away, my assurances that all was going well so far and also my idea for the next step in our little game.

She thought it a clever plan and at once had Van Helsing awakened. She then suggested to the professor, as her own idea, that he should try to hypnotize her in order to discover my location through the mental bond that our exchange of blood was known to have forged between us. From a faked trance she soon reported darkness, and "the lapping of water. It is gurgling by, and little waves leap. . . ."

Mina's imitation of the hypnotic state was superbly done, or at any rate done well enough to make Van Helsing take the bait. He soon pronounced that now he knew:

what was in the count's mind when he seized that money, though Jonathan's so fierce knife put him in danger . . . He meant escape. Hear me, ESCAPE! He saw that with but one earth box left, and a pack of men following like dogs after a fox, this London was no place for him. He have take his last earth box on board a ship. . . . Tally Ho! . . . Now more than ever we must find him if we have to follow him to the jaws of hell!

This was not the hoped-for reaction and Mina grew paler as she asked faintly: "Why?"

"Because," Van Helsing answered solemnly, "he can live for centuries, and you are but mortal woman. Time is now to be dreaded—since once he put that mark upon your throat."

And Mina, not knowing how else to reply, fell down in a faint beneath the professor's bright-eyed scrutiny. She was game, though, and tried him once more, later in the day, after the men had learned about *Czarina's* departure carrying an odd box placed aboard her by a vampirish man.

I asked him if it were certain that the count had remained on board the ship. He replied: "We have the best proof of that—your own evidence when in the hypnotic trance this morning." I asked him again if it were really necessary that they should pursue the count, for oh! I dread Jonathan leaving me, and I know that he would surely go if the others went.

Again Van Helsing's answer was yes. I paraphrase, omitting some five hundred words.

Mina persisted: "But will not the count take his rebuff wisely? Since he has been driven from England, will he not avoid it, as a tiger does the village from which he has been hunted?"

Van Helsing, who had now somewhat modified his earlier ideas of my "cunning more than mortal," would not entertain the thought. "Look at his persistence and endurance. With the child-brain that was of him he have long since conceive the idea of coming to a great city . . . the glimpse that he have had, whet his appetite only and enkeen his desire. . . ."

The other men, except for Mina's outraged husband, who was ready to take any risk to be avenged on me, were as I had expected losing their enthusiasm for the chase. Certainly by October fifth, only two days after I had supposedly fled the country, Seward for one was already having second thoughts:

Even now, when I am gravely revolving the matter, it is almost impossible to realize that the cause of all our trouble is still existent. Even Mrs. Harker seems to lose sight of her trouble for whole spells; it is only now and again, when something recalls it to her mind, that she thinks of her terrible scar. . . .

That damned scar hung there on her face, an ominous red warning to us all. The goings-on in Mina's subconscious—remember that at the time we did not know that word—had been channeled by Van Helsing's mesmeric powers into producing this stigma. And that the scar nearly matched the one I had received at her husband's hands must have been more than sheer coincidence—there's that profound or perhaps meaningless word again. And no one who could see both scars seems ever to have remarked upon their similarity—except for Mina, and one other, as I will shortly relate.

Van Helsing, now that the tiger had been—as he thought—driven far from the village, and perhaps beyond the hunters' reach forever, was, perhaps impelled by his own subconscious, looking for other potential game. "Our poor dear Madam Mina is changing," he confided to Seward at a moment when the two of them were alone. "I can see the characteristics of the vampire coming into her face. It is now but very, very slight; but it is to be seen if we have eyes to notice without to prejudge. Her teeth are some sharper, and at times her eyes are more hard . . . there is to her the silence now often, as it was with Miss Lucy."

Whilst Seward nodded, wide-eyed, the professor went on: "Now my fear is this: If it be that she can, by our hypnotic trance, tell what the count see and hear, is it not more that he who have hypnotize her first, and have made her drink of his blood, should compel her mind to disclose to him what she know of us?"

Seward had to agree, and it was decided to again reverse policy and exclude Mina from all councils of war. On that evening, before they had been forced to break this sad news to her, "a great personal relief was experienced" by both doctors, as Seward wrote, when "Mrs. Harker . . . sent a message by her husband to say that she would not join us at present, as she thought it better that we should be free to discuss our movements without her presence to embarrass us." Mina of course had caught some hints from Jonathan as to which way the wind was blowing, and had also caught from me a mental signal that I was a-thirst to visit her that night.

Actually my small, furry shape alighted on her bedroom windowsill just as she was packing her husband off to join the other men in their deliberations below. She closed the door of their sitting-room behind him with a sigh of relief, and came tripping gaily into the bedroom. Her face brightened further as she caught sight of the transformed count with bat nose pressed against the pane, impatiently awaiting audience.

She moved at once to open the window for me—that I might avoid the inconvenience of a shape change to get in—but her first glance at the bat-form as it hopped inside was not without an admixture of repugnance. I made haste to swell into human shape as soon as I was well within the room.

"Think of it as a mere disguise," I murmured when we had kissed. "No more than a suit I sometimes wear. But tell me, why such a joyous dance step, fair lady, as that with which you crossed the sitting room just now?"

"Besides the joy of seeing you again," Mina answered, "it was just sheer relief at not having to endure another of their meetings." She told me how she had just anticipated her re-exclusion by their leadership, and sighed as if at the removal of an ill-fitting shoe. "They all sit there, scowling or open-mouthed, listening to Van Helsing rant on about how hideous vampires are, as if that had no connection at all with me. That is, until one of them remembers the mark of Cain upon my forehead, and sneaks a look at it; and then his eyes slide almost guiltily away as soon as they come near to meeting mine. Even—even Jonathan is no longer quite willing to look me steadily in the face. He loves me still, I think, but it is as if—as if he has grown somewhat ashamed of me."

She raised her fingers to the red scar that marred her beauty. "Vlad, speak fully and honestly, as your love for me is full and true. What can be done about this? Is there no way to make it disappear?"

I was now sitting on her bed, my legs crossed, swinging one of a pair of stylish new English boots. I supposed I might possibly have applied some hypnotic powers of my own to rid her of the scar, but it had been my experience with similar hysterical manifestations that if they were suppressed in one form, without the root cause being removed, they were likely to reappear in some new form even more discomfiting.

"Not without considerable risk to you," I answered. "Not at present, anyway. Remember, Van Helsing would probably be gravely suspicious that you were truly turning vampire if the scar, or the small marks on your throat, were to suddenly disappear. But take heart, in time we shall find a way."

"But, Vlad, why should Dr. Van Helsing's touching me with the Host have left this hideous stain for all to see? I still cannot understand; be patient with me. Why must I bear this mark if—if I am not in fact . . ."

"Unclean and evil? Be assured that you are not. That mark can have come only through Van Helsing's mesmeric power, whether under his deliberate control or not, acting on your body through a part of your own mind that is not conscious."

"But how can a mind that is not conscious act?"

"I do not know how." In that year of 1891 a

young doctor named Sigmund Freud was only beginning his researches into hysteria. "But I have seen similar things before. Mina, I myself may be evidence of a superior kind of hypnotic power."

"What do you mean, Vlad?"

"I mean a power basically similar to hypnotism, but carried to an extreme degree, far beyond what Van Helsing or Charcot or any of the regular practitioners of today can hope to accomplish. Surpassing their best efforts—or the best efforts I could consciously make—even as the steam locomotive transcends the power of the boiling tea kettle.

"I should have died of sword wounds, Mina, in the year of Our Lord 1476. My lungs stopped, and my heart, but I feared neither death nor life . . . do you know the writings of the American, Poe? Or of Joseph Glanville, your own countryman? 'Man doth not yield him to the angels, nor unto death utterly, save only by the weakness of his feeble will.' It was no vampire woman's embrace that made me what I am."

She stared at me so strangely for a little while that I had to smile to reassure her. "But it is frightening, Vlad," was all she said.

"Any human life can frighten the one who lives it," I told her softly, "if he or she will let it do so." Still smiling, I caressed her cheek. "Then simply trust me. To frighten you again is the last thing that I want. In good time both our scars will disappear. Come, now, will you not smile again for me? Ah. That is one ray of bright sunshine that I find most pleasant."

After we had talked of happy matters for a little

time I said: "I am very glad to have you with me now. But at the same time I could almost wish you were below at the men's council, that we might be fully informed of all their plans. Is your latest exclusion from their meetings permanent, do you think?"

"Oh, pooh! I can find some way to rejoin them, if you think that there is something truly vital I might learn."

"There are several questions whose answers may be vital to me. For example, when and by what means do they intend to pursue *Czarina Catherine*? I am sure they mean to do so somehow. And, have they telegraphed ahead of her, to authorities at the Bosporus, say, or perhaps somewhere nearer my homeland, in an attempt to have the box investigated or destroyed? Godalming is influential and they will not be above using bribery to hunt me down."

Mina was now sitting on my knee, rubbing her face against mine, then tilting back her chin so her long throat passed against my lips. "I will try to make certain, of course—ah. But as for telegraphing ahead, I think not. I think they want the satisfaction of destroying you with their own hands."

I held her at arm's length, and spoke with utmost seriousness. "And you had best take care, my sweet, that they never turn on you with the same thought in mind. I have seen things in Van Helsing's eyes, and heard things from his lips . . . his own wife's not in a madhouse for nothing, in my opinion. Give him any evidence that he can interpret as just cause and he'll be delighted to hammer a stake through your soft heart and watch you jump with every blow. Or, more likely, he'll talk dear Jonathan into doing it for your own good whilst he and the others watch. As he convinced Arthur to send his beloved Lucy on to her reward."

"I have thought about it." But now Mina did not seem especially frightened. She nodded, narrow-eyed, at me and smiled. "There is one almost infallible way by which a poor simple girl like me may turn away strong men from almost any course of action."

I loved her. "And that is?"

Her smile widened. Were her teeth, in truth, a very little sharper now? "Suggest it to them as my own idea, and keep on reminding them that it is mine."

And true to her word, a few days later she got all the men to swear that they would kill her should they ever decide she was so changed toward vampirism that such a move would be best for all concerned. She told me later that whilst she made her moving plea, Van Helsing for once rather sulked in the background. Needless to say, is it not, that the act never came near accomplishment?

She was able to pass on to me also some matters which were meant to be kept secret from her but which she was able to learn without difficulty from a servant who had been sent to arrange for railroad passage.

"They are going overland, Vlad, departing from Charing Cross station for Paris on the morning of October twelfth; in Paris they plan to board the Orient Express. Exactly how far they mean to go by rail, or what are their plans for intercepting you at their destination, I have not yet been able to learn. Oh, what will they do, what will I do to explain my faulty visions when it is discovered that the box is empty?"

"Mina, I have been giving the matter long thought, as you may well imagine. We must face facts. From what you tell me, Jonathan seems more mad than sane with the wish to do me harm, and if that were not enough to keep the others going, there is the professor, who will not let them turn back from the hunt. Nothing but evidence of my death is going to satisfy this crew. That box, when they open it, may not be empty after all."

TRACK SEVEN

The lynching party departed London on schedule one foggy morning, and reached Paris via boat-train on the night of the same day, October twelfth. Mina had talked the men into bringing her along, in her capacity as a hypnotic medium, by which they might hope to keep track of my whereabouts. With a somewhat altered appearance, and of course traveling under an assumed name, I was on the same train as their expedition left Charing Cross station. As I and my enemies crossed the Channel more or less together, the *Czarina Catherine*, going the long way round, was traversing the Mediterranean toward the same distant goal. I was sending her whatever favorable winds and weather came easily to hand, and turning aside a squall or two that threatened some delay.

I of course brought no coffin half filled with

earth along in my compartment. But in the baggage car rode a steamer trunk, capacious and fashioned of cattle hide nearly half an inch thick, which three strong porters had groaned to load aboard the train. It was labeled as the property of Dr. Emile Corday, going on to Bucharest.

On the first leg of our journey, before reaching Paris, I made no effort to see Mina, being content to exchange wordless mental reassurances with her a time or two. I had some concern that the men would recognize me, despite all I had done to alter my man-form appearance. My hair I had combed down over my forehead scar, I had shaved off both beard and mustache, and was cultivating rich brown sideburns that gave my face a fuller look.

The shape of my nose, and the usual hue of my skin, which my foemen kept describing variously as "pallid," "greenish," or "waxen," were somewhat harder to disguise. To alter the former materially proved impracticable, and to change the latter to a ruddy, healthy, trustworthy glow required massive daily doses of mammalian blood; beef and pork were generally the most readily available.

By the evening of October twelfth, as I have said, my foemen and I were both in Paris. We stood not far apart inside the Gare l'Est, I squinting behind dark glasses in the glare of the station's new electric lights. Around us, with measured dignity, preparations went forward for the departure of the most famed vehicle of the Compagnie Internationale des Wagons-Lits et des Grands Express Europeens, or indeed of any other railway establishment before or since. The Orient Express had then been in operation for some eight years, and was at the peak of its considerable elegance, if not yet of its fame. The baggage allowance per passenger was ample for Dr. Corday's massive trunk. I was assigned a cabin deluxe in a car next to that wherein my five hunters shared two. Ladies in that era were usually sequestered in their own *voitures-lits*, and at least during the customary hours of slumber; and I rejoiced to discover that Mina would be in a compartment alone when I could come to her.

Departure was timed to allow full serious Gallic consideration to be accorded to the evening meal aboard. Oozing from the window of my cabin as the Orient Express chugged east across the darkened countryside toward Strasbourg, I retained man-form—a bat would have been blown away at once in the gale of sixty miles an hour created by our motion—endured coal smoke and flying cinders, climbed to the top of the swaying, speeding car, and made my way from one car roof to another toward the rear of the train.

Hanging over the side of the train to peer into windows as I passed, I soon located the dining car, and studied its interior to see whether my enemies might be at table, and whether I could catch a glimpse of my beloved. I might have been looking into the dining room of a fine hotel. Waiters wearing breeches of blue silk, white stockings, and buckled shoes were pouring chilled champagne. The light of fine lamps, swaying only gently with the motion of the train, fell upon mahogany paneling and heavy furniture of solid oak.

And there indeed was Mina, lovelier than ever in a new open gown. Beside her at table sat her husband, gray and changed even as she had said, staring fixedly into space. With the now oddly matched couple dined Drs. Van Helsing and Seward; across the aisle, Lord Godalming and Quincey Morris, both in tweeds that might do well as shooting costumes, made hand gestures that suggested they were discussing the flight paths of game birds, or mayhap of bats, over their veal cordon bleu.

All seemed to be going according to plan. But judging from the fresh, full condition of the plates, Mina was not likely to be back in her sleeping compartment for some time. Meanwhile I could try to ascertain just which cabin was hers, and this I proceeded to attempt, making my way to the ladies' sleeping car and peering down as well as I could into its series of windows. Unfortunately these apertures were all so heavily curtained that I could learn nothing; the noise of the train was such that I could hear no sounds from inside the car. At last I came to one window with curtains open enough for me to see that the compartment inside was untenanted at the moment. I moved to slip inside, but found my way suddenly barred—it was the old familiar block against entering a domicile unasked.

Mumbling imprecations to myself, and wondering if Mina would realize that I needed another invitation to be able to come to her, I crawled on to the end of the train. The last car, as I soon learned, contained a smoking lounge and library, and its end was graced by a small observation platform.

Anxious to be out of the rush of wind and greasy smoke, I gave this platform only the most cursory look before swinging myself down onto it, and missed seeing the dark form of a man who stood motionless in a corner and gazed out at the scattered lights of farms and hamlets that flew by us in the night. In the surrounding roar of air and iron I could not hear his lungs or heart, and the glowing signal of his cigar became visible only when he turned to face me. I realized that I had been an instant too late in taking my own stance at the rail, as an interested observer of the countryside; yet I looked back at him as insouciantly as possible, daring him, as it were, to believe the evidence of his own eyes concerning my arrival.

He was a man about thirty-five years of age, of middle height, with a small, well-trimmed beard and brown, liquid, intelligent, and somehow powerful eyes. He removed the large, black cigar from his mouth and stared at me with the frank astonishment of one who could indeed believe his eyes' report that I had come down from the roof.

Casually I snapped my collapsible hat back into shape and replaced it on my head. Then I nodded affably to my companion and prepared to engage him in conversation; it was necessary to learn whether my own survival was going to require throwing this unfortunate person from the train, or whether he could be brought around to the belief that he had not really seen what he had seen at all.

"Bon soir, monsieur," I offered, and switched to German when his rather hesitant reply came in an accent that betrayed his greater familiarity with that tongue.

"Good evening," he answered, and had to stare

a moment longer before blinking and offering an apology. "Pray forgive my staring. But—but I was lost in thought here, and it seemed to me that—that you arrived here on the platform . . . as if from nowhere." Hesitant though his words were at first, they soon acquired a tone of firm dominance that was evidently more natural for him.

"Quite understandable," I murmured. "Allow me to introduce myself. I am Dr. Emile Corday, of the Akademie der Wissenschaften, in Vienna."

He was nonplussed again; once more I had blundered. From behind my glasses I scanned the passing scenery, looking out for a haystack into which I could toss him, thus getting an inconvenient observer out of the way for an essential day or two, if not forever. It was beginning to look as if his departure from the train would be required, but I was loath to take his life.

"The Akademie . . . ?" he muttered. "But I myself . . . that is, I thought I was fairly well acquainted with all . . ."

"Ach, of course I have not been active there for some years. I am at present in the employ of a London firm . . . no, thank you, no cigar, Herr—?"

He reached to grasp my hand by way of self-introduction, and opened his mouth to announce his name, but at that moment we plunged into a short tunnel and his words were lost on me.

After such intensive dousing in engine smoke as the tunnel had afforded us we moved by common consent to re-enter the interior of the train. It was of course the smoking car we entered; I froze momentarily, anticipating immediate and desperate action, when I recognized two of the—exclusively male, of course—inhabitants as Arthur and Quincey, who seemed to have just seated themselves and lit cigars.

I contrived to sit with my back to them as my new companion and I took seats not far away; he had his own cigar new-lighted and was likely to wish to remain in this car for some minutes. Nor did I wish to leave him until I was sure how much he had seen, or thought he had seen, of my inhuman acrobatics.

The voices of Quincey and Arthur were pitched too low for ordinary ears in my position to have picked them up, but I had little difficulty.

"In Texas we call a who-er a who-er," Quincey was whispering with some vehemence. "You sure that li'l red-haired piece is one, whyn't we up and put the question to her? Ask her if she's got a girl friend aboard, too. Things'd be more comfortable that way."

"It isn't always done that directly and bluntly, old fellow, as you never seem to learn. This is not Africa, after all, nor the South Seas."

"That's what you said in London, too. And matters there worked out pretty well, the way I handled it. Right?"

"The woman there was absolutely terrified, dear chap, after you claimed to see a bat, and fired your Colt out the window for target practice. . . ."

"My practice is at present rather limited," my new friend was saying, closer to my ears. He seemed in a way attracted to me, as one unusual person is sometimes drawn to another even when neither knows the exact quality of the other's strangeness. "I have devoted so much energy

lately to these researches on the effects of co-
caine, and on the energies of the mental process
as they may affect the physical health.''

This last caught my attention with a jolt. ''Most
interesting, Doctor,'' I said with feeling. I had
surmised his title by now if I was still ignorant of
his name.

My companion had fallen silent, pondering
something, letting his cigar go gray.

''Shouldn'ta had that las' brandy if this's to be
my night to howl, but t'hell with it. Now I'm
gonna mount that red-haired catamount or know
th' reason why . . . Art, you are sure she's a
who-er?''

''Quite, quite. One can learn from listening to
the servants, you know, even as they learn from
us. One must conduct negotiations through them,
I'll wager, for the favors of this auburn-haired
charmer and any companion she may have
aboard. . . .''

''And did you say you had a practice now in
London, Dr. Corday?''

''Ah, not precisely, Doctor, no. Rather I am a
consultant there on various physiological and
medical matters . . . for several firms. . . .''

My processes of invention, never very strong,
were flagging rapidly. I did, however, by speaking
slowly and with thoughtful pauses, manage to
stall my interlocutor until Quincey and Arthur
had got up again and left the car, evidently to
begin negotiations. I thought Arthur trailed rather reluctantly behind his friend; Lucy had been in
her grave for only three weeks, and dead for only
two. Perhaps I was naive, but it came as something of a surprise to me to learn that ladies of the

evening regularly rode the *wagons-lits* in luxury across the Continent. But why not? Money and boredom both abounded on the Orient Express, and I believe there is something intrinsically exciting in the quick motion of a train.

When my new friend and I did leave the smoking car I arranged matters so that he preceded me through the train, opening doors as we came to them; thus I was given an invitation into each sleeping car that I had not yet visited. At this early hour of the night the ladies' car was of course still passable by gentlemen. Inside it, only glass panels and a frame of wood separated the compartments from the more or less public aisle; but damask curtains covered most of the glass, and I still did not know in which compartment Mina was going to lodge.

"Ah, it is an extravagance, this train," my unwitting benefactor murmured after we had passed on into a gentleman's car and were pausing before the door of a cabin that was evidently his own. "For myself, that is. But I wanted to be alone, and in peace for a time, to think . . . there is so little time for thought."

"I have noticed that in my own affairs," I rejoined sympathetically. "Well, I trust I have not unduly distracted you from your thoughts, Doctor. Your research sounds immensely interesting and I look forward to hearing more of it in the near future."

"You are going to Vienna?" he asked.

"A much greater distance. Business will eventually take me as far as the Black Sea."

"Well, we shall certainly have time to talk tomorrow . . . at breakfast, perhaps?"

"Why not?" I would always be able to plead some minor indisposition while at table; and if it became necessary I could even swallow some bland food, to be regurgitated later.

"As for interrupting my research, distracting me, Dr. Corday, do not give it another thought. No, you have given me . . ." He broke off with a little laugh. "Food for thought," seemed to be the unstated conclusion of his sentence. "Do you know, when first I saw you on the platform there tonight, I fancied you had . . ." But at that point he had to break off again, with a little smile followed at once by a very serious look of intro-spection. What he thought he had seen out there was too ridiculous for casual, social discussion.

I answered his smile. "I look forward to hear-ing of it in the morning." And I bade him good-night and went on to my own room.

Once in, I locked my door and of course went out again through the closed windows. Hat folded into my pocket against the blast, I worked my way aft again toward the women's quarters. Intelli-gent, practical Mina had contrived to open her window curtains enough for a cinder-scorched wayfarer hanging from the train roof to see inside, where she and Jonathan now sat primly tête-à-tête.

Primly is perhaps not the right word, for as he sat there he was whetting his huge, murderous new knife, the weapon with which he hoped to send me to eternal punishment. It was a type of knife called Kukri, as I recall, favored in those days and earlier by the Gurkhas of Nepal, and acquired by Quincey or Arthur in their travels. As I stared at this evidence of how stubbornly my enemies still relied on metal to accomplish my demise, my plan for their deception began to take its final form.

Shortly Jonathan rose and, with a few words to his wife, which I could not hear, thrust the keen blade into a scabbard underneath his coat, bade her a chaste goodnight, and left. As soon as he was gone and the door of the compartment locked Mina came over to the window. Her face was wan but the sight of my own visage, inverted just outside the glass, brought some animation to her countenance, and she remembered to beckon an invitation to insure my ability to enter. A moment later and we were in each other's arms.

Mina reported that, as far as she could tell, the men were still all firmly convinced that I lay as inert cargo aboard *Czarina Catherine*. She had been doing what she could to reinforce this opinion, with her changeless reports of watery noises and darkness, at her regular morning hypnotic sessions with Van Helsing when she pretended to be entranced after he had made a few mesmeric gestures.

"It will take us at least three full days to reach Varna, where they plan to intercept the box," she told me. "Vlad, are you sure that your presence aboard the train can be kept secret from them until then? When and where will you rest?"

"I am getting off at Bucharest," I explained. "And I have made provision, too, for resting whilst on board." And with scarcely a qualm I told her of the great leather trunk that rode in the baggage car, half filled with good Transylvania earth. I felt scarcely a qualm, as I say, in telling her; not for centuries had I trusted any breathing

FRED SABERHAGEN

soul with knowledge so vital to my survival. To lose my trunk or be deprived of using it would place me in a desperate strait—though admittedly not quite so desperate as if I had been wrecked in the North Sea on my way to England. The Express was hurtling eastward, hour after hour; and from near the Franco-German border it might have been possible for bat, wolf, and man, traveling sequentially, to regain the homeland before being destroyed by exhaustion and the sun.

When Mina and I had pleased each other as best we could that first night in the swaying train we lay companionably together side by side upon the narrow bed; I with my acute hearing found some amusement in parts of a conversation that penetrated train noises and thin partitions to reach my ears from a neighboring compartment. The persons talking were a young lady, who I suspect had auburn hair, and a young man who by daylight probably wore blue silk and white stockings in the dining car, and by night evidently served in a more enterprising and lucrative capacity as the lady's business agent.

"What is it makes you smile so, Vlad dear? I confess that my own heart is heavy, whilst your life and Jonathan's remain both in grave danger."

"I am pleased that Arthur and Quincey have plans for less destructive work tonight."

"Really? What do you mean?"

Mina was quite interested as I explained. Perhaps because of the nature of our special relationship, she discussed openly with me matters she would have been reluctant to mention to her husband.

"At least it must distract them from their cruel thoughts of harming you," she murmured. Then shortly I said it was past time for me to go, if I was to manage to dine on beef blood and to get some rest before the dawn.

"Now do be careful," she warned, "especially going atop the moving train."

I kissed her hand. "I shall take care. But really, I am no more likely to fall from the train top than you would be to topple over when crossing a level and unmoving floor. And for your sake too it is time I left; for you must rest. The good professor will no doubt come round for his usual report before dawn, or have you brought to him to deliver it."

"And what am I to tell him in the morning?"

"Let it be the same report as before—wind and waves, and the darkness of the hold."

The kitchen or galley portion of the *voiture-restaurant* was not deserted even at that hour. Bakers and scrubbers worked industriously so that the passengers should dine and sup in serenity and plenty on the morrow. But after biding my time at a window I entered in mist-form and abstracted some beef and lambs' blood—congealed, but better than nothing—from carcasses kept in a massive icebox toward the rear. Then, hunger appeased and ruddy cheeks preserved for a few hours more, I sought the privacy of my great cowhide trunk.

Getting into the unpeopled baggage car presented no problem at all. Alas, what with my unusual fatigue, and what would now be called jet-lag, or weariness compounded by changing time zones, getting out again did become a problem. The fact is that I overslept, and woke past dawn, to find with some concern that I could not change my shape to get out of the box.

I managed to force open the trunk's lock from inside, and then, exerting all the considerable strength of my fingers, tried to close it again once I had got out, so that it should appear to be normally locked. Some of the train crew came blundering into the car whilst I was thus employed. I tried to take shelter behind some piles of luggage; but the cunning of centuries, if I could in fact lay claim to such, was set at naught by the mere limited geography of the confined space; and in fact I was soon accidentally discovered.

There began at once an excited argument. Conductor, porters, trainmen of all description seemed to appear from nowhere to press inquiries upon me, in a dozen languages, as to who I was and what I was doing in this place unthinkable for a passenger to enter. I kept calmly insisting that I had merely entered by mistake, that the door after all had been unlocked, and that they had better take care to lock their doors if they wished to preserve these regions sacrosanct.

I might have browbeaten my way free at once, had not the sharp eye of one of my interrogators happened to fall upon the bright metal of my own trunk's mangled lock. A string of multilingual expletives, and we were off again. This fine trunk, the man insisted, had not been so vandalized on his retirement from the car on the preceding evening—I had done it, I was a thief and worse.

This outcry I could only stem by claiming the trunk as my own; naturally I could produce a document or two identifying myself as the Corday whose property the trunk was labeled as. Before these arguments of mine could have any conclusive effect, however, the conductor had taken it upon himself to fling open the leathern lid, with a dramatic gesture that seemed to hope for a dismembered body, at least, to come to view within. All stared nonplussed at my mere load of earth.

"And how is this explainable, monsieur?"

"If you are referring to your rudeness, my good man, you must know the answer better than I."

"I refer, sir, to the conditions of this trunk and of its contents." He peered in once more, eyes lighting up. Might there be, after all, a corpse or two beneath the mold?

"It is my trunk, monsieur conductor, and its conditions my affair."

We adjourned shortly to the next car, where the conductor had his command post, as it were, commanding a view of the car's corridor and the doors of the passenger's compartments. Above his desk hung a small mirror that, had I not been immune to fear, might well have given me a moment or two of apprehension. A little stove at the conductor's feet as he sat there enthroned gave off a grateful warmth against the autumnal dawn.

If he had sought to keep me standing there as a supplicant he was mistaken. Monarch though he might be in his small, wheeled domain, my own rulership was vaster and more practiced, and I more skilled even than he in the tones and gestures that best serve to overawe. Without seeming to exert great physical force I still moved resistlessly through his entourage of lesser train-

men and walked deliberately to my cabin. One or
two of them followed at a little distance—the
affair of the trunk was not yet really over, and
what was I to do for a resting place now?—but
for the time being no further effort was made to
detain me or force questioning.

I had barely got into my room and started to
relax when a light tap came at the door.

"Who is it?"

"Dr. Floyd," I thought the answer came, which
sounded like an English name, and seemed to be
spoken in that tongue; but it was undoubtedly the
voice of my German-speaking acquaintance of
the night before.

Much to my surprise on opening the door, I
beheld Mina standing there at the Viennese doctor's side. When we two men had exchanged
greetings, the doctor, speaking English in defer-
ence to Mina, introduced me to her.

"In the course of a certain professional matter
I met Mrs. Harker rather early this morning, and
she has graciously consented to breakfast with us;
when I mentioned, Dr. Corday, that you too were
from London, she was most interested to meet
you."

"I am flattered, Madam Harker." And I managed to slip her the slightest wink as I bowed to
kiss her hand.

The "professional matter," as Mina informed
me later, had been a result of a disagreement in
one of the gentlemen's cabins during the night.
Colt revolvers and bowie knives were brandished
but fortunately not much used. There was evidence, in the form of certain articles of clothing,
that at least one young woman had been on the

premises. Dr. Floyd—as I then understood his name—had treated Quincey Morris for scalp lacerations and a certain young waiter for moderately serious but not disabling head wounds and facial contusions.

All right, why should I now be coy and indirect? What with Arthur changing his mind at the eleventh hour about his need for female company —he had begun tearfully and drunkenly lamenting Lucy—and Quincey too actively disputing the bill for services rendered, an altercation had arisen, and bandages as well as banknotes were required to smooth things over.

Harker had heard the commotion and burst out from his compartment adjoining, glaring madly and waving a huge knife; luckily he calmed quickly on discovering the true nature of the problem. Seward and Van Helsing had already gone in search of Mina to hypnotize her for the morning communique, and Jonathan told the conductor he had better cast about for some other physician to tend the wounded. As luck would have it, my friend of the smoking car was domiciled nearby, and came to volunteer his services. His accent, and perhaps something in his physiognomy, caused dear Jonathan to drop some half-audible remark about a "sheep-headed Jew" when Quincey groaned with the discomfort of getting a stitch or two in his thick scalp. Mina, finished early with her seance, had already come on the scene; authentically gracious as always, she left the men to argue and nurse their wounds, and came to breakfast with the good Samaritan as a token of reparations. She was delighted to have me as an unexpected bonus; her husband seemed

FRED SABERHAGEN

glad to get her away from the scene of sordid combat for any reason.

We three sat down in the dining car together. I ordered only cafe au lait, which I could swallow if there were compelling cause to do so.

"And are you too, Mrs. Harker," I asked, "traveling only to Vienna?"

"Ah, no. My husband's plans are grander. He has arranged a holiday for our party, at some spa on the Black Sea or nearby. His plans are still somewhat mysterious."

"I love a mystery, madam. Would that it were possible for me to join you."

"That would indeed be pleasant—doctors. Both of you."

The man I thought of as Floyd had been pulling at his beard and glancing intently from Mina's face to mine and back again. I realized belatedly that my hair had fallen aside from the center of my forehead.

"Dr. Corday," he began hesitantly, "I hope you will not think me impertinent—I really have some professional interest—would you think me rude if I were to inquire how you happened to come by the small scar on your forehead?"

"Not at all, Doctor. I incurred that peculiar mark some five months past, at the hands of an acquaintance of mine." As I spoke I realized how much my conversational English had improved since I first encountered Harker in Castle Dracula. "Guest in my house at the time; given to nightmares, unfortunately. Chap became quite violent on one occasion, and we were both of us in good luck that no more serious injuries occurred."

"Thank you. I--I was emboldened to ask because . . ." His eyes drifted again to the mirror image of my scar, that stood in bold red upon the fairest brow in all the world.

"The scar upon my forehead is a sensitive subject with me," said Mina boldly. "If you are curious, know that it is the result of a physician's faulty treatment. I wish to speak no more about it."

"Your pardon, madam."

"Not at all, Doctor." Mina's voice was reasonably gay again.

"Dr. Corday." The Viennese turned to me, obviously with a change of subject in mind. "You were telling me of your consulting service in London." Blocked in one investigation, he would pursue another. And his voice now held a hint of command: how could I refuse to answer his queries directly now, when such a change in the conversation would serve to cover a lady's embarrassment?

Coming toward our table were two waiters bearing food and drink through the car; one had a black eye. And behind these, as a ship of the line was wont to enter battle behind a screen of skirmishing destroyers, came my old foe the conductor. Doubtless he was just passing through the car—not even a wanted murderer would have been interrupted in mid-meal on that train —and meant to bide his time before confronting me again. But the presence of Mina inspired me, and I launched into a sudden speech that was as much for the conductor's benefit as it was for my possibly dangerous breakfast companion.

"You see, my friends," I announced rather

loudly, "in London I function chiefly as a consultant for Moule's Patent Earth-Closet Company."

"Moule's—?" Floyd dabbed uncertainly with a napkin at his fine brown whiskers.

"Earth-Closet Company, of Covent Garden. Moule's Company now make earth closets for the garden, closets for shooting boxes, closets . . ."

A look of refined social horror, I saw with concealed jubilation, was now welling up in the doctor's face. The same expression was mirrored in Mina's countenance, and in the conductor's lordly visage as well, where, as I saw to my relief, there was also the dawn of a certain understanding.

"Closets for cottages, closets for anywhere. Earth closets complete are now made, fitted with pull-out apparatus; fitted with pull-up apparatus. . . ."

I did not see then, and do not now, why subject matter fit for the front page of a respected newspaper should be abhorrent at table; doubtless this attitude is a result of my irrepressible medieval barbarism. Giddy with success and relief, however, I pressed on, driving the foe metaphorically before me:

"Closets made of galvanized or corrugated iron, to take to pieces for easy transport. Can be put together in only two hours. To work satisfactorily only require to be supplied with fine and dry mold. Closets built on this principle never fail, if properly supplied with dry earth; of which, for demonstration purposes, I am carrying a supply of superb quality in my trunk in the baggage car at present. . . ."

* * *

At Ulm the train crossed the Danube and I thought briefly of getting off and trying to make the rest of the journey by water. Breakfast had concluded in morose near-silence and I was not sure that Mina would be willing to speak to me again for some time. But my calculated boorishness had had the desired effect, where any amount of suave verbal fencing might well have failed; the Viennese had broken off his questions, and whenever the conductor passed me he now made sure to avert his gaze. I was a social time-bomb liable to explode again at any moment aboard his train.

But my ticket read through to Bucharest, and to get off sooner would draw even more attention to myself. Enough was enough. No one would bother my trunk now, by day or night.

At Vienna, my young doctor-friend with the so-thoughtful eyes got off the train. He was courteous to stop to offer me a handshake before we parted, at which time he also raked me with one more friendly but penetrating glance that showed I would not soon be forgotten.

"*Auf Wiedersehen*, Dr. Corday. It has been a fruitful journey for me—a most fruitful journey in some respects. . . ."

I returned his handclasp warmly and with mixed emotions. I would under other circumstances have enjoyed his company and delighted in his penetrating thoughts, but at the moment I was quite glad to see his back.

Budapest was only a short stage farther on our journey, and by the evening of October fourteenth we had passed the stops at Szegedin and Timisoara, the latter once the Hunyadis' headquarters. Yes, I was now nearing home. Again and again I breathed the air, simply to catch now and then, through numbing coal smoke, the living odors of the dear land of my youth.

I visited Mina at night and brought her up to date on all my plans before it came time for me to leave the train. To my relief, she accepted with her usual intelligence my apologies for my performance at the breakfast table.

"For the present," I then counseled her, "continue to give them their reports, darkness and water, and so forth, as before."

"And when the ship lands at Varna, Vlad? Will they not haste to board her, and by bribery or force find means to open the box? And when it is found empty, will not your plans be ruined, and I fall under the most serious suspicion?"

"I mean to see to it that they do not board Czarina at that port. I must get them to chase the box; with your help I must keep it moving ahead of them, by land or by riverboat, but not so far ahead that they fail to keep following. The deeper they penetrate my territory, the greater my advantage; for there the knowledge of geography, language, and custom is all mine; they will be strangers in a strange land indeed. Also I will be able to enlist auxiliaries as required."

"Vlad." She was very serious. "As I have pleaded with Jonathan for your life, as much as I dared to do so, so now I would plead with you for his. I ask you, for my sake, to spare him, should the time ever come when he is fully delivered into your hands."

"Far greater gifts than his life would I gladly grant you, if you did ask for them." And once again I kissed her hand.

TRACK EIGHT

By about five o'clock on the afternoon of the fifteenth my enemies and Mina were ensconced at the Odessus Hotel in Varna. Had I taken the train that far with them I should then have been about five hundred kilometers, or three hundred miles, from home, as the bat flies. But I had been resting snugly in my trunk—the lock forced together firmly from inside—when it was unloaded on schedule, in broad daylight, at Bucharest. By getting off the train there I had reduced the distance to my home by about one third from the Varna figure, which enabled me to feel somewhat more secure. Besides, there would have been little for me to do in Varna, beyond dalliance. I had decided that the ship was not going there after all.

At any rate, *Czarina* was not even due to reach the Dardanelles till the twenty-fourth. There was plenty of time, and I decided to go home at once, there to arrange some reception for my guests.

In Bucharest I knew where I could obtain a cart and horse that I, in native clothing, could drive myself without attracting any particular attention. Dressed once more in costume of my homeland, and with the leather trunk as almost my sole luggage, I took the road back to the high Carpathians. Dozing by day at the side of some small, seldom-traveled way—already home was near enough that the common roadside earth would let me get a kind of rest—and traveling steadily by night, in three days I won my way so far up the slowly climbing roads that with the third sunset I felt sure that I would need my trunk of earth, and therefore my wagon, no longer. The horses I soothed and sent to stand in the yard of a poor farmer, who when it came time for plowing in the spring would bless the hand that had sent them to him. The cart, a poor thing, I left by the roadside, still holding the trunk, from which I had spilled and scattered the earth, lest such cargo here give rise to too much speculation. I do not often bestow largesse upon the lazy world, but considered that my homecoming deserved some unusual celebration.

Before going to the castle I stopped at a spot some miles distant, where the *Szgany* sometimes camped. A few were there, with their wagons and barking dogs and ragged children. The counterfeit ruddiness of my days on the train had faded; my hair when it blew before my eyes looked lank and gray, and the *Szgany* knew me at once. I frowned to note that the first to see me gave me hangdog, sullen almost reproachful looks. When they called Tatra out of a wagon, matters were different. His leathery face worked with joy as he beheld me, and he came forward at once to fall on his knees and kiss my hand.

"Master! Long have we waited for your safe return. My wife and seventh daughter have worked the spells three times, at dark and full of moon. . . ."

"Yes, yes. Well, here I am. How are things at the castle?"

His face took on some of the others' sullenness. "We were not welcome there."

"Not welcome? In my home? Who has told you so?"

A hint of coming satisfaction touched his lips with a smile. "The ladies three who dwell there, master. They said they spoke with your full knowledge and authority. I doubted them . . . but I am only mortal man."

"You will be welcome now, my friend. But first there is another matter I must discuss with you." I informed Tatra of the approach of my enemies, and of the effort I was soon going to require of him and his men. I did not tell him that I was not going to be inside the box at the time when he received it downriver; I could not expect him or his men, if they knew that, to defend the box as wholeheartedly as might be necessary. Tatra in turn told me of certain things that he had witnessed in the castle, before being excluded therefrom, and I was frowning when I took my departure from the gypsy camp.

Anna, Wanda, and Melisse knew of course by this time that I was coming home, as they would have known across the vast miles had some sharp stake of English yew been forced into my rib cage to drive my spirit out. They were waiting on the battlements when the chief bat came down out of a rainy midnight sky. Anna, fairest and boldest of the three, actually put out her wrist for me, with a mocking smile, as if she thought I might perch there like some pet bird.

Melisse, tall and dark, and Wanda, her shorter, fuller-breasted sister, were in the background, not quite daring such impertinence but brave enough to give out nervous little laughs when Anna was not punished instantly. I wanted to see exactly how matters stood here before I acted.

In tall man-form I stood with my back to the rainswept parapet and looked down at the three white faces looking up, and soon the laughter stopped.

"I am informed," I stated then, "that you are molesting the local people here. That you have abducted young men from the villages and held them prisoner. My orders were that you take no lovers nearer than a score of leagues, and that you take none by force—"

It may be that I have an extra sense for danger. Or it may have been some combination of hearing, subtle mental alarms, and the sight of unconcealable anticipation in the women's faces that warned me to spin round on guard. A peasant youth with lank blond hair and straggly, sprouting beard was rushing at me just inside the parapet, charging with a stout wooden spear, its sharp point fire-hardened, leveled at my midsection. I pushed the thrust aside with one hand, wrenched the weapon from him, and seized him in a killing grip.

But before my hands put on the force that would have crushed his spine I looked into his face. No secret agent of Van Helsing, this. Only a farm lad, strong as a young horse and handsome as a god, or had been before his strength was drained away through the six small red points that now marked his throat. He had spent almost his last strength in rushing to kill me, and now his eyes gazed back at mine almost indifferently.

I let him drop to the stone walk, picked up his weapon, broke it to splinters in my hands, and threw them into the abyss. All the while I was looking at the women.

Anna sighed, then raised her chin proudly as ever, returned my gaze, and waited. Melisse suddenly brought hands up to hide her face. "Oh, Vlad," cried Wanda, "he did come from more than a score of leagues away!" Then in a breaking voice she said: "I warned them not to try to kill you."

"Your cry of warning just now *to me*, my dear," I answered, "was so soft that I heard it not."

Then I went on, almost as if nothing had happened: "The *Szgany* are returning. And there come also some English folk, whom you are not to touch. As for your punishment, for disobeying my orders and then trying to take my life, the first part of it is this—to wait." Memories of old happiness with these women came to me as I looked at them, and made me smile; and first Wanda and then Melisse began to whimper in the rain.

Hardly a word more did I hear from any of them. I carried the peasant youth below, to what had once been Harker's room, and examined him. Despite all the blood that had been taken, he was not yet *nosferatu*, or at least his case was still doubtful. I pondered the situation and realized, with a sigh, that it was my duty as lord of Castle Dracula to restore him as best I could to his own home. There was not another living soul at hand whom I could entrust with such a mission, and after obtaining a horse and cart from Tatra I set out to do the task myself, despite the days that it must occupy.

Meanwhile there was my daily chore of keeping track of the *Czarina Catherine* at sea, by means of her splinters and dust that I kept in my possession. I continued to see to it that her winds were favorable, as if I were in fact depending on her in my race for home. Since the enemy were waiting for her at Varna, I had decided not to land her there at all, and so blew a few more well-chosen winds about the ship, with fogs so that her crew would be at a loss to know which way to steer and I could drive her where I willed.

By the time the crew knew fully what was happening to them they were in the mouth of the Danube at the port of Galatz, somewhat closer to my own domain than I had been in Bucharest.

The docks at Galatz were new and efficient, having been begun only in 1887, and the place was a thriving port. The unloading of the boxful of earth was seen to by my unwitting agent, one Immanuel Hildesheim, slurred by Harker in his journal as "a Hebrew of rather the Adelphia Theatre type, with a nose like a sheep." Hildesheim, acting under written instruction from a Mr. de Ville of London—a near relative and close friend of Dr. Corday, of course—gave the box over to Petrof Skinsky, whom I mentioned earlier in connection with my departure from my homeland.

The posse, when they learned of the ship's arrival in Galatz, lost no time in entraining there from Varna, a comparatively short journey of some three hundred miles by rail. They of course brought Mina along. As the train passed through Bucharest she stared out through its windows, hoping unreasonably to catch some sight of me.

In Galatz the adventurers interviewed *Czarina Catherine's* captain, a superstitious but opportunistic Scot who had suspected that something more than natural good luck was behind the astounding swiftness of his voyage, yet had clubbed his restive crew into submission and enjoyed the ride as being good for business. Information gleaned from the captain led Van Helsing and his men to Hildesheim, and thence to Skinsky, whose body with its throat cut was found in a nearby churchyard just as they were asking for him. I suppose he had tried to cheat the Slovaks in some way, and was killed by them, but of course the implication in my enemies' records is that I was responsible for his death.

Exhaustion was setting in among the hunters, who for a time lay about disspiritedly in their several rooms at the Galatz hotel. Quincey nursed his scalp wound, that was somehow never mentioned in any of their journals. Mina began to fear that they might not, after all, push on to the conclusion she and I were trying so hard to arrange. She therefore decided to spur them on by drawing up a logical—though of course fallacious—chain of reasoning, showing where the box that had become their grail was now most likely to be found.

Although I had no hand in formulating Mina's report it was quite accurate about the coffin's location. Of course its usefulness to my foe rested, as she knew full well, upon two false premises: first, that I could not move, or chose not to move, toward my home by my own efforts, but preferred to be conveyed by others; and second, that I was within the box that had come by ship. When she had finished presenting her report and logical analysis to the men they were delighted by it and reinvigorated for the chase, and she promptly got out of their way again. Van Helsing himself paid her intelligence a verbal tribute which was perhaps somewhat tarnished by the words with which he closed his speech: "Now, men, to our council of war . . ."

Mina's conclusion was that my box was being shipped by water closer to Castle Dracula, and so Arthur and Jonathan were detailed to take up the pursuit by chartered steam launch, ascending the river Sereth toward its junction with the Bistrita, which latter stream, as Mina had noted, ran "up round the Borgo Pass. The loop it makes is manifestly as close to Dracula's castle as can be got by water." Quincey and Dr. Seward, accompanied at first by two men to look out for their spare horses, were to follow generally along the right bank of the Sereth, being ready to take action on land wherever the box carrying the vampire might be put ashore.

As for Van Helsing, he had his own goals in view and after a short rest in Galatz was ready to pursue them:

I will take Madam Mina right into the heart of the enemy's country. Whilst the old fox is tied in his box, floating on the running stream whence he cannot escape to land . . . we shall go in the track where Jonathan went, from Bistrita over the Borgo, and find our way to Castle Dracula. Here, Madam Mina's hypnotic power will surely help . . . there is much to be done, and other places to be made sanctify, so that that nest of vipers be obliterated.

Harker was ready to leave his wife, to go himself aboard the launch, where he assumed the chances of coming to grips with me would be the best; but he was not at once convinced that Mina should be taken toward my castle any farther. "Do you mean to say, Professor Van Helsing, that you would bring Mina, in her sad case and tainted as she is with that devil's illness, right into the jaws of his death trap? Not in the world! Not for heaven or hell!"

But his sales resistance could not hold out against the old maestro of obfuscation:

The professor's voice, as he spoke in clear, sweet tones, which seemed to vibrate in the air, calmed us all: "Oh, my friend, it is because I would save Madam Mina from that awful place that I would go. God forbid that I should take her into that place. There is work—wild work—to be done there, that her eyes may not see. We men here, all save Jonathan, have seen with our own eyes what is to be done before that place can be purify

. . . if the count escape us this time . . . he may choose to sleep him for a century, and then in time our dear one"—and he took Mina by the hand—"would come to keep him company, and would be as those others that you, Jonathan, saw. You have told us of their gloating lips; you heard their ribald laugh as they clutched the moving bag that the count threw to them. You shudder; and well may it be. Forgive me that I make so much pain, but it is necessary, my friend. Is it not a dire need for the which I am giving, possibly my life? If it were that anyone went into that place to stay, it is I who have to go to keep them company."

The vision of Van Helsing as a vampire is one before which my imagination balks; this is doubtless only a shortcoming on my part; he may have been well fitted for the role, since as we have seen he had already the power, by means of speech, to cast his victims into a stupor. At any rate, Harker in his confused anxiety was made to feel that it was he who was somehow endangering his own wife: "Do as you will," said Jonathan, with a sob that shook him all over. "We are in the hands of God!"

Mina's own feelings were very complex at this point. But she was stirred to see how the men threw themselves and their fortunes into the preparations for their final assault on Castle Dracula and its dread lord: "Oh, it did me good to see the way that these brave men worked. How can women help loving men when they are so earnest, so true, and so brave! And, too, it made me think of the wonderful power of money!" That is my girl, as they say, in a nutshell.

On October thirtieth the three-pronged drive of my enemies was launched. Van Helsing took Mina by train to Veresti, where the professor planned to buy a carriage and press on to the Borgo Pass. Jonathan and Arthur, the latter an amateur steamfitter of some standing, to judge by the skill with which he effected several repairs en route, started chugging up the Sereth. In two days they reached the Bistrita, meanwhile receiving from the river folk occasional reports of the Slovaks' boat that was carrying my box ahead of them. Quincey Morris and Seward meanwhile had rather a dull ride of it, trotting across country with no real excitement until they joined forces with the river-borne party near the end . . . or what they all took to be the end.

Van Helsing's journey with Mina was somewhat more lively, though nowhere near as eventful as it would have been if I had been as intent on his destruction as he imagined. The professor recorded in his diary that their carriage "got to the Borgo Pass just after sunrise" on the morning of November third. The several closely following entries are rather muddled and probably unreliable, for he records that they did not come near the castle itself until the sun was "low down" on the afternoon of the following day. This would seem to mean that nearly two full days of driving were needed to cover a distance which I as coachman traversed in a couple of hours with Harker as my passenger, on a night when I did some deliberate doubling back and made frequent stops looking for treasure. Perhaps the professor and Mina—both of them by now, for different reasons, in peculiar psychological states —actually dozed in their seats through many of the daylight hours, whilst the horses stood idle, or sought their own path among the few available.

This daylight-dozing theory may be strengthened by Van Helsing's statement that he was awake most of the night of November third to fourth to keep a fire going. Mina seemed to have given up eating, he wrote, "and I like it not." During the night he several times nodded into slumber, each time awakening to discover her "lying quiet, but awake, and looking at me with so bright eyes." At the same time she was in general "so bright and tender and thoughtful" that his fears were somewhat allayed.

Still, by the night of November fourth to fifth, he again "began to fear that the fatal spell of the place was upon her, tainted as she is with vampire baptism." And now Castle Dracula was indubitably in sight, even in reasonable hiking distance, and he set up a sort of base camp.

Mina still professed not to be hungry, and—though she really made little effort to do so—apparently could not cross a circle of crumbled host that she watched him make around her. This, he told Mina, was for her own protection. Van Helsing himself of course was armored by all his usual freight of herbs and religious paraphernalia.

After dark the horses screamed, and amid snow flurries the three women of the castle appeared, taking form slowly in the outer reaches of the firelight. From Harker's descriptions Van Helsing "knew the swaying round forms, the bright hard eyes, the white teeth, the ruddy color, the voluptuous lips. . . ." For some reason *voluptuous* was a favorite word of the professor.

Alas for Anna, Wanda, and Melisse. I had warned them against touching any of the expected "English," and now, too late, they were being obedient to the letter of my orders. But still of course they must go out and gibber at Van Helsing in the night, and drink his horses' blood, and call to Mina to come and join them as a sister. Perhaps they thought to send Van Helsing screaming in panic and fleeing like a peasant down the mountainside, rushing over a precipice in blind terror. They did not know his name, of course. I had not told them that. . . .

They were disobedient subjects, not once but again and again. In the old days such behavior would quite likely have brought them to the wooden stake whilst they still breathed . . . has it occurred to you that impalement is the one punishment equally enforceable upon a vampire and a breathing man or woman? Some say now that I was known as Vlad the Impaler whilst I still breathed. Bah, to be remembered for mere gory butchery, no matter how just or necessary, and to have all guiding purpose and ideals forgotten . . .

Never mind. I had tolerated far too long the three women's disobedience, which had then culminated in treachery to me and assaults upon the innocent. Certainly if things were to fall out so that Mina had to join me at the castle at once, I did not want those three around to spit with jealousy and bother her.

Seward at dawn on November fifth "saw the body of *Szgany* . . . dashing away from the river with their leiter wagon. They surrounded it in a cluster, and hurried along as though beset." This was indeed Tatra and some of his most faithful men, who, according to my orders, had taken the box unopened from the boat and were rushing it toward the castle. By this time Jonathan and Arthur had seen their vessel suffer its final breakdown, had somehow commandeered horses, and were riding in pursuit as well.

Meanwhile I had returned to Castle Dracula from my errand of duty with the unfortunate peasant, arriving just before dawn; and now, congealed in man-shape by the morning light, I squinted against the sun's rays to make out a human figure that was climbing alone toward my forbidding walls. When I recognized Van Helsing my grip tightened on the edges of the embrasure through which I watched until the old stones gave up flakes into my hands. But I meant to let him have his way, convince himself that he had sterilized my house. Mina was far more important to me than any thing or person he might destroy within that gloomy pile.

I remained in my high, comparatively sunny observation post, where I thought he was not very likely to come looking for me. Soon after he reached my front door far below a hollow booming began to reverberate up through the courts and rooms between. Later I discovered that the professor had been prudently knocking loose the hinges of those great entrance doors, not wishing to be trapped inside by any misfortune, or vampirish plan. He used a handy hammer that he had lugged up in his bag, and for which he meant to find other employment as well.

As he wrote later, he was working on the doors when he thought he heard "afar off the howl of wolves. Then I bethought me of my dear Madam Mina. . . ." He had left her sleeping alone in the snow, wrapped in rugs for warmth but protected by nothing else more substantial than his ring of crumbled Host. If she had never drunk from my veins she very likely would have perished from exposure. And had those wolves been looking for their breakfast . . . but as matters stood they were sent by me to find her and stand guard.

Van Helsing of course did not know this. The dangers Mina might be facing put him, as he wrote, "in terrible plight. The dilemma had me between his horns." Though he expected that his Holy Circle would guard her from vampires by day or night, "yet even there would be the wolf."

But he was not the man to let the wolf's real fangs on Madam Mina's skin, or the dilemma's figurative horns upon his own, turn him aside from his objective now so near at hand within the castle.

I resolve me that my work lay here, and that as to wolves we must submit, if it were God's will. At any rate it was only death and free-dom beyond. So did I choose for her.

As for himself:

I knew that there were at least three graves to find—graves that are inhabit; so I search, and search, and I find one of them. She lay in her vampire sleep, so full of life and voluptuous beauty that I shudder as though I have come to do murder.

Now, Professor, why on earth should you have felt that way, do you suppose?

Ah, I doubt not that in old time, when such things were, many a man who set forth to do such a task as mine found at the last that his heart fail him and then his nerve. So he delay, and delay, and delay, until the mere beauty and the fascination of the wanton Un-Dead have hypnotize him; and he remain on and on, till sunset come, and the vampire sleep be over. Then the beautiful eyes of the woman open

In my time I have known an ugly vampire wench or two; theirs is a sad lot.

and look love, and the voluptuous mouth present to a kiss—and man is weak. And there remain one more victim in the Vampire fold . . .

No such weakness for Van Helsing himself, of course; though he admitted that he:

was moved to a yearning for delay which seemed to paralyze my faculties . . . I was lapsing into sleep, the open-eyed sleep of one who yields to a sweet fascination, when there came through the snow-stilled air a long, low wail, so full of woe and pity that it woke me like the sound of a clarion. For it was the voice of my dear Madam Mina that I heard.

This yowl seems to me more likely to have issued from the throat of one of the guardian wolves than from the lady herself; however that may be, the professor did not bother to check on Mina's position vis-a-vis the wolves, but turned back to the "horrid task" from which he had been distracted. He soon:

found by wrenching away tomb tops one other of the sisters, the other dark one. I dared not pause to look on her as I had on her sister, lest once more I should begin to be enthrall; but I go on searching until, presently, I find in a great high tomb as if made to one much beloved that other fair sister . . . she was so fair to look upon, so radiantly beautiful, so exquisitely

Guess what?

voluptuous, that the very instinct of man in me . . . made my head whirl with new emotion.

Of course he was not put off by human instincts. After desecrating another Host by dropping it within my own disappointingly empty sarcophagus, he nerved himself to face his "terrible task . . . had it been but one, it had been easy, comparative. But three! To begin twice more after I had been through a deed of horror . . ."

He does not record the order in which he took

his victims, but I can testify that fair Anna was the last. It bothered me that at the end she screamed my name. And when I felt something within me trying to move and melt at that mere sound, I knew I had already changed; that my sojourn to England and my love of Mina had not been without profound effect . . . but whether this changing, softening, in me was for good or ill I could not have said.

So the professor thrice dutifully endured "the horrid screeching as the stake drove home; the plunging of writhing form, and lips of bloody foam. Then before leaving the castle he "so fixed its entrances that never more" could the rightful proprietor "enter there Un-Dead." It is hard to imagine what means he employed toward this end. Surely particles of transsubstantiated bread would have ceased to resemble bread, and therefore ceased to be the body of God, within a few months at the most. At any rate, I noted no impediment when I went out or in.

There remains but little to be told. Weary from daylight, from my long though indirect exposure to the sun, I descended from the castle and waited in the last light of afternoon beside a rocky outcropping, along the road by which the *Szgany* soon must come. From the distance my ears brought me the sounds of their flight with their wagon, and from farther still I heard the hoofbeats of the Furies who had pursued them all the daylight hours. As I waited, my wolves came now and then to give me dumb report, by howls, and head pointings, and flashing wordless thought. I saw how the chase must end, and smiled. And I knew also of Mina not far away, now with the professor back at her side, both of them watching the approaching chase.

I called great blasts of wind and snow about me as I stepped out into the road before the gypsies' wagon, halting their horses more with my felt presence than any sight they could have of my upraised arm.

"Master!" cried out Tatra, joyful in the driver's seat. "I thought—" He turned in puzzlement to look at the heavy box that rode behind him. The *Szgany* around him reined their plunging horses in.

"There is no time to explain now, my loyal ones," I said, springing up into the wagon. I set my fingers beneath the box's lid and opened it, wrenching screws and nails free. "Drive on! And as we go, do one of you nail this down again. Above all, remember, they must not uncrate me till the sunset."

I flattened myself down within the box, upon the alien earth that gave no rest nor peace, and waited, calling down blessings on my loyal men. How, in cold alien England, could I ever have set such an ambush for my enemies? Willing arms beat down the lid above me whilst the wagon lurched underway again and gathered speed.

As we sped I called more wolves together and set them running on the heels of my pursuers. There I held them, for a diversionary attack at the last moment should one be needed.

I know when sunset's coming, even if the day be overcast, or black as night with clouds. That day was partly cloudy, with the snow coming and going like curtains drawn across the rocky, piny landscape. Believe me well, I knew to the mo-

271

ment when sunset was due upon that day. After four centuries' dependence on it there was no way that I could fail to know.

Our horses labored. Those of the foe grew nearer and nearer still. Then all at once and nearly simultaneously two voices, Harker's and Morris's, cried out in English: "Halt!" Through the wooden lid above me I could hear contending voices, those of my foes and friends, and then the wagon stopped. I needed but a few moments more, a very few . . . I decided to risk it without calling in the wolves.

The astronomer, the meterologist, the artist, each have their own definitions of the precise moment of sunrise or sunset. For me, sunset occurs when the mass of intervening earth grows great enough to sharply attenuate the flow of neutrinos—or whatever the proper title of this flux should be—that, emanating from the unshielded sun, hold in partial paralysis the deep nerve centers of the vampire brain and body.

At the moment when the first of my enemies sprang upon the wagon the mass of an intervening mountain already blocked me from the sun. Mina, then at a slightly higher elevation and looking down with Van Helsing at the scene of struggle below, noted that "the castle of Dracula now stood out against the red sky, and every stone of its broken battlements was articulated against the light of the setting sun."

It was Harker himself who had boarded the wagon, and at once "with a strength which seemed incredible raised the great box and flung it over the wheel to the ground." Quincey Morris, though sustaining in the process a knife wound that was shortly to prove fatal, bulldozed his way through the *Szgany* and joined Harker in prying off my lid. Seward and Lord Godalming were now at hand, sitting their weary horses with leveled Winchesters, against which my knife-carrying gypsies were powerless to interfere. As the lid fell free I looked toward the western sky, from which the sun had just that moment gone, and felt my powers come. My timing had been fine; nay, I boast quite truthfully that it was perfect.

Mina shrieked as she saw her husband's knife cut through my throat.

whilst at the same moment Mr. Morris's bowie knife plunged into the heart. It was like a miracle; but before our very eyes, and almost in the drawing of a breath, the whole body crumbled into dust and vanished from our sight.

I shall be glad as long as I live that even in that moment of final dissolution there was in the face a look of peace such as I never could have imagined might have rested there.

And so shall I, my dear; for that look meant that my body, lanced with metallic pain at heart and throat, found anesthesia in the balm of victory as I changed form to mist, which, flowing away unnoticed amid the flurrying snow, was soon invisible to all who might have watched it. . . .

I had thought that Van Helsing or Seward or even one of the others might be bothered by the metallic means—involving no wood, nor garlic —with which I had been, to all appearances, so easily dispatched. There was also a lack of "screeching," "plunging," and "lips of bloody foam," all of which phenomena had accompanied each of their previous lynchings of my race. But I need not have worried. My hunters were emotionally and physically worn out, one and all, and more than ready to find the play utterly satisfying as it stood. Even Mina's subconscious mind had been satisfied—for, even as she screamed to see my death—not knowing at the moment whether or not it might be real—the mark of the vampire vanished from her forehead, never to return. She was able to run out of Van Helsing's Holy Circle at last, to comfort Morris in his dying moments and throw her arms about her husband. The gypsies had scattered and fled, and I, in mist-form amid the blowing snow, took my own leave. . . .

For a few hours . . . .

The snow ceased shortly after sunset, and the ensuing night was bitter cold. My enemies made camp in the open—their own fears and perhaps the consciences of some of them would hardly have let them rest inside the walls of Castle Dracula that night. They built up a fire against wolves—my disturbed children were still howling in the distance—and planned to take turns standing watch. But one by one they all sank into fitful sleep around the ebbing flames, till one person only remained awake, she who had begun to learn to make the night her day.

I deepened the slumber of the others and then I came and stood in the far firelight, where her restlessly watching eyes could not fail to see me.

Automatically at her first sight of me her hand

went up to her forehead once again, to reassure itself of unmarked smoothness there. She looked around at all the men, then got to her feet and came toward me, placing her sturdy boots carefully upon the frozen ground. I could tell even at a distance that something had changed. What, precisely, I could not say. But suddenly I was wary.

"Vlad," Mina said, briskly and without preamble, as she came up, "you have given me your assurance that I have nothing to fear in the way of—of permanent physical consequences, as a result of our relationship to date. Is that not so?"

"It is." I bowed, without taking my careful eyes from hers.

"It is a matter of some importance that this should be so, now," she went on, and paused to emit a faint belch. "Excuse me."

"You have been reluctant to eat? That should vanish soon, as your stigma has already done. I told you these manifestations in you were merely the result of Van Helsing's hypnotic—"

"*This* has nothing to do with Van Helsing, or with hypnotism," she interrupted brusquely. "The fact is that I am pregnant."

My mouth opened but I could find no words.

"I am pregnant, and I intend to take no chances with the welfare of my child-to-be. I am saying goodbye to you now, Vlad. Do you understand?"

I could but nod.

It was the summer of 1897, I believe, when Mina and her good Jonathan, along with Lord Godalming and Dr. Seward—who were by then encumbered with their own wives and infants—and of course with you-know-who acting as mentor and guide, journeyed once more to my fair land. I suppose that, as before, the peasants waggled fingers and blessed themselves with prayers and incantations upon learning the pilgrims' destination as they passed; that sort of thing does not change much in six or seven years.

Although by now, of course, Castle Dracula is almost obliterated, from truthful memories as well as from the landscape, the tourists in 1897 found it but little changed. I am sure that Mina had to put forth some effort to persuade them—to persuade her husband, at any rate—to make the journey; if I were he I would not have chosen Transylvania for my holiday.

I knew that she was on her way, across the miles . . . I knew. And of course I knew it also when she walked into the ruined courtyard of the castle on a day of birdsongs and summer light and here and there a climbing flower.

After chatting with the others of her party for a while over this and that item of the architecture she descended alone toward what I might call my public tomb—which is the one Van Helsing had already found. There was and is another, much more private, and not far away.

With all the sunlight up above, even the dim underground chamber was almost bright as day. Before the impressive monument that bears my name, Mina stood for a long moment with her head bowed. Then turned—and I was waiting for her, sitting casually upon a lesser slab nearby.

"You startled me," she said, raising one hand

toward her breast in a Victorian maiden's gesture that she gave up on halfway through, beneath my gaze. Then she asked: "How is it with you, Vlad?"

"Well enough. I continue to—pursue my destiny." I made a vague gesture, not knowing, myself, quite what I meant. "And you?"

The voices of the rest of her party were audible somewhere above, a childish treble among them. A slight shadow crossed Mina's face and I divined its meaning, and went on: "The child is innocent of me and mine. The bloodstreams do not mingle in the womb." So I thought then; latterly, men of science are no longer quite so sure.

"Two children, Vlad. I have borne twins."

"Then both are innocent. But what if they were not? There are worse fates in this world than to be a vampire." On Lucy, Mina's daughter, I will have no comment now, for she was still alive the last I heard. But certainly Quincey, her son, kept to breathing all his short life; he needed bayonets and hand grenades to drain the blood of others, and it was German iron that drank his, in 1916 at the Somme.

Mina's face cleared and we stood looking at each other, and she seemed to be wondering what to say next. But gradually she began to smile and shook her head at me. "Vlad, Vlad. There have been times in England, in the bright sunshine, when—forgive me, but when I have doubted your very existence."

"Oh? But that is all right. Every year there are fewer and fewer people who believe in me. But if they all forget me I will be here anyway, like an artifact of some lost civilization."

"Oh, Vlad! Your life is such a lonely one. And for six years you have been here waiting." I had not been waiting entirely unaccompanied, but saw no reason to correct her estimate.

Above, sharp careless footsteps of a small throng resounded on stone vaulting, drawing closer now, and a high voice was raised: "Mummy! Mummy, are you down there?"

I reached Mina in one silent bound, planted a kiss upon her lips, and pressed something into her hand. I was held in man-shape by the daylight, but still those were my grounds and I knew them well. By the time two children came racing into the vault I was out of sight, but watching.

"Mummy, mummy, there you are. Ohh, what's this? Tombstones!"

Then Harker himself, gray and solid and growing a little portly, strolled in and came to a sudden stop as he realized what chamber he had entered. "Lord," he murmured, "I never thought to see the day when we could stand here in calm safety."

"I came to offer up a prayer, Jonathan," his wife said. "For *him*." Her husband was not looking at her, and her eyes flicked in the direction where I had disappeared. "That we may meet someday in—in a happier place than this."

"How lovely of you, my sweet, to pray for him," Harker murmured, and gave her hair a little proprietary touch, which must have disarranged it, for a small restorative fingering by her own hand followed in a moment. "What have you there in your hand, Mina?"

"Why, it's a gold ring. It was here in a crevice

between the paving stones, and I picked it up. Do you think I might be allowed to keep it?"

"I don't see why not, my dear. I believe the proper owner is not likely to come looking for it now. Ha, hum. Quincey, Lucy, show some respect, do not sit on the tombstones, please."

Have I seen Mina since? Why yes, I must admit, a time or two.

Jonathan died of apoplexy, raging at Neville Chamberlain in 1938. Mina lived to be ninety-five, and breathed her last in an Exeter nursing home in 1967, and was interred in her family's plot nearby. In St. Peter's Cemetery, as a matter of fact, not far from this very snowdrift where we sit . . .

Van Helsing, God rest his own perturbed soul, was right about one thing at least. . . .

When I have mixed my blood with theirs, often enough, they all must walk after they appear to die. Exceptions are extremely rare. Some, like Lucy Westenra, bestir themselves in a mere three days or less. With some it takes three years or more. Modern embalming methods are to be considered, for if the vampire heart is nearly destroyed it needs a long time to regrow. But it will do so, if destruction is not utterly complete. But after that regrowth, more healing time will pass, time in which the buried body, still quiescent, restores itself inexorably to youth. And after that . . .

The bond has stretched twixt Mina and myself, but never broken. And I have come here tonight to welcome her into a new life. A life in which I trust she will find, despite its continuation of earthly sorrows, some great joys too, unknown to those who merely breathe . . . Mina!

The tape ends shortly, the only sounds on its remaining length being the hissing of snow and wind around the windows of the car, and what some listeners describe as faint and distant peals of laughter, one feminine and gay, one masculine and deep.

FRED SABERHAGEN

THE BEST IN SCIENCE FICTION

GREG BEAR

GORDON R. DICKSON

☐ 53577-4	ALIEN ART	$2.95
☐ 53578-2		Canada $3.95
☐ 53550-2	BEYOND THE DAR AL-HARB	$2.95
☐ 53551-0		Canada $3.50
☐ 53221-X	GREMLINS GO HOME	$2.75
☐ 53222-8	(with Ben Bova)	Canada $3.25
☐ 53068-3	HOKA!	$2.95
☐ 53069-1	(with Poul Anderson)	Canada $3.50
☐ 53562-6	THE LAST MASTER	$2.95
☐ 53563-4		Canada $3.95
☐ 53581-2	THE MAN FROM EARTH	$2.95
☐ 53582-0		Canada $3.95
☐ 53572-3	THE MAN THE WORLDS REJECTED	$2.95
☐ 53573-1		Canada $3.75
☐ 53570-7	ON THE RUN	$2.95
☐ 53571-5		Canada $3.50
☐ 53564-2	THE OUTPOSTER	$2.95
☐ 53565-0		Canada $3.50
☐ 53575-8	PRO	$2.95
☐ 53576-6		Canada $3.75

Buy them at your local bookstore or use this handy coupon:
Clip and mail this page with your order.

Publishers Book and Audio Mailing Service
P.O. Box 120159, Staten Island, NY 10312-0004

Please send me the book(s) I have checked above. I am enclosing $_____
(please add $1.25 for the first book, and $.25 for each additional book to
cover postage and handling. Send check or money order only—no CODs.)

Name _____

Address _____

City _____ State/Zip _____
Please allow six weeks for delivery. Prices subject to change without notice.